HOME is EAST

HOME is EAST

MANY LY

delacorte press

Published by
Delacorte Press
an imprint of
Random House Children's Books
a division of Random House, Inc.
New York

Visit us on the Web! www.randomhouse.com/kids
Educators and librarians, for a variety of teaching tools, visit us at
www.randomhouse.com/teachers
Library of Congress Cataloging-in-Publication Data
Ly, Many.
Home is east / Many Ly.
p. cm.
Summary: After her mother moves out, a ten-year-old Cambodian American girl and
her old-fashioned father leave their home in Florida to begin a new life in San Diego,
experiencing turmoil and change as they slowly adjust to their new circumstances.
ISBN 0-385-73222-8 (trade) — ISBN 0-385-73223-6 (glb)
1. Cambodian Americans—Juvenile fiction. [1. Cambodian Americans—Fiction.
2. Fathers and daughters—Fiction. 3. Mothers—Fiction. 4. Divorce—Fiction.
5. Friendship—Fiction. 6. San Diego (Calif.)—Fiction.] I. Title.
PZ7.L979555Ho 2005
[Fic]—dc22
2004014969
The text of this book is set in 12-point
Adobe Caslon.
Book design by Angela Carlino
Printed in the United States of America
August 2005
10 9 8 7 6 5 4 3 2 1
BVG

acknowledgments

Each step I took with this book was a step closer to finding home, and how lonely the journey would have been if I'd had to take those steps alone. I thank the following people:

The Squirrel Hill Writers' Group, especially Isabel Alcoff, Bonnie King, Maggie Martin, Cindy McKay, and Pat Schuetz. Lori Keefer and Matt Hackler, for your generous reading. Barbara Paonessa, Marcia Bradwick, and Bettie-Love Downs, for being inspiring teachers. Jamie Benjamin, for your wisdom and company.

My agent, Jodie Rhodes, and my editor, Stephanie Lane, for your guidance, and your love of Amy.

My family and family-friends: Davin and Julie Pin; Sivun Sao; Sihourn Um; Manith Mann; Song Cheng and Suzanne Chea; Nancy Chun and Thorn Kim; Sengkry Nay and Thach Nhon; and Im Tran, my mother, for giving voice to Peera.

And my husband, Danith, for being my compass.

For all parents who have
traveled so far

PROLOGUE

Thailand, 1980

THE AMERICAN WOMAN who interviewed my dad had very light hair, and her skin was almost transparent. She, Dad, and the Khmer interpreter sat in a large, open room with a wood plank floor. The air was hot and dry, and Dad could feel sweat beads forming on his forehead. The room was quiet enough that he could hear three different heartbeats. His was the loudest; it beat in his head and rang in his ears. He politely smiled at the two people across the desk. Then Dad looked down at his feet, wondering if all Americans were this pale.

Dad was nervous, and rubbed the scar on his left cheek. Ever since he had fled Cambodia for the refugee camp a year before, he'd been waiting for the day when he could go to America. For four long years, he'd been laboring in a farm cooperative run by the Khmer Rouge, who had barged into his family's home and ordered him, his parents, and his sisters and brothers deep into the countryside at gunpoint. In the cooperative, Dad rose before sunup and worked until the stars shone, digging canals, planting and harvesting rice fields, and doing anything else the Khmer Rouge ordered him to. He was never given enough to eat, so when he could he caught bugs to eat later in the night when everyone was asleep. One moonless night, he dug up a rat that he'd hidden earlier, and built a small fire to roast it. Dad had become so skinny and weak that it was hard for him to stand, and the smell of the rat's fat hitting the flames churned his stomach until he couldn't wait any longer. As he was about to pull his food off the skewer, two drunk Khmer Rouge men came upon him. They clumsily aimed their machine guns at my dad, and he felt himself wet between his legs. They laughed madmen's laughs, and as their bodies shook, the machetes they carried along their legs glowed. The two men saw my dad's fire and kicked a burning branch at him. As he dodged the fire, Dad tried to calm his heartbeat. Sure that they were going to kill him, he wanted to think good thoughts before he died. But all he could think about was the rat he'd been hungry for. Then Dad felt a piece of metal run down his cheek and heard the two men walk away. Something warm trickled down the side of his face, and soon he tasted his own blood and tears. He couldn't find the rat that night, so he lay on the ground, with his knees to his stomach, and thought about the days when his mother had rocked him to sleep.

Now, sitting before the woman, my dad was so close to America. All he had to do was answer her questions correctly. Before meeting her, he hadn't thought the interview would be difficult, but now, facing the person who would determine his future made him feel as if his head would explode.

Finally the American woman pushed up her glasses and asked slowly, "What is your name?"

Dad went to school in the evening to learn English, and

at the familiarity of the question, his neck loosened a little. "Peera Lim," he said.

The interpreter translated the second question, which was about his history, and Dad answered that he'd been a student. When asked what happened to his family, my dad looked at the woman's pen and quietly said they had been killed by the Khmer Rouge. A wave of sadness overtook him as he watched her write down his answer and check off a couple of boxes, the black ink finalizing his past. He'd been separated from his family, and while he was in the cooperative, news of their murders had traveled down to him. During the first couple of months in the camp he'd ask anyone he came into contact with about his family. Those people who were certain of the fate of his parents and siblings corroborated the sad news. Some said they had seen the executions; others said they had seen the corpses. Then the people would go into detail about the deaths of their own loved ones. Dad knew that each member of his family was dead, but he'd never really considered them gone, never to come back. Not until the woman's pen had put an end to his family.

When Dad looked at the woman again, he tried to smile. Then the interpreter asked why he wanted to go to America. For a moment, my dad was relieved. *This is it,* he thought, *the question I've been waiting for.* But as he tried to form the words he thought the Americans would want to hear, his head became light. The room was suddenly cool, and he felt far away. He tried to focus on the two people before him, but he couldn't. His mind was filled with the picture of the lake behind his childhood home.

He saw the huge mango tree that had grown beside the lake, its green branches brushing the water when there were strong winds. When the mangoes at the top branches ripened, he and his brothers would wait for them to fall into the lake. Then they would jump into the water and swim to the fruits. While still standing in the water, they would bite into the mangoes, tear off the skin with their teeth, and eat the sweet golden flesh as the juice trailed down their chins and dripped into the water. Afterward, when they were full and drying at the bank of the lake, they would all agree that they could live forever if each day were like this one.

"The American is waiting," the interpreter said to Dad, interrupting his memory.

My dad blinked and stared at the woman, wondering whether he would ever be happy or full again. He didn't know what awaited him in America. Could it promise him another day when he thought he could live forever? No, Dad solemnly realized, nothing could. Nothing could make up for all he'd lost. No matter how much he wanted it to be different, his family was gone. Only he was left. Only he was left to keep them alive, despite the fact that the interviewer had already marked them as dead.

Dad cleared his throat. The woman in front of him became clearer than before. She wasn't pale like a ghost but pink like a newborn baby. "I want to go to America to go to school and get a good job. I can work hard and build myself a future. I need to move on," he said. As scared as he was, my dad was certain that he hadn't lived through the past five years only to fail now.

Several months after the interview, Dad received notice that he had been granted refugee status to enter America. He would be sponsored by an American couple who would help him adapt to his new life in his new home. Dad always told me that when the day came for him to leave Thailand, he returned half of his heart to Cambodia and brought with

4

him only the other half. That half was for the wife and family that he would have in his new home. When I was younger I would get frustrated at the idea that I couldn't have all of him. But now, now I understand that he hadn't left any of himself behind. He had brought his entire being, along with his family and everything he'd ever loved about Cambodia.

1

As a child I lived with my mother and father in St. Petersburg, Florida, a hot and sticky city that has only two seasons: spring and summer. In the summer months we would get heavy thunderstorms that were both a gift and a curse. For a couple of hours we were cooled by the rain pellets that attacked our roofs, windows, and lawns. But when the storm passed, the heat quickly seeped out of the ground and overtook us. It crawled up our legs, oozed through our clothes, and stuck to our armpits. When the overwhelming weather passed, the bright yellow sun would blind us again. I couldn't stay outside too long, not even after school. The sun was so intense that a spoonful of oil and two eggs would make a late breakfast on the sidewalk in front of our house.

Mom and Dad rented a small one-bedroom house with a red roof and an oak tree in the front yard. Our house sat on the edge of a largely Cambodian neighborhood on the south side of the city. We didn't have many luxuries—no new car and no soft bedsheets—but we were still considered well off by some other families because we had our own dwelling.

Our neighbors lived in duplexes or triplexes, or even worse, on top of each other in tiny apartments. The lack of personal space created a familiarity among our people that could be suffocating.

In the evenings and on the weekends we spent most of our time with my parents' friends and their children. They came to our home or we went to theirs, either walking across the street or driving down the block in our maroon Oldsmobile. There were always excuses to have get-togethers: birthday parties, New Year's parties, parties just for the heck of it. No matter what they celebrated, I dreaded them.

When I asked Dad why we were always with his friends, he said that there wasn't anything else to do. I told him that the American kids in my class went to movies and ate at the mall. He refused to try these things because he said Mom didn't like American food. This was true, but I also knew he looked forward to the get-togethers because he enjoyed being around many Cambodians. Dad had known most of them since before I was born and even before he met Mom. When he had first come to the States, he had lived with two American sponsors. They were nice people who gave him a room in their large house, fed him cheese and potatoes, and took him to church. But Dad said life wasn't the same without *his* people, that if you didn't share the same history, then there couldn't be true understanding. Luckily he was able to find a job in a shrimp factory where a lot of Cambodians worked. Every day they stood side by side snapping off shrimp heads.

One day in May, Mr. Yen invited us over for his younger daughter's birthday party. The ground was hot and the air was muggy, so we drove to his house. They lived two blocks down from us, and their house was the nicest and biggest of all the Cambodians'. Their daughter Janet, who was in my third-grade class, was turning nine. At their party, like at every party, I stayed around my parents for as long as I could before joining the other kids.

That afternoon, the men's conversation followed a familiar and dreadful route. One of Dad's friends asked in Cambodian, "Peera, when's your wife going to leave you?"

Unfailingly, the men, with beer in front of them and cigarettes between their fingers, started laughing at *Phou* Ret's question, once in a while elbowing each other in the side or nodding at each other, as if to say *One of these days*. For as long as I could remember, this was the joke about Dad— when his wife was going to leave him. He would politely smile at his friends, but I never found the joke funny.

"It's been ten years. If she were going to leave, she'd be gone by now," Dad said quietly. His response was always calm, never angry. But when he ran his hand down the side of his face, I knew he was a little upset.

Dad had a round face with thick bushy eyebrows that met right above the bridge of his nose. He was a couple of shades darker than Mom, and his skin felt like soft leather— like the wallet that he'd had for many years. And on his left cheek, along his ear, lay a scar that reminded him of the awful years in Cambodia. I would often see him touch it when he was uncomfortable.

Mr. Yen said simply, "It won't last." He was the first Cambodian Dad had met in America, and immediately Dad had been impressed by him because he wore a suit and spoke English like the Americans. That day Mr. Yen shook his head and spoke slowly and thoughtfully in English, as though he had just come to this conclusion about Dad's marriage.

"Look at you," Mr. Chen chimed in. "You're so old. Sooner or later she'll be bored, and she'll want to have fun. She'll find someone younger and smarter than you, and go." From what I understood, they all thought Dad was too serious and proper. He was sixteen years Mom's senior. He didn't smoke, not even when they offered him their cigarettes. He was in his forties now and wore old people's clothes, not the cool pants and shirts the younger men were wearing.

I bit the inside of my left cheek and wished I had the nerve to spit in those men's faces. Mom and Dad loved each other and had me, so wasn't that proof that they would stay together forever? On the walks back home, I would promise myself that I'd never let those men and women make a joke of us anymore. I thought that I might stare at them until they flinched or shake my finger in their faces until they looked away. But each time they started in on Dad I couldn't find the courage to keep that promise.

"I have a daughter, don't I?" Dad asked, looking at no one directly. The men continued to laugh. None of them backed him up.

"It's the least she can give you, you fool," Mr. Yen said. He spoke this way to many people, and I never understood why they put up with it.

Frustrated, but scared to do anything about it, I stood and left to find my mom. While Dad seemed at ease in the company of the other men, Mom usually stayed quiet with other women. She knew most of them believed that she'd only married Dad for a free ticket to the States. Dad often encouraged her to speak to them more, so that they would accept her. But knowing that these women and their husbands were a part of Dad's life even before she came into the picture, Mom never trusted that they sincerely welcomed her. And she had less trust in the older ladies who didn't have husbands but doted on Dad, and would sometimes look at her questioningly. So she never seemed to care to make friends with them. This was fine with me because, except for a couple of the ladies, I didn't like them much, either. I hated how they said things about my parents and then laughed in front of us, glancing slyly at each other, as if they were sharing a private secret.

I found Mom with the other women at the back of the house in the kitchen, where they busied themselves with food preparation and gossip. I could smell beef stew cooking in a soy sauce and tomato paste broth. Standing alone near the refrigerator, Mom picked me up and kissed me. "Amy-a," she whispered into my cheek. No one else pronounced my name with three syllables. It was beautifully soft every time she said it, as if she were almost out of breath.

"You two don't even look like mother and daughter— more like sisters. I wish I could look as good as you," a young woman said to her.

She was right. My mom was the most beautiful woman alive. Her long black hair made her look like a mermaid from the deep Asian water, and her skin was as smooth and dark as the shell of a brown egg. Her eyes were so black that Dad sometimes said he could drown in them. Men would ask her why she married an old man like him. And women would tell her that she would always be safe with Dad because he couldn't possibly go after a younger woman. Like Dad, Mom would just smile and nod until the topic passed.

An older woman walked up and slapped the back of the young woman, laughing. "You can't look like her. None of us can. We don't have an old man to take care of us!"

The women in the kitchen laughed, the ugly laugh of green jealousy. Even the young woman joined in. I thought that the woman would be offended—she'd been told she could never be as beautiful as my mother. Instead, she seemed to have taken the comment as sympathy and shared pleasure in mocking my mom. Men and women were so alike.

Mom looked at me, smiled, and kissed me again on one cheek, then the other, and then all over my face. I laughed in pleasure until I saw sadness in her eyes.

"Don't you want to play, Amy-a?" she asked.

I shook my head. Someone had to be with her, to let her know that she was not alone in the midst of these mean women. I would be the person to stand by her side and protect her.

"There's my little girl," a voice said. It was Mrs. Yen.

I greeted her by folding my hands under my chin, slightly bowing my head, and telling her hello. *"Chumreab suor, Ohm,"* I said.

I called both Mrs. Yen and her husband, and anyone else who was older than my parents but not old enough to be my grandparent, *Ohm.* I called a woman younger than my parents *Meing,* for Aunt, and a man younger than them *Phou,* for Uncle. They were titles that we kids used for all older Cambodians. Dad said it was the respectful way, not like the Americans—who called each other, young or old, by their first names.

Mrs. Yen patted my head. I could never understand why a nice lady like her was married to such a loud, rude man. She was a skinny woman who looked old enough to be my mom's mother. Her smile always looked sincere because her eyes would smile, too. Dad said that eyes never lie. And her eyes were always nice to me.

"Amy, go play with the other kids. I think some of them are outside," she said.

I still didn't want to leave, but I wanted to be polite to Mrs. Yen, so I looked at Mom for permission. She nodded. "Thank you, *Ohm*," I said.

I didn't like spending much time with the neighborhood kids because in some ways they were meaner than the American kids. At school I was always picked last for kickball or group work. Janet and the rest of the Cambodian kids on my street sometimes didn't even pick me for games they played at home. She and her friends would call me a baby and tell me to go back to my mom and dad . . . or worse, tell me to go back to the American girls, who didn't talk to me. So often I stayed in the house and read the books Dad had bought for a dime each at a church bazaar. I liked reading, but it was lonely when the only places you could go were the ones in your head.

"Look, the baby finally woke up," the girls said when I found them near a bush beside the house. I ignored the burning in my cheeks and pretended not to hear them.

Janet looked at me and rolled her eyes. *Nope, she is not in a good mood*, I thought.

"Hi, Janet," I said. Janet was a tall Cambodian girl, and very dark-skinned with long curly hair. She had a round white birthmark the size of a quarter in the middle of her forehead, and she was always pulling her hair forward to cover it.

Janet, Melissa, and Lulu were cutting up "vegetables," a cooking game that all of us girls liked to play. We would pull weeds or pick leaves for the ingredients, and if we were lucky, someone would sneak some vegetable scraps that our moms hadn't used in the real food. I noticed today that they had gotten hold of yellow celery sticks.

"Hi, Melissa and Lulu." They were Janet's cousins, and

they took their cues from her. They could be nice girls when Janet wasn't around.

"Can I play?" I asked Janet. After a few minutes of waiting, she finally told me to go under the orange tree and bring back the windfall oranges.

Janet placed her left hand on her hip and pointed at us with her right. "Lulu, go with her, and Melissa, you stay with me."

Lulu and I left the cooking station and walked across the vegetable garden to the orange tree in the corner of their yard. The oranges were green and only the size of golf balls. Every time there were harsh winds, some of the fruits would fall off the branches and land on the ground, embedding themselves in the grass like Easter eggs. I was searching for a couple of them when Lulu told me to stop moving.

"Listen, Amy." I stood still. "Can you hear it?" she asked me. I shook my head. "Well, listen hard, then." I listened hard. It was the sound of chirping.

"Baby birds," I whispered to her.

"Let's go tell the others, but no matter what, don't tell the boys," she said to me, and put a finger to her lips.

We ran across the yard to Janet and Melissa.

Then the four of us stood under the orange tree trying really hard not to make a sound so that the baby birds wouldn't be scared. Besides, we couldn't risk letting the boys find out. We wouldn't be able to control them if they found the birds first.

Janet gave each of us an area of the tree to be responsible for searching. I studied each branch separately so as to miss nothing. About three feet above me, I found the small nest of twigs and jumped up and down in excitement. Finally locating the nest would make Janet happy.

"I found it. Hurry," I whispered, and signaled for them to come my way.

Janet shushed me. I pointed to the branch, and Lulu began to jump up and down, too, until Janet pushed her to stop. We stood on our toes to see what was inside, but we didn't get lucky until a few minutes later, when the mother bird flew into her home of twigs with a worm in her beak.

"Look!" I pointed. We all stared at three tiny beaks poking out of the nest and trying to peck at the worm.

"How cute," Melissa cooed. "I wish I could take them home." After the worm was eaten, the mother bird flew away again.

"Where's the daddy?" Lulu asked.

Janet, as always, had the answer. "He's probably far away, taking care of his other kids."

"Really?" I couldn't tell if it came from Lulu or Melissa.

"How do you know?" I asked Janet.

"Well, if he's not doing that, then where is he?"

"I don't know. Maybe he's the one on the ground finding the food, and the mother is the one who goes to pick it up and bring it to their kids," I said. Melissa and Lulu nodded in agreement. I didn't know if I was right, but what I had said sounded so much better than what she had said.

I should have known that my answer wouldn't satisfy Janet, who stood glaring at me. "You always think you know everything, Amy," she said. I began to shake my head and tell her not to get mad, but it was too late. "And since you know everything, you must already know that your dad isn't *really* your dad."

In a million years, I never would have expected to hear those words. It felt as if someone had hit me in the neck, causing my head to spin. "I don't know what you're talking about. So stop making up lies," I said, and stared at her.

"What? You don't know that your *real* dad is still in Cambodia?" she asked. She gave a hollow laugh, the kind you hear from a smirking soap opera villain.

"Shut up," I ordered, balling up my hands.

"Melissa, am I wrong?" Janet asked. Melissa and Lulu shook their heads. "You see, Amy, I'm right. He's not your real dad, and everybody knows it. Your dad came here first. And then your mom came to join him, already pregnant. Don't you get it?" she said, pointing to her house.

I didn't want to *get* what she was implying. "Who told you?" I asked.

"Nobody had to. Everybody knows. You're just too dumb to figure it out."

"Shut up, Janet, before I get mad." But I was already mad. She just stood there with a smug look on her face, and when she didn't break away from that look—the one that showed how much she was enjoying hurting me—I thought she might not be lying at all. But she had to be. My dad was *here*, just across the yard from me.

"Say you're sorry for lying," I ordered as I stepped closer to her. I could see Melissa and Lulu out of the corner of my eye edging away from us. Janet didn't budge.

"Sorry for what? Sorry that I told you the—" I didn't let her finish. I tightened my right fist, feeling the sharp fingernails poking into my palm, and swung at her face. The next thing I saw was Janet on the ground with a hand covering her nose. The blow—or the surprise of it, more likely, because I didn't have much of a punch—had knocked her to the ground.

After that couple of seconds, I knew that Janet and her

little clique would no longer call me a baby, and no one would say bad things about my parents again. I had kept my promise to defend my mom and dad.

On the short car ride home, Dad lectured me about how he did not raise a daughter to go around fighting. Mom had made me apologize to Janet and her parents. I was scared to face Mrs. Yen because apologizing would be admitting my fault, but not doing so would be disrespectful. I wished I could tell her what her daughter had said about my dad. After my apology, Mrs. Yen told my mom that kids would be kids. Playing around would sometimes lead to injuries.

Dad shook his head as he drove up to our house. Mom turned around in her seat and looked at me. "Why did you hit Janet?"

"I don't know," I said, and looked out the window.

I couldn't block Janet's smug face from my mind, or her ugly voice, and the harder I tried, the more I started hearing other voices, voices I had heard many months before and wanted to forget. Mom and Dad were in their bed, and hoping that I could sleep in the middle, I had tiptoed to their room. They were whispering.

"I'm sorry. You are a good man, and you deserve a good wife. I am not that person," Mom said.

A few seconds passed before Dad spoke. "We have a family. We've been a family for ten years. I don't understand how you can just forget about that."

"I don't see myself growing old with you."

I couldn't hear what else they said because there was shuffling. There was more moving, and I quickly tiptoed back to my bed, pulling the sheet over my head. Their bedroom door opened and closed. Then the front door. Then the car door. Then the car roared away.

Now I turned away from the window and saw Mom still looking at me. She was waiting for a better answer to her question, but I didn't know what to say. I wanted to bury what Janet had said and pretend I had never heard it. It was at that moment that I realized there was so much I didn't want to know. I knew about those evenings when Mom didn't get home from her English class until late, when Dad begged her to watch TV with us but she refused to and instead stayed in her room, when Dad and I laughed about a gray hair we found on his toe but she couldn't find it funny enough to join us. When Dad and I were happy, and she wasn't. I knew these things, but I didn't want to know what they might mean. All I wanted to know was that my parents were okay, that they were happy being a family. Dad often told me how he and Mom had met, and each time the story sounded like a fairy tale.

After he had been living in America alone for ten years, Dad had decided to find himself a wife. He wanted a real Cambodian wife—one who wasn't Americanized. He said that the single Cambodian women here had started adopting the American ways, going on dates and having multiple boyfriends. When he told Mr. Yen and the others of his plan to return to Cambodia to get married, they all tried to talk him out of it. They said that any person who married him would only do so to come to the United States. He didn't listen to them, and Mr. Yen called Dad a fool.

One day while in Cambodia Dad stopped on the roadside for lunch. There were lines of carts from which vendors sold noodles, rice wrapped in fragrant lotus leaves, dried fish, roasted hens, and fresh coconut juice and fruits. But he had eyes for only one—a small cart to the side tended by a girl who was brushing away the flies with a rag. She was young and beautiful, wearing a sprig of jasmine in her hair.

Dad went up to her and started talking. For the first time since he'd lost his family he wasn't shy. He told her about why he'd had to leave Cambodia and how much he missed it. She listened and encouraged him to talk more about himself. He went back every day to see her, and shared with her his dreams and hopes for a family. Most of the time she kept quiet, so he didn't get to know much about her or her history. But he didn't care. One day when he handed her his empty rice bowl, he just came right out and asked her to marry him. He promised to bring her to America and give her a happy life.

For their wedding they burned sticks of incense at temple. Dad apologized for not giving Mom a proper ceremony, but she said it didn't matter.

When it was time to return to the States, Dad had to leave his new bride behind. Because of all the legal paperwork, it would take at least six months before Mom could join him. While they were apart, Dad counted the long days without her. And the days became even longer when she wrote him that she was pregnant, and to expect her to be big when she joined him in St. Petersburg.

Dad continues to tell me his story. The story has remained the same, but the face and voice that he tells it with have changed over the years. Each time, there is less pain in his eyes and less strain in his speech. This gives me hope that one day I, too, will feel less pain and strain, in my heart.

2

EVEN WHEN IT was just the three of us, Mom didn't talk much. Dad was the one who was always full of jokes and stories. Mom liked to look out her window during car rides, and many times Dad would have to repeat himself because she didn't hear him the first time. She'd turn to him then, give a small grin, and turn back to the window. Sometimes, I turned to see what she found so fascinating. But all I saw were other cars.

When Mom did speak, it was usually about what I should and should not do. When I was in the second grade I told her about a boy in my class who all the girls had a crush on. I wasn't sure why I did this, except that she was driving me to a store, and the radio was playing a fun song that all my classmates were talking about. It was sunny outside and she wore a sweet-smelling perfume, so I felt as if everything inside me was as beautiful as the scent she had sprayed herself with.

When the song was over I said, "There's this boy at school who is *so* cute." As I repeated the words I had heard so often, my cheeks felt as if someone had pinched them. I could feel myself smiling.

I didn't realize Mom had turned the radio off until she spoke to me in a quiet, sharp voice. "You're a kid. What do you know about that?" I was suddenly embarrassed for having smiled and wished my cheeks would feel normal again. I didn't want to get in trouble for talking back, so I didn't answer her.

Mom shook her head. "You go to school to learn, not to look at boys. Don't say that to anyone. They'll laugh at you." I knew that "anyone" meant the people in our community, and I also knew that "they" weren't to know anything that went on in our house.

Mom was rarely angry with me, and I was sorry I had upset her. I reached out my left hand to touch her right one, which curled around the steering wheel. But she moved her hand as if she didn't want mine on top of hers. Slowly I put my hands under my thighs. I can't remember what store we ended up going to; I just remember that the ride there was long.

What I liked best about Mom were the times we spent by ourselves in her room. When Dad was hypnotized by a football game on television, she and I would spend the few hours in their room brushing our hair and painting our toenails and fingernails. She would comb my hair with her long thin fingers and braid it. I loved the feel of her nails gently rubbing my scalp. After she painted my nails light pink and the polish had dried, we would climb under the bedsheets and nap. I would spread myself out in the queen-size bed and roll around, something I couldn't do on my twin bed in the living room. Once I nestled myself against her warm body, I was out. And each time I woke up, I would find one of my arms around her waist. She was mine to keep.

As all-around beautiful as my mom was, her hair especially stood out to me. It had a life of its own. Even when her face was as lifeless as a blackboard, her hair seemed to flow like soft waves in the ocean. She often let me brush it, and each stroke seemed to give it more life. I made my hands swim in that dark sea and let them get lost.

"I want your hair, Mom," I said one afternoon as I put away her brown brush.

"What's wrong with yours, Amy-a?"

"Yours is different. It's thick and shiny and long. When's mine going to get long?" I reached to feel my hair, which grew just past my shoulders.

She walked out of the room and returned with a pair of scissors and a small white envelope.

"No, don't cut it!" I exclaimed, thinking that she was going to cut her hair off just because I was upset that mine wasn't like hers.

"I'm not, you crazy little kid." She reached for a lock of hair from the back and snipped if off with the scissors. She then tied the lock with a red thread from her sewing kit and placed it in the envelope before handing it to me. "Now you can always have my hair, Amy-a."

"Seal it with a kiss," I begged.

She kissed the back of the envelope, leaving the waxy print of her lips on it. I took the envelope and tucked it under my mattress for safekeeping.

●

Our daily ritual was easy. With only one car, Dad would drop Mom off at the Bakers', whose home she cleaned, and since their house was close to my school he would drop me off next before he drove to Exxon, where he'd been working as a mechanic ever since he'd left the shrimp factory after four years. After school I would take the bus home and wait for my parents. But one frigid late-October day, there was a change.

Before Mom stepped out of the car, she turned to me and said, "Amy-a, don't go on the bus today. I'll borrow one of the Bakers' cars to pick you up and you can help me finish the cleaning." I stared at her, thinking that something about her was different. If possible, she looked even more beautiful than other mornings. "Amy-a, did you hear me?"

I nodded. It was unusual that she would let me help her on a school day, but I was thrilled.

Only a few kids were still outside when I arrived at Jefferson Elementary. The cold bit at my ears and froze my nose as I raced indoors, straight for the office.

"No running!" a safety patrol kid yelled behind me. I slowed to a skip.

"Hi, Amy," Mrs. Robinson said. "It's cold today, huh?"

"Yes . . . ma'am." It took a while for me to say the two words as I tried to catch my breath.

"What can I do for you today?" Like Mrs. Yen, she had a truly nice smile. She was the school secretary, and everyone liked her. Mrs. Robinson was the only adult in the entire school who knew all of our names, even us Cambodians.

"My mom is picking me up today, so I won't be on the bus."

"Okay, but make sure you let Mrs. Wallace know." I thanked her and headed for my classroom.

In my class the big topic of the day was whether it was going to snow. I couldn't imagine that I would be so lucky.

My mom was going to pick me up, *and* it might snow. I might actually be able to touch snow. I had heard that it was soft like cotton. Maybe if I could gather up enough of it, I could cover it in mango syrup and eat it. Nothing could be more delicious.

Only half of the students were present, and we were restless as we waited to see if more kids were coming. Nobody wanted to sit down, even when Mrs. Wallace threatened us with extra homework. The boys talked about the snowmen that they were going to build, and the girls, who looked more special today than they usually did, talked about the snow angels they were going to make. One girl, Brittany, wore a white furry coat with these fluffy things around her ears. I heard her tell her friends that they were earmuffs. She looked like an angel.

After seeing the array of pretty jackets everyone had on, I quickly took my brown one off and hung it on a chair near the bookcases in the back of the room. I had had that jacket for three years. When I'd first worn it, it was so big that it covered my bottom. Now it was so small that it barely covered my wrists.

Melissa walked up to me. Her jacket was off, too, but I noticed that her sweater was new. "That's pretty," I said.

"Thanks. Janet's not here because her dad let her stay home. They should have closed school today. They do it for hurricanes, so they should do it for cold days," she said. Melissa wasn't too good at school, so she was always happy when it was canceled.

We didn't do much work in class that day. When no more students showed up, Mrs. Wallace made it a silent reading day. The temperature remained low, but the snow never came. We kids kept hoping, but every time we looked out the window we only saw gray clouds.

In the afternoon the cheery atmosphere in the room turned somber and angry. A couple of the boys started fighting over comic books, and Brittany accidentally drew on her white jacket with a black marker. I looked outside to see that the low-hanging clouds had turned even darker, like black charcoal. It felt as if they were ready to swallow me up. Even though it was only one o'clock, the dark of night was almost upon us.

Once the school bell rang, we rushed to get in a straight line and waited for Mrs. Wallace to let us out. I walked Melissa to the bus circle, and then watched her wave to me from her seat. Teachers were pushing students onto buses, parents were honking at cars in front of them to move forward, and kids were huddling in groups and stomping their feet to keep themselves warm. Leaves were swirling from their branches. The clouds remained low over our heads, and the cold air became thicker, as if they were ready to spill their guts on us. I waited out in front of the school near the flagpole, proud to be one of the few who were waiting to be picked up by their moms.

I saw Brittany standing next to Mrs. Wallace and walked over to them. It was Mrs. Wallace's week to wait with us kids for pickups. The rest of the teachers were already in their cars, probably on their way to a warm home and chicken soup. She had an arm around Brittany, whose face and ears were as pink as strawberry bubble gum. I pulled the arms of my old brown jacket down to cover my wrists.

"Hi, Mrs. Wallace. Hi, Brittany."

My teacher nodded at me and asked, "Are you sure your mom is picking you up today?"

"Yes, ma'am," I said.

Brittany didn't look at me. In fact, she had her eyes closed. Poor thing, she was too fragile for the harsh weather.

At that moment I wanted nothing more than to be her friend so that I could put my arms around her, too, and warm her. She and her friends looked special in everything they did, whether it be twirling their hair around their fingers or chewing on their pencils in class. They sat on the side closest to the windows, so when the sun was out, it would shine on their heads, turning every strand of hair into corn silk. I knew that Brittany and her friends were different from me and mine, but I didn't understand why they were packaged so much better than we were.

I was going to tell Brittany how pretty she looked, but Mrs. Wallace exclaimed, "Thank the Lord, your mom is here, Brittany. One more minute and I think you would have frozen to death."

After Brittany left, there were only two of us, myself and Ricky, a second grader who couldn't get enough of the cold. At one point he was running around with his jacket off until a teacher yelled at him to put it back on. I moved in closer to Mrs. Wallace. I thought that maybe she would put her arm around me to keep me warm, but she put her hands in her coat pockets instead.

"Amy, we've been here for thirty minutes. Your mom should have been here at two-thirty," she said. I could see puffs of steam coming from her mouth. I didn't want to make her mad, but I knew my mom was coming.

"My mom's coming, Mrs. Wallace. I promise." Why wouldn't she? She probably had problems borrowing Mr. Baker's car.

Five minutes later, Ricky's dad came for him, so Mrs. Wallace decided to take me inside. We met Mrs. Robinson in the school office, and Mrs. Wallace told her bitterly that it was nice of parents to think of them as babysitters.

Mrs. Robinson told my teacher to go home, and then she stepped into her office to call my mom at work. A couple of minutes later she walked back out and told me that my mom wasn't there, so she would call my dad. When I heard her footsteps coming toward me again I almost didn't look up, knowing that things weren't quite right.

"Amy, your dad will be here in thirty minutes," she said.

"Did someone say where my mom is?"

"No one picked up the phone, okay?"

"Okay," I said. What else was I going to say?

At three-thirty, Mrs. Robinson walked with me to the parking lot. When the wind blew at us, I could smell the soft scent of Shalimar. My mom wore the same perfume. We talked about how cold and gloomy the day was, and then she pointed across the street. "Look, Amy, there's the sun."

I turned my head to look in the direction of her finger, and there I saw the sun trying to peek through the clouds, shooting a ray of light onto a pretty white house across the street from Jefferson Elementary. Then, just as easily as it had come, it went away, covered by the dark, heavy drapes of clouds.

As Dad pulled up it started to drizzle, and I knew that harder rain was in store for us. He got out to shake Mrs. Robinson's hand, thanked her for staying behind with me, and apologized for the problems our family had caused. She squeezed my hand and headed off to her own car.

Dad was quiet in our Olds, probably thinking about Mom's whereabouts. "What time was she supposed to come?"

"Right after school."

"Well, what time was that?" he asked. He wasn't yelling, but he was louder than usual.

"Two-thirty." I could feel tears in my eyes. Dad rarely raised his voice to me, especially for something I wasn't responsible for. Even the year before when I had left his best shoes outside by mistake and they had gotten soaked in the rain, he didn't yell at me. All he said was that I should be more careful. And now I didn't know why he was mad. Maybe he knew what might have happened to Mom. I didn't want to, but I was beginning to know, too. And it made my stomach feel like ants were biting it from the inside.

When we reached home Dad immediately went to the kitchen phone and called Mom's boss. "Hi, Mrs. Baker." There was a hesitation from him. "Yes, yes, she's getting better. I'm sorry I didn't call earlier. . . . She might not be able to come in tomorrow, either."

I ignored the rain that was now thumping hard on our roof and anxiously waited for Dad to get off the phone.

After he hung up the phone he stood looking at it on the wall and said to me, "Your mom didn't go to work today. She called in sick this morning." His voice sounded drained. Yet what he said didn't surprise me.

The next minute was the longest I have ever known a minute to be. I was cold, shivering, with goose bumps on my arms and legs. I looked at Dad, needing him to turn and offer me a smile, even if it was just a small one, and tell me that I was wrong. That Mom had not left us.

I broke the long silence. "Why did you tell them that Mom's not going into work tomorrow?"

He finally turned away from the phone. "Amy, stop asking so many questions."

I kept quiet for a long time after that.

But when the six o'clock news came on, I said, "Dad, we should call the police."

I held on to the hope that because I was a kid I must be wrong. On a regular day, my mom would have been home an hour before. And by now she would be taking a shower while Dad watched the news. *The only reason,* I thought, *that she is not doing that now is that something bad happened to her. Maybe she got hit by a car. Maybe someone grabbed her. Maybe she is lying unconscious somewhere.* Maybe anything, except that she had left us. As I came up with reasons, Dad shook his head and walked into the kitchen.

I went into their room again. Earlier he and I had checked to see if any of her things were missing. Nothing. Her clothes were still hanging and her shoes were still stacked neatly in the corner of the closet. The bed was untouched, and her comb and brush set still lay on her dresser. Everything was the same in her room, but everywhere else something had changed for good.

Hearing a growl in my stomach, I headed for the kitchen, knowing full well that I would have to do the cooking if I wanted dinner. Dad was sitting at the table staring at the refrigerator when I walked in. I rinsed three cups of rice and plugged in the rice cooker. Next I put three Chinese sausages in the oven. I cooked an extra one for Mom in case she changed her mind and came home that night.

I sat down at the small secondhand dining table that was discolored with all shades of brown scratch marks. Mom had hated it when we bought it. She told Dad we needed a new one and we had money for it, but he said that extra money was for savings. I had felt sorry for her then. She wanted many things: clothes, furniture, even a house. But Dad always insisted that they save their money.

As I waited for the sausages to cook, I looked at Dad, wondering why we didn't give Mom the benefit of the doubt; why we weren't up and screaming, knocking at neighbors' doors, posting flyers, or calling the police? Wasn't that what people did on TV? Why were we still home when Mom was missing? But deep down I knew why, and I knew I needed to accept it. Even though Dad and I never said the words, we knew the truth as we sat and listened to the clock ticking and the Chinese sausages sizzling in the oven. He couldn't have said to me, "Your mom left us, Amy." And I couldn't have said it to him. So instead, I said, "Dad, can't you call your friends? Maybe she's at someone's home." These words felt as hollow as an empty well.

"No, Amy, you can't tell anyone. I'll call the police if she doesn't come home tonight. But at school tomorrow, you don't say anything to anybody. Understand?"

I nodded, although I knew that we would never call the police. I also knew why I couldn't tell anyone. We couldn't risk having the news of my mom's leaving us spread around the neighborhood. Dad would look bad, and I would look pathetic. We couldn't let the things those awful men and women said about my mom be true!

My mom didn't come home that night. I sat on my bed in the corner of the living room, and Dad sat on the small tan and brown couch, both of us waiting, until one o'clock. We hadn't said much to each other after dinner, only listened to the rain. At one o'clock he turned the television off and walked to their room. I turned onto my side and watched him. I felt as if I was truly seeing him for the first time.

Before that day, he was Dad, and that was all I needed to know about him. He was the strong and handsome dad he was supposed to be. He was Heathcliff Huxtable and Danny Tanner. But with his back to me and only the moonlight piercing our one living room window, he was just a man, just as Mom was just a woman. And that revelation scared me. I suddenly imagined him leaving me, too. If Janet was right, and Dad wasn't really my dad, why wouldn't he leave? Mom was really my mom, and she left, so what would stop him? It was then that the tears began pouring out.

I cried for my mom, and how unhappy she must have been with me and Dad, and I cried for Dad, who would also be unhappy with me, and I cried for myself because I knew I would be alone. At first they were soft sobs I muffled in my pillow. Then the sobs and cries roared in my ear. I was angry that she had left me. I hadn't done anything to her! I loved her and protected her. Wasn't I the one who stood with her against all those women? And after Dad left me, where would I go? I couldn't stop crying even though I already felt the dryness in my throat and eyes.

I didn't know Dad had come to me until he picked me up and took me to the couch. As he rocked me against his chest, he whispered to me to tell him what I was feeling. I didn't know where to begin. It was like the time I had gotten lost on the first-grade field trip to the science museum. When it was time to go back to school, my classmates were suddenly gone, and I didn't know which bus to get on. I felt stranded among all the first graders, strangers from different schools. I saw teachers with their single-file lines of kids already boarding buses but didn't know who to turn to with my problem.

Now I knew I was in Dad's arms, but I was still unsure of everything else. After my body quieted down and the hiccups that followed subsided, I told him about Janet and Melissa and Lulu. "They said that you're not my dad. And that my real one lives in Cambodia." The chance that he might say they were telling the truth terrified me so much that it brought on fresh tears.

Dad rubbed my back. Then he laughed softly and kissed me. "Amy, you are my little girl."

"Really?" I asked, laying my head against the side of his neck, which smelled of grease and sweat. If Mom had been here, she would have sent him to the shower already.

He laughed again and said, "Really. Your mom told me. Someday you'll understand why someone might say something cruel like that. But for now, just know that I am your dad."

I didn't think I would ever understand why someone would be cruel on purpose, but because he told me it was so, I believed him. A tear formed at the corner of his left eye and stayed there, turning the eye glassy and making his entire face look a little bit older. His hair was thinning on the top of his head, and Mom had sometimes joked that he was balding. But I didn't care; I thought he was handsome and loved it when people said I looked like both my parents. I ran my fingers down his thin, four-inch, milky white scar. Then I looked into his eyes, searching for any lie, but there wasn't one. I wiped away the tear that now rolled down his cheek with a finger and licked it. It was salty like my own.

3

I was late for school the next morning. Dad nudged me awake at nine o'clock. When I finally sat up and stretched, I listened for the sizzling of the fried eggs Mom usually made for breakfast. I looked around and didn't see either of my parents, and I didn't hear anything from the kitchen. Then I heard Dad in the bathroom dropping the toilet seat before saying, "Amy, go get ready for school. We're late and I have to stop by the bank before I drop you off."

I wondered why no one had woken me up sooner, but then I remembered why I wasn't hearing any eggs frying.

My mom was gone.

I pulled back the window curtain and saw that the sun had finally found its way out from behind the clouds. Where had it been the day before, when I needed some light in my life? I didn't want to go to school; in fact, I didn't want to go anywhere. I wouldn't know what to say if someone asked me about Mom. I knew I didn't have much compared to other kids at school, since Mom was only a housekeeper and Dad was a mechanic. The American girls regularly came to school with new brand-name skirts or tops. But like most of the girls from my neighborhood, I rarely owned anything expensive.

What I *had* had that not all kids on my street had was a family, a mom and a dad who loved me the way I wanted them to, and I had held on to that knowledge as my most valuable possession. Though it would embarrass me later, I showed my parents off to the kids in our community like a first-place prize. Whenever Mom planted kisses on me or whenever Dad held me in his arm, it was as good as sucking on a cherry lollipop, knowing that those who were watching wanted a lick, too.

But that had changed. I couldn't stand the thought of not having Mom, and knowing that the world would learn about my loss both scared me and made me shiver with anger. If those people hadn't gone on and on about her leaving us, she might never have done it. I went over in my head what I would tell people when they figured it out. How could I explain that it wasn't my fault she left?

"Amy, let's go," Dad said.

"Can I stay home today?"

"What? No, you can't stay home by yourself," he said absentmindedly.

"I've stayed home by myself before."

"Amy, don't talk back and hurry up."

I walked to my three-drawer chest and took out a pair of jeans and a Mickey Mouse sweatshirt that I had gotten for my birthday the year before.

In the bathroom mirror, I looked at myself. I had always hated that I had brown freckles and not soft, baby-doll skin. My big round eyes were too far apart, and my nose was square on my small head. The one thing I had going for me was my big eyes, but now, after having cried all night, the area around them was puffy, the skin pink and bloated and tight, revealing only two small slits for my pupils to peer through. I looked awful.

There wasn't anything for breakfast, so I ate cold rice and the leftover sausage that had been saved for Mom. I bit into the sausage and saw cubes of fat inside. In my mouth it no longer tasted sweet and salty but gritty and cold. It got me thinking that for the rest of my life, all I would have to eat were fatty pink Chinese sausages and cold hard rice. And a lump filled my throat.

After the harsh rain that had followed the chill of the day before, the ground was soaked, the roads overflowed with water, and the sky was far away, making everything around me feel distant and unreal.

Dad and I first stopped by Bank of America to see if Mom had left us any money. "Go sit over there near the plants," Dad said when we entered the building. Seeing that there were already three women there, I shook my head and grabbed his hand. I was not ready to see anyone and risk having them ask about me and my family.

I turned to see an old woman getting in line behind us. She wasn't much taller than me and had white curly hair and tiny red lips, which she attempted to open as I quickly turned back around. I could feel my heart thumping. *She knows about my mom*, I thought. Finally it was our turn to be helped, and I was thankful to be called away from her.

"I need to know my balance, please," Dad said to the teller, handing the young woman his checkbook. She wrote the amount on a sheet of paper, and then he asked when the last withdrawal had been made.

"Yesterday, Mr. Lim."

Dad thanked her, and she handed me an apple Dum Dum. I was careful not to look at the old lady as we walked away. But on our way out she tapped my shoulder, and I felt the tips of my ears blaze.

"Little girl," she squeaked, "you are very cute. How old are you?"

I didn't say anything, so Dad told her that I was almost ten and thanked her. In the car, he told me that Mom had taken almost all the savings and left us only a small part of it.

"Is that okay, Daddy?"

"Yes and no. It's good that she didn't take everything, but it's bad because we don't have much money left.

"And, Amy, you were rude to that lady back there. I've taught you to thank people when they compliment you."

Dad was right; he'd told me that rule many times. But didn't he understand that there was a lot on my mind?

"I'm sorry I forgot, Dad," I said in Cambodian. I had learned that whenever I apologized in Cambodian, Dad forgave me much more quickly than when I did it in English. A few seconds later I asked, "What do I say if someone asks about Mom?" He didn't answer me, so I asked again.

"I don't know. But don't say anything at school."

I had to stop by the office for a late pass before going to class. Mrs. Robinson asked if everything was all right, and I nodded. I knew the kids would all look at me once I entered class late, and the thought made me sick. Already it was hard for me to breathe, and my heartbeats only grew louder and harder inside my chest.

Sure enough, when I walked in, Mrs. Wallace was at the front of the classroom going over the week's spelling words, and all heads turned toward me. "Class, you've seen a late person before. Now turn around," she said. I gave her my late pass and went to my seat, where Melissa and Janet both turned to look at me.

While we worked on the spelling words, writing them out five times each, Mrs. Wallace called me to her. *Oh, my God, she's going to tell me in front of everyone how bad she feels about what happened to Dad and me.* If I could have run out of the room without causing another commotion, I would have.

Instead, she gave me a wax smile and asked, "What time did your mom come yesterday?" I didn't know what to say, especially since Janet, who I knew was listening, sat so close to the teacher's desk. If Janet found out, she would surely tell her dad, and the entire neighborhood would know. If only there were a fire drill to save me. "Amy?"

"My dad came, ma'am."

"When?" She was no longer smiling, and I knew that she was still upset about not getting home early the day before like the other teachers.

"At about three-thirty. He was very sorry that you waited so long with me."

"Did you tell your dad when school ends?" I nodded.

"Good. Now, do you have your math homework?" I shook my head.

"Why?" she asked.

I looked up and past her shoulder and saw that Janet was looking at Melissa. I knew that the glances they were giving each other were about me, and I hated it. Then I saw Brittany talking to a girl next to her, and for some reason I wished it were me they were talking about.

"Amy?" Mrs. Wallace asked. I turned away from the girls and stared at the floor. I didn't dare to face my teacher, because I was in trouble and she was an adult.

"Amy, I am talking to you. And look at me when I do. It is impolite not to look at the person who is talking to you." Each word she spoke hit me like a hammer.

At home, I was never allowed to look directly at my parents when I was in trouble. The one time my mom had slapped me was when I had looked into her eyes to tell her that I was sincerely sorry for having left my clothes on the bathroom floor. She said that I was challenging her. Now Mrs. Wallace was yelling at me for not looking at her. There were so many things I couldn't understand, and no one tried to make anything easy for me.

I did as she said. In my feeble voice I apologized, and heard the entire class laugh at me.

When it was lunchtime, I tried desperately to talk to Janet and Melissa, to act normal, to discredit Mrs. Wallace, and to eliminate any ideas that they might consider taking back to their parents.

"Janet, did you have fun yesterday?" I asked in the lunch line. She didn't reply but kept talking to Melissa.

I finally gave up. I wished I could bring lunch from home like Brittany and her friends. They didn't have to stand in line with a pink free lunch card, so for the entire thirty minutes, they sat and ate and talked and laughed.

As soon as the last bell of the day rang and Mrs. Wallace opened her door, I raced to the bus. When I got on it, I felt again as if I were floating between two worlds, one real and one fake. It was only twenty-four hours before that my world had started to change. It was only a day ago that I had stood outside waiting for my mom. Now I was on the bus finding a seat, as if it was supposed to be just another day. Yet I knew it wasn't, and I also knew that I would never have a regular day again.

I decided to take my last shot at talking to Janet and Melissa. When they got on the bus, I waved my arm to show them that I had found us an empty row in the back of the bus. Janet saw me but pushed Melissa into a front row. Some more kids got on, the big ones finding their way to the back. Two fifth graders sat with me, pushing me against the side of the bus.

I was surprised to find Janet and Melissa waiting for me when I stepped off the bus. The usual heat was finally enveloping us again, so they took off their jackets and tied them around their waists, and we walked down our road together.

"Why were you late, Amy?" Janet asked.

"Oh, my dad forgot to set the alarm." I knew telling lies was wrong, but I figured a tiny one wouldn't be so bad. They quickly glanced at each other and then playfully pushed me from side to side between the two of them. Maybe they didn't know anything after all.

During our dinner of rice and fried eggs the phone rang. "Hello, Mrs. Chea," I said. It was Melissa's mom.

"When did your mom leave?" she demanded. How did she know? And why was she so blunt about it—didn't she know that it would hurt less if the needle was smaller and sharper?

I should have been polite and answered her; instead, I hung up on her and sat back down to finish my dinner. Dad looked at me but didn't say anything.

Slowly he drank water from his glass and got up to call her back. "Sorry," he said, "Amy dropped the phone." He always had to be polite. Although I admired that trait in him, it infuriated me that he was his normal self that night. I wanted him to tell those nosy people that they were wrong to butt into our business. I wanted him to show them that it was their talking that had chased my mom away.

I went to watch TV and turned the volume high to block out their conversation. How could Dad so easily let someone like Mrs. Chea in on our problem and risk having her tell the entire community? Did he think they would care about us? I didn't. I was certain that the only thing they cared about was being right about my mom.

"Lower the volume," Dad called from the kitchen. I didn't. I decided he could do it himself if he wanted to. I hated him and I hated my mom and I hated everyone else, too.

After he hung up the phone he told me to wash the dishes. I stayed put on the couch and placed my finger on the remote control's volume button to turn it up even more, but at the last minute I didn't dare to.

"Amy!" he yelled.

I didn't answer him, and I could tell that he was about to yell at me again when the phone rang. Great, now the entire neighborhood was going to call.

At nine o'clock Mr. Yen came over with beer. I opened the door for him but didn't bother to greet him. He and Dad spent the rest of the night drinking, smoking, and chewing on dried squid at the kitchen table. I couldn't believe how rude he was. My mom had left us, and all he seemed to care about was pushing Dad into smoking. He knew my dad didn't smoke. But what I had an even harder time believing was that Dad was actually doing it.

I tried not to listen to their conversation, but it was hard not to. It was difficult to understand everything they were saying, so I turned the volume down a little when Mr. Yen began to talk about girls.

"Most of them are useless and a waste of time," he said. I smacked the remote control on the coffee table, but neither of them seemed to notice. Then I sat quietly. I'd always known how surly and disrespectful Mr. Yen was, but I didn't know until then how mean he was. It must have been hard to live with him, to hear him say that sort of thing every day. Poor Mrs. Yen and Janet.

After they quieted down from laughing, Mr. Yen's voice became more serious. "We all told you to be careful, didn't we? I care for you like a younger brother, Peera, and I told you not to marry someone like her, someone you didn't even know. You didn't listen, though."

"I know," Dad said resignedly. I felt so sad for him. He was a strong man; it was not part of who he was to give up like that.

Then more softly Mr. Yen said, "She wasn't all that bad. I expected her to be gone much sooner. Ten years. That's not bad. Others don't stay even that long. They come here, and everything is so new. They see the fast ways of the Americans. They want to try it, you know?"

Dad didn't answer him.

Mr. Yen went on. "Now look at you. You're stuck with a little daughter without a mother. For all you know, she might not even be yours. Maybe that wife of yours had another man before she came to America." Then in English he said, "Nothing's written in stone to show you otherwise." My heart stopped beating, and the seconds went by slowly as I waited to hear what Dad would say. All I could think was *Please, please*.

"No," Dad said slowly. "Amy's mine." I opened my mouth and gulped in as much air as I could.

"You can't be sure. You left that woman in Cambodia by herself for almost six months."

"You know that was because I had to come back to work. She would have come with me, but she had to wait for clearance before entering America."

Mr. Yen didn't give up. "It was bad news when she got here and was already pregnant."

"*Bong*," Dad said, calling Mr. Yen *big brother*. "I know that child is my daughter." His voice was firm and deliberate, and for once, Mr. Yen didn't have a comeback.

I had believed Dad without question when he said he was my real father. And now that Mr. Yen knew, the truth seemed somehow even truer. No matter what people might say or do to try to erase it, the truth would always be there, written in stone.

Several minutes later Mr. Yen chuckled and said in Cambodian, "Women are still useless." And Dad laughed with him.

4

WHEN THE REST of the community found out about Mom, everyone said "It was bound to happen sooner or later" and "She must be a truly heartless woman to abandon her only child." Then they shook their heads at me in sympathy, as if they were agreeing with *me* that my mom was cruel and horrible.

For the next couple of months, Dad and I remained the center of attention; nobody could stop talking about how unfortunate and wretched we were. Soon after that cold day in October, neighbors regularly visited our home, bringing warm stir-fried noodles or freshly wrapped spring rolls. They always brought enough so that we would have leftovers for breakfast. On Friday and Saturday nights, families would have us over to their homes, insisting that we needed at least a couple of "real" meals. A few of the women came over to wash our dishes and straighten the rest of the house, claiming that I was too young to be saddled with that responsibility.

"Amy, we are lucky to have people who care about us,"

Dad told me one night as I chewed the meat off a spare rib that a lady down the street had brought.

My feelings were different. I appreciated having delicious food and a clean bathroom, but after a while those luxuries weren't worth the gossip and the pity. People didn't sympathize with us because they understood but because it made them feel superior to us—their mission was to save the forsaken father and daughter. Only Mrs. Yen helped us because she cared. One difference between Dad and me was that it took him longer to see the real picture, to chip away the layers of gloss and see what truly lay beneath the paint. But when he finally saw what I saw and felt what I felt, it hit both of us in the face like a fastball.

In mid-December the Yens came over to celebrate my tenth birthday. After dinner, Mr. Yen handed me a twenty-dollar bill and asked what I was going to do with it. I still hated him, but I knew that if I gave the money back I would be in deep trouble. "Aren't you happy with the money? We remembered your birthday. Too bad your mom didn't." Then he patted my head.

"You didn't have to come, *Ohm*," I said. "I'm only a day older than I was yesterday." I gave him my sweetest smile and looked straight into his eyes, just long enough that only he saw me doing it. He knew I despised him and didn't want him there. I had a feeling that if no one else had been in the room with us, he would have smacked me.

Before they left Mr. Yen cleared his throat, and we turned to look at him. "Peera," he said, "throw a Christmas party."

"No, we have no women to do the cooking. Plus, we're not Americans. Christmas is for Jesus people, anyway," my dad said. We were Buddhists, although I didn't really know what that meant. Each time we attended service at temple, Mom said I had to be clean and have good thoughts. Mrs. Yen and most of the old people we knew attended service regularly, but Dad said that we didn't need to go to temple every day to know right from wrong. "That comes from here and here," he said, pointing to his head and heart. So most of the time we visited temple only on holidays or for someone's funeral. But I still knew the difference between hell and heaven well. If I helped a homeless person, I could go to heaven; if I didn't respect my parents, I could go to hell.

Mr. Yen persisted. "Who cares. I'll have my wife do the cooking."

"I don't know. We don't have extra money for something like that."

"That's no problem. I'll take care of it. You just need to relax. I'll worry about everything," Mr. Yen said.

The party was scheduled for Saturday, four days before Christmas. Mrs. Yen and a few of her friends came Friday night to start preparing the food. They went straight to the kitchen and laid old bedsheets and newspapers on the floor before sitting down Indian style to begin cutting up the meat and vegetables. We were going to have fried catfish with pineapple and tomato sauce, noodles in a fish broth I didn't like, lemongrass-seasoned beef skewers, stuffed chicken wings, and a roasted twelve-pound turkey for us kids, who were hoping for a real Christmas dinner.

Janet and I were responsible for dusting the television and the knickknacks around the living room and for staying out of the kitchen. The dusting was easy, but the other part was hard since we had nowhere to go. There had been a thunderstorm earlier in the day, making the ground too wet and cold to sit on, and Dad's room was now a storage area for our sofa and my bed. For most of the night, Janet and I stood against the kitchen doorway watching the ladies and once in a while bringing them a cup of water or handing them a knife.

They were so skilled. The sharp knife barely touched the cutting board as they sliced the London broil into thin strips and the lemongrass into rings.

"We're going to have a lot of food tomorrow," Janet said to me.

One old lady whom I had never met before pointed her butcher knife at us and said, "Good, you two girls stay put there and learn from us. Someday you'll need to do this so that it'll be my turn to sit back and do nothing."

"I'm never going to cook. I'm going to go to restaurants every night," Janet said in her broken Cambodian. She crossed her arms on her chest, and the woman snorted.

"Fine, as long as you have a boss as a husband." Then she turned to me. "What about you? Is this too good for you, too?" She pointed to their work area, which was filled with meat and vegetables and smelled like limes and oyster sauce.

I was about to answer her, but someone else beat me to it. "She's the one without a mother, the one I told you about." It was the young lady who had laughed at Mom at Janet's birthday party.

Then the old lady nodded and said, "She'll be lucky to grow up into a young lady and find herself a decent husband. I don't have much, but at least I have a husband."

"Amy just turned ten," Mrs. Yen said from the sink. "She'll have plenty of time to worry about that. First, she's going to college." She turned around and winked at me.

Janet whined, "So will I, Mother," and left.

I studied the old woman who didn't think I would have

much of a future. She had black teeth from chewing tobacco, and a bad perm that frizzed her hair. Her cheeks were hollowed and her fingernails were yellow. I didn't think she was lucky. In fact, none of these women were lucky. Even Mrs. Yen, who was the nicest person in the world, wasn't lucky. I didn't want to wake up each morning and put on the same uniform to go to work only to return home to a husband who would tell me to bring him beer. I wanted to wear a blouse and a jacket with a matching skirt that came to my knees and high heels. And panty hose. And I wanted a husband who would bring me something to drink.

All the adults sat in a circle on the living room carpet with food in the center for everyone to share, and we kids had our own small area in the corner. Everyone seemed to be having a good time. The women were talking and the babies were crying. The men were loud, screaming even though they were sitting right next to one another. Mr. Yen, as usual, was the loudest.

"See, Peera, didn't I tell you this was a good idea?" he asked. All the men agreed with him, raising their beer cans. But Mr. Yen didn't stop there. He looked at the circle and said, "You see, he told me that he didn't have the money to throw a party, so I told him that I would throw one for him."

I was so embarrassed I stopped eating. Everyone nodded, as if they *understood* that my dad and I were now so lost and poor that Mr. Yen had to save us. I had my dad to take care of me, so I certainly didn't want Mr. Yen's help. Then, to my amazement, Dad insisted, "You wanted the party."

"It's okay. Remember, your wife just left," *Phou* Ret said.

No one laughed, but I still thought they took pleasure in being right about Mom. Some of the men said they would never allow their women to run out on them. "Don't even think about it," they warned their wives, who sat across from them. Those wives rolled their eyes, and everyone except Dad and me found it funny. As their laughter subsided, I heard some of the women whisper to each other that some girls just forget their children; they just get up and go without thinking. As true as those words were, I didn't want to believe them. I refused to believe that my mom had forgotten about me.

Mr. Yen raised his right arm and signaled for everyone to quiet down. "You're crazy, Peera. If I wanted a party, I would have done it at my house."

I stood up to look at Dad and found that he was expressionless. I couldn't listen to any more of what these people had to say, so I pushed my way out of the living room and went into the bathroom. I pulled down my pants and sat on the toilet, forcing myself to go to the bathroom. I wanted to get rid of everything these people had brought into our home.

●

For the next several months Mr. Yen continued to visit us regularly, and we continued to eat at his home. The women, however, stopped bringing us food and cleaning up our house. So all the cleaning was my responsibility, while the cooking was Dad's. His food wasn't fancy at all; most nights we ate instant noodles or rice and sausage. Dad would joke about how kings and queens wished they could eat as well as we did, and we would laugh until it hurt.

Whenever Dad laughed like that with me, holding his

stomach with both hands, I thought that he and I could do it, could make it on our own. But the feeling never lasted. He would suddenly turn quiet again and not say another word for a long time, sometimes nothing all night. Or some evenings he would stay out with his friends and leave me by myself. I would then go to my parents' bed and lie on it, sniffing the air for any lingering scent.

One night I waited for Dad until ten o'clock. He had asked earlier if I wanted to go with him, but I didn't. I couldn't, day after day, listen to his friends' fake sympathies. "Dad," I asked softly when he returned, "why don't you stay home with me? Why do you always hang out with your friends? Don't you get mad when they make fun of us?"

"That's adult stuff," he said. "You just worry about being a kid."

I was a kid, but I didn't think that mattered when it came to understanding their jokes. Every time my dad was the butt of a joke, I was there with him, whether or not he felt the pain of the jokes with me.

One ripe summer evening we walked to the Yens'. I held Dad's right hand; in his left he held a large brown envelope, which I could hear rubbing against the side of his old khakis.

"What's that in your hand?" I asked him. He looked straight ahead without blinking. I turned my eyes to what he was looking at and saw a group of shirtless boys fighting to get hold of their single basketball. "Dad, what's that big envelope for?"

He glanced down at it. "Nothing. Just something I need to show Mr. Yen."

"What is it for? Is it important?"

"I'm tired of all of your questions," he said, and let go of my hand.

I was thinking about grabbing his hand again when a swarm of mosquitoes found us. When I stopped to scratch my ankles, Dad said, "Amy, you should wear pants."

"It's too hot."

"You're just lucky you're in America. If you were in Cambodia, you would have on a long sarong whether it was too hot or too cold. No girl could walk around in shorts."

"Well, we are in America, Dad."

"You're beginning to sound more and more like Janet. That little girl needs a whack or two." I thought Dad was beginning to sound like Mr. Yen.

Any other time I would have agreed with him that Janet needed manners, but I was too excited to see her that day because, surprisingly, I missed her. Since it was summer, I stayed home all day by myself and had no one to play with because both she and Melissa went to summer school for extra help in math.

Mrs. Yen opened the door and pulled me into her arms, calling me Daughter. "Janet's in her room. Maybe you can help her with her homework," she said.

I walked into the room Janet shared with Becky, her older sister. The room was hot and stale, and the only relief came from an old portable fan that whined and buzzed.

"Amy, come and look at the shirt in my new magazine," Janet said. She held up a page with a picture of a hot-pink halter top her dad would never allow her to wear. Becky told her to shut up.

"*You* shut up, Becky," Janet said. "Amy thinks I would look good in it."

Becky scrunched up her face. "You're so annoying, and no one said you'll look good in it. Where's your homework? You should be looking at that instead of those pictures. That's why you're going to summer school. You're stupid."

"Shut up!" Janet yelled, and threw the magazine at her sister. It hit the wall and slid beside the bed. From outside Mr. Yen told all of us to shut up, and Becky got up and left. I sat quietly on the edge of her bed.

"Hey, Amy, can you keep a secret?" whispered Janet, whose face was still flushed from screaming. I nodded.

"Are you sure? No one knows."

I crossed my heart.

"I have a boyfriend."

I blinked at her. This was worse than the halter top. "Who?" I asked. She told me it was Eric, a skinny Cambodian kid with big knees who didn't live very far from us. "Aren't you going to get in trouble?"

She gave me an "I know" look. "Yes," she said. "That's why it's a secret. Duh." She began to explain how it had all happened, and I wanted to pay attention. But I couldn't. I was too stunned by the fact that she trusted *me* with such important information.

Janet then pulled out a piece of paper that was folded in the shape of an envelope from her Girls Rule folder. She carefully unfolded the paper and showed me the big heart that she had drawn in red around the misspelled words *I Love Your*.

"Aren't you kind of too young?" I asked her.

"Amy, everyone has a boyfriend. You're too different, and you talk like you're my mom."

I was about to tell her what I meant when we heard loud voices from the living room. We couldn't make out the exact words, but Mr. Yen and Dad were yelling. Then we heard Mrs. Yen's soft voice and Mr. Yen telling her to go away.

Dad called for me. "Amy, come on, let's go home," he said. I was scared to move. Something told me that things would change if I moved.

Janet looked scared, too, as she sat motionless on her bed, staring at me. "I wonder if they're fighting because your mom hired a lawyer and everything to divorce your dad."

"What?"

"Honest. I heard my dad telling my mom," she said, and held up her right hand. But I didn't want her honesty. Who said she had the right to be honest at my expense?

"Come on, Amy," Dad said once more, and I hurried out of the room.

I found Mr. Yen standing at the doorway of the kitchen holding a Hennessy bottle in one hand and pointing at the front door with the other. "Go, you dumb fool, and don't ever come back. Who's stupid enough to go after a woman who doesn't even want him?" he yelled at Dad, and glanced at me. I would never forget those eyes—dark with intensity and shining with anger. They landed on me for only a second but sent chills down my arms.

Mrs. Yen, blocked by her husband, was running back and forth with a plastic bag in her hands. When Mr. Yen started toward us with his liquor bottle up in the air, she rushed in front of him, handed me the bag, and pushed me outside.

"Amy," she began, and just to hear her say my name made me cry. Something was wrong, for sure. "I'm sorry we didn't eat tonight, but there's fried rice in this bag for you and your dad. Don't cry, Daughter." She wiped my eyes. "I don't think I'll see you for a while, but if you ever need anything, I want you to come by. Mr. Yen isn't a bad man. He's a tiger on the outside but a mouse in the inside."

Tears flowed from my eyes by the gallons, and my body began to shake. Dad followed us and thanked Mrs. Yen. He took my hand, but I yanked it away. Then he grabbed my arm, and with my other arm still reaching out for Mrs. Yen, he dragged me from the only family we had left.

5

BEFORE WE HAD gone over to the Yens', the air had been still. Now the wind was howling, and the palm leaves above us were flapping madly against their skinny tree trunks. Fallen leaves swirled in a circle as if they were possessed by a spirit, and those still intact on the tree branches rustled against one another like the disks on a tambourine. As the tightness in my heart grew, I joined forces with the wind and leaves and cried louder for Mrs. Yen.

"Hush. People are watching," Dad said as he continued to pull me home.

I didn't want to hush. What did it matter, I thought. The same people he was worried about now had been watching us since long before that night; he was just slow to see it.

"Why didn't you tell me?" I cried.

"Amy, if you don't quiet down, I'll really give you something to cry about when we get home." His voice was like a freshly sharpened blade cutting into steel.

One of my flip-flops tore in half and eventually fell off, leaving my foot raw against the rough concrete sidewalk. At one point something cut into my heel, and even though it was nearing night I could see the tiny trail of blood I was leaving. But no matter how much it hurt to be yanked and scraped, I couldn't walk on my own and just leave behind any hope for a mother.

Dad and I finally got to the house, but I refused to go inside. "Do you see that!" he threatened me. He pointed to the oak tree that grew in front of our home; it was about half the size of the house, and in the summer it flourished beautifully. I wanted to answer him, but I didn't have the courage to show him that kind of blatant disrespect.

The neighborhood kids and I had many uses for our thriving oak tree. In the winter, when there were some bare branches, we would break off twigs and play pick-up sticks with them in the house. In spring when baby lemony-green leaves started to sprout, we would pluck them off the branches and cook them in our make-believe kitchen. And in the summer and fall, we would use it as a refuge from the heat or as home base in our hide-and-seek games.

But that night, Dad used the oak tree for something else.

Still pointing to the tree, Dad said, "I'm telling you for the last time to stop. And if you don't go in the house, I'll have something to show you."

My crying had turned into hiccups, and when I could I began screaming. Even though the screams scratched my throat and rang in my ears, it felt good to release them. Each one left me with a sense of power that I had never felt before.

"Amy, go inside," Dad ordered.

"No!" I yelled. I knew that since Mom had left, Dad and I had changed. But I would have never imagined us fighting in front of our house for just anyone to see. He remained quiet, his mouth tight, his eyes giving me no idea of what he was thinking. My throat ached, but I forced myself to continue screaming anyway. There were no words in particular, just shrills of anger and frustration. How could I be so unlucky in this world! No mom. No Mrs. Yen. I hadn't done anything to deserve this. I wanted someone—whoever was responsible—or anyone, for that matter—to just give me an explanation, please.

Dad left me at the door and walked over to the oak tree. Although he'd never done it before, I knew what he was planning. But I wasn't scared. The knowledge of what was going to happen actually brought me peace. I no longer wanted to hurt inside, so maybe a different type of pain would make the other kind go away.

"You need to be taught a lesson," Dad said, nodding in my direction and pointing a finger at me. "You don't listen anymore. You walk around here like you're the boss. You give me no respect. Just because you grew up here you think you're American, doing whatever you want. Not caring if you bring me shame. Kids in Cambodia don't do this. They don't talk back and look at their parents as if they were nothing." He was tramping around the oak, in one direction and then another, with his arms up in the air.

Dad snapped off a thin branch about three feet long and shucked off the leaves. I stopped screaming. Just like that, I lost my inner power and didn't even care.

Instead, I focused on something larger, more powerful. I asked God not for help but for answers. There must be a reason why in less than a year, my world had changed so much, why my mom had left me, why my dad was about to punish me, why I was so alone. If no one was going to tell me, couldn't he? *You have the answer, don't you?* I asked, looking up—where he was supposed to be. But by the time I searched for him night had taken over. And when I turned my eyes back down from heaven, it was just me and Dad.

Dad pushed me inside the house and slammed the door. He ran his hand down his cheek. "Amy, I'm going to just say this once: take off your shirt and lie flat."

I did as he said, quietly lying down and parallel to the coffee table. I shut my eyes, and I again remembered the night I'd overheard Mom and Dad arguing in their room. I hadn't thought much of it at the time; it was one of those things you hear people say and hope they didn't mean—no matter how earth-shattering it may be. Mom loved me, and I didn't want to believe she would actually leave us, even if she wasn't happy. Dad told her that we'd been a family for ten years, and those ten years were so long to me. They were the years of my life. I held back my tears as I realized that those years didn't matter to her, not even one.

I could hear Dad's breathing, and my head, which had been swirling with their voices, began to clear. As I looked inside myself all I saw were clouds, and I was lost in a place without hurt or love, a place that reminded me of the time Janet and I had competed to see who could withstand holding an ice cube to her cheek longer. At first, the cold from the ice cube stung my cheek, but soon there was only numbness.

The numbness now felt so good that I could feel the center of my being rising and floating. I saw my naked back and the cut on my heel, the blood from it smeared all over my calf and foot. And I saw Dad standing above me, the thin branch in his hand. He looked tired, and in pain. His shoulders drooped, and his face was dark and lonely. At that moment I was not mad at him; I only felt sorry that I hadn't been a better daughter.

Ever since that October day I had been thinking only of

myself. Not once had I thought about Dad or the hurt he was going through. Lying flat now, I knew I didn't deserve what he was about to give me, but I also knew that he needed to deliver it—if not for me, then for himself.

I don't know when I stopped crying that night. When I woke up the next morning it hurt to open my eyes, and my body ached as I shifted in bed and tried to pull the worn sheet off me. I felt the sun coming through the window and saw tiny red veins in my shut eyelids. The house was hot, the air was still, and the sweat that collected around my neck and on my back made my skin itch and burn. The memory of the night before weighed upon me like a huge rock.

I heard Dad in the kitchen opening and closing the refrigerator door. I smelled the once-so-familiar Chinese sausages, heard them sizzling in the oven. I wanted so badly to get up and pee, but I didn't want to risk having to talk to him. I knew what he had done to me was important to him, and I was almost happy for him. But at the same time, I was embarrassed for him and for myself.

"Amy, it's noon. I made porridge and sausages." His voice was soft and cheery. I squeezed my eyes tighter. "Amy, get up and wash up so you can eat. I'm hungry." I would have turned to the wall if my back hadn't hurt so much.

"Amy?" I felt his breath on my cheek, and he smelled like Head & Shoulders. "Amy, I know you're not sleeping. Sit up. I brought you breakfast." He put one hand behind my neck and the other underneath my legs before moving me up in bed. I cringed as he moved me.

When I gave up and opened my eyes, I was surprised to see Dad's eyes twinkling as he sat before me. He took my pillow and fluffed it before putting it behind me. Then he moved the fan to the foot of my bed, and the cool air slowly cleared my head.

"I'm going to feed you just like when you were a baby, Amy. Remember? Open up." Even though the previous night was over and done with, I was determined not to eat, and I was now ready to make him feel bad for what he had done. But my stomach betrayed me. I did as he said, and although the rice porridge was still too hot, my insides welcomed the food.

Dad had a lot to say that morning. I only started listening, though, when I heard about my own room. "I think you and I should move. Maybe California. I heard that there are a lot of opportunities there. We need to get away from here and start fresh. You know what I mean? Isn't it a good idea? You can live in a nice house with your own room. I should have given you mine. That's right, my daughter's going to have her own room *and* pretty clothes to wear to school every day. What do you think, Amy, just you and me in a brand-new place?" I didn't know what to say.

After breakfast Dad took me to the bathroom and made a bubble bath using dish detergent. "Don't take too long. We're going for ice cream down at the beach." He bent down and took off the bandage that he must have put on my heel the night before.

When he left I undressed and climbed onto the counter and strained my eyes to see my back in the mirror. It hurt, but I had to see. There were ten thin, soft pink slashes.

The bubbles didn't last long, but I stayed in the bath anyway. It was cool to my back and legs. Dad hadn't apologized for what he had done, and I didn't expect him to, even though he was sorry. For Cambodians, apologizing is a huge deal. Children, because they are young and subservient, are expected to say "I am sorry" in English for minor things and in Cambodian for everything else. Parents, however, rarely leave their superior positions, even if they hurt a child's feelings. Even with one another, I'd never heard adults say "sorry" in Cambodian. Once in a while they might say something like "Sorry I knocked over your drink" in English. As they said those words, they would wave their hands gently in the air to show that it was a trifling matter, but what the heck. Because I was a Cambodian, I accepted that fact and forgave my dad for hitting me. He made me breakfast and a bath, and he was going to take me for ice cream; that was the best apology he could give me.

Dad was ready to move on, and so was I. I thought of the bedroom he promised me. For as long as I could remember, I'd slept in the living room, where my bed was out for everyone to see. I couldn't keep the sheets neat and pretty because someone always ended up sitting on my bed, or lying on it, without permission. Soon, though, that would be over. I would have my own space, something I didn't have to share. But did it have to be so far away? California was on the other side of the country. Couldn't Dad find a place closer to St. Pete so that if we needed help, we could call on Mrs. Yen? I grew cold in the bath, and shivered at the thought of being even more alone.

●

Once Dad was set on moving he decided we should sell everything except the Olds because we would need it to take us across the country.

"How long is the ride to California?" I asked him.

"Not that long. We'll have fun driving." His manner had become calm and easy again, like when Mom had been living with us. He even moved differently, as if he were gliding from one place to another. Seeing him like this, I was optimistic about our future.

"I know, but how long do we have to be in the car?"

"Maybe four or five days."

"Can't we take an airplane?"

"That costs too much. We need to save up as much as we can. Once we get to Gali it'll be just you and me." Like many Cambodians, he called California Gali, with a hard *G* and an accent on the second syllable. I always thought they'd come up with the nickname because the whole word was too long for them to pronounce. "There'll be no one there to help us," he continued. *Considering everything that has happened in St. Pete, maybe that won't be such a bad thing,* I thought.

Dad and I hadn't been invited to anyone's home for parties or visits since his fight with Mr. Yen. For the Fourth of July, as neighbors gathered and barbecued, we ate Kentucky Fried Chicken and drank Coke, my mouth watering all the while at the smells coming from their homes.

Dad spent most of his free time at home watching TV. Initially, after the fight, I continued to play with the kids outside. In fact, I rose to a great popularity among the boys, who were fascinated with the whipping that Dad had given me.

"Did you get whipped bad?" one kid asked me.

"No," I answered.

"Did you bleed?"

"No."

"Did he chain you up?"

"No."

"Did he throw you across the room?"

"No."

"What did he do, then?"

I shrugged.

Disappointed, they walked off. I continued to get those

questions. My answers never changed, so after a while the boys left and never returned.

Even with Janet and Melissa, I received a certain respect that was new to me. We no longer had to play what Janet wanted to play. If I didn't want to run around and instead wanted to play Mother, May I? and be the mother, then that's what we did. It was wonderful to have things done my way, and I started feeling sad about the move to California. I had visions of the three of us spending time together at school once fall came around. Several years later, though, I learned that all great empires collapse. Mine only lasted for two weeks.

One day we were down the street near Melissa's home. "Come on. I'm thirsty," she said, and Janet and I followed her upstairs to her apartment. Mrs. Chea was straightening their living room.

"Janet, what's your mom doing today?" Mrs. Chea asked, looking up from picking scraps off the carpet.

"Probably just sewing," Janet answered.

"It's already one o'clock. Aren't you girls ready for lunch?"

"Yes, yes, yes, Mom, please," Melissa squealed.

"Fine. Finish what I was doing while I make you sandwiches." And she walked off.

The three of us went on our knees and started working immediately, picking up as many scraps as we could with one hand and holding them in our other, cupped hand. We picked up anything from sewing thread to rice crumbs. Janet found a quarter under the couch, but Melissa said it was hers since it was her apartment.

I didn't care whom it belonged to; I was more interested in how the sandwich was going to taste. I already knew it wasn't going to be something simple like a PB&J. Mrs. Chea was known to make the best French hoagie, stuffed with roast marinated pork, pickled carrot slices, and cilantro. The thought of the combination of salty meat and tart carrots weakened my knees.

Mrs. Chea called from the kitchen, "Go wash your hands. The food's ready."

We three scrambled to the tiny bathroom. We spread out like a fan, with Janet standing on the toilet, me on the bathtub, and Melissa right in front of the sink. We gently pushed each other side to side with our hips, fighting for the water and the Ivory bar, giggling all the while. Then we dried our hands on our T-shirts and shorts.

"You go first, I have to go to the bathroom," I told them.

They were at the round kitchen table wedged in the corner between the refrigerator and the oven when I came out. Janet and Melissa each had a plate with a sandwich and a glass of water. The aroma didn't disappoint me at all, but I didn't see a third sandwich, not on the table or on the counter.

I said, "Hey."

Since their mouths were full, they only gave me a small wave. I wondered if Mrs. Chea had saved the third sandwich in the oven . . . or even in the fridge. But I couldn't just start opening their things. Could I? Maybe it was in the living room. But I didn't find anything in there, either, except for Mrs. Chea, who, by then, was watching a Cambodian movie. I stood in the archway for a couple of seconds just in case she saw me and asked, "Amy, why aren't you eating?" And I would then gently say, "I don't know where you put my plate, *Meing.*" But she didn't say anything, so I went back to the kitchen table. I figured that if I stood at the table and

Melissa saw that I wasn't eating, she'd tell me where my sandwich was. So I rested my stomach against the table, smelling the pickled carrots that churned my stomach into agony.

After five minutes of standing, I said, "Well, I have to go now."

"Bye," Janet said with her mouth full.

Before I closed their front door I also said good-bye to Mrs. Chea, but she didn't respond.

When I stopped playing outside in the following days, Janet and Melissa knocked on my door. They wanted to know what I had been doing inside. "It's too hot outside," I said, and closed the door on them. They would never understand the truth: I no longer needed them as friends when I felt so bad with them around.

Other than that quick visit from Janet and Melissa, no one really came to our place, not until we had the yard sale in late July. One Friday night I made three YARD SALE signs. On them I colored red balloons and purple streamers with markers. We'd never had a sale before, but I'd been to so many with Mom that I knew what needed to be done.

"Dad, these signs will need to go at the right places or we won't get anyone to come."

"Sure, boss," he said, and saluted me.

I woke up very early the next morning and helped Dad move small items out onto two big sheets we had thrown over the small yard. We took out Mom's clothes, some kitchen things, and some tools, and carefully laid them out in different sections: WOMEN'S CLOTHES, KITCHEN, TOYS. I found Dad's Bible, which was a gift from his sponsors, and his Cambodian/English dictionary, both of which he told me to put in the fifty-cent box. While I was outside straightening things, he went back inside to polish the furniture that was also for sale and then prepped the Olds for the long drive ahead of us. I was still tagging the items when our first customer, a Cambodian lady who lived on the next block, came by around eight-thirty.

"How much does your dad want for this?" she asked, pointing to my mom's dresses.

"They're each three dollars, *Ohm*."

"For this? You are joking." She held up a yellow one with green flowers that my mom had worn to a wedding. She picked up each dress with two fingers as if the garments were dirty, and after looking at them, dropped them in a heap. I didn't want this lady or any other lady to have my mom's clothes.

"Where's your Dad? Tell him I'll give him a dollar for each dress."

"He's not here," I fibbed. After Dad had finished moving the for-sale items outside and working on the car, he remained in the house, sitting in a corner, with his knees pulled up to his chest. When I went in to check on him, he told me to leave him alone. I felt sorry for him, sitting in the middle of an empty room in what used to be our home.

The old lady went to the kitchen section next. "How much for the pot?" I pointed to the sticker that said $1.50. She opened her purse, pulled out a dollar bill, and dropped it before walking off with the pot.

I went to my mom's dresses, refolded them, and changed all the stickers to $7.00. No one would pay that much for them, so they were safe.

By midday I told Dad that almost everything was sold.

"You mean stolen." He was mad that he got only half price for everything. "And why did you make your mom's things so expensive? They're still here. We can't keep any of those. There's no room in the car for them. We need as much money as we can get," he grumbled. He didn't understand that those who had asked about her things didn't deserve them.

An American lady walked up later in the day. She had two girls with her, probably her daughters. All three were bony and had oily hair. The mean kids at school would have called them scrawny.

"Hi," I said.

They each smiled and said hi back. The mother held up a dress against the taller of the two girls. "What do you think?" The girl nodded and said it was pretty.

"How much do you want for this?" she asked me.

"Uh, it's seven dollars."

"That's kind of expensive for a yard sale, don't you think? How much do you want for all of these?" She pointed to everything in Mom's section.

I knew Dad was right. We couldn't take these things with us. And if I didn't sell them to this lady and her daughters, then surely one of the Cambodian ladies would have them at the end of the day. "I'll ask my dad."

He came out and told her that she could have everything, including the shoes and belts, for twenty dollars. She handed him the money, and I gladly put all the items in bags for her. I was waiting for her to ask whom everything had belonged to. Because if she did, I would say, "My mom, but she doesn't live with us anymore." And for the first time I felt as if I wouldn't cry saying it.

By six that evening, nothing was left except for knick-knacks, which we ended up throwing away, and my dresser.

"I can't believe no one wants to buy this," Dad said, running his hand over it. I hardly heard him speak as he slid his hands over the surface of the dresser.

"Dad, that's because there are no handles. And the second drawer has no bottom, see?" I pulled it out to show him.

"I guess I'll take it out for the garbage man. Be sure you pack everything. Once we leave tomorrow, we're not returning, not for anything."

"We don't have anything we can't leave behind," I said, trying to be funny. But he didn't get the joke and walked away.

As he took out the dresser, Mrs. Yen and Janet walked up to the door. Since the incident at their home, I hadn't gotten to see Mrs. Yen except for brief moments when the Yens visited the neighbors next door. Once in a while Dad and I had found dinner left in front of our door, and we knew it was from her. One time I had found a yellow shirt-and-shorts set.

I rushed to the door. "Hi, *Ohm*."

"I packed up some food for your travel tomorrow, Peera," she said. "There are beef jerky and pickled vegetables. They should be okay for a day or two, at least." Dad took the packages and gave them to me. "We can't stay long. I have to start on dinner in a little bit. You know how my husband likes to have a big meal on Saturdays." She started to smile but quickly added, "Make sure you drive out early tomorrow while it's still cool."

"Come inside," Dad said. All four of us moved inside and sat on the brown and tan carpet.

"You and Amy had a nice place here, Peera," Mrs. Yen said, looking around the bare walls, which had holes from where we had hung pictures.

Janet and I moved over to a corner and played tic-tac-toe. We spread ourselves out and lay on our stomachs.

"So, you know what school you're going to?" Janet asked.

"No, we don't even know where we're going to live."

She shrugged and gave a loud sigh before telling me about the new boy she had fallen in love with.

"I hate it when he acts like a kid," she said.

"That's because he is one, Janet."

"Oh, you don't know anything." But I didn't let that bother me. Actually, I was sorry for her because she was the one who didn't know anything.

Soon it was time for them to go. Janet and I stood up and looked at each other, and in her face, I read what I was feeling. I didn't want her to go. When would I see her again? I completely forgot about all the times she had ignored me and hurt me. For that minute, she was my best friend, and I would never have another one like her.

"Well, at least you won't have to see your *favorite* teacher, Mrs. Wallace, next year," she said sarcastically.

"No, but I also won't see Mrs. Robinson, and I never told her good-bye. Will you tell her for me?"

"Yeah."

We all walked to the door. "Amy, be good like you've always been and listen to your dad. And remember me," Mrs. Yen whispered in my ear as she bent down to kiss me and stick something in my pocket. She didn't have to tell me that. I would never forget that she called me her daughter, that she loved me, and that she thought I was smart. She took Janet's hand, and they walked out past our yard and then down the sidewalk. I put my hand in my pocket and felt the gift she had given me. I didn't have to look at it to know it was money.

It was past dinnertime, and the street was quiet as we watched Mrs. Yen and Janet walk to the corner and then turn. I was glad that we were leaving in the morning. And I was gladder that I didn't have to see the neighbors before leaving. Dad would have told me to be polite and give my farewell to them, but they didn't deserve anything from me. I was relieved not to ever have to see them again. But then my thoughts went back to Mrs. Yen; I would never see her, either, not unless we met somewhere far away from St. Petersburg. But that wouldn't be anytime soon. I decided to tuck her asleep in a corner of my heart, and every time I needed love, I would wake her up with a thought.

"Good-bye, Mrs. Yen. I'll miss you," I hollered to her, knowing she was too far away to hear me.

BEFORE WE STARTED out I promised Dad I would stay awake in the car so he wouldn't fall asleep at the wheel. When he said I wouldn't last for more than five minutes, I should have believed him. As I climbed into the Olds, the neighborhood was just waking up, too—the ground was damp and a mustard yellow sky hung over our yard, the houses across the street, and the road we turned onto. How appropriate that everything before me was just a hazy picture. Each time I closed my eyes, Dad would ask, "Don't you want to see Florida before we leave it?" I didn't. Not because I was tired and couldn't keep my eyes open, but because I wanted that hazy picture to fade to white like a photograph that had been put in the washing machine by mistake.

When I finally woke up we were driving on a long stretch of road with tall, skinny trees on both sides. Once in a while I saw black and white cows lazily grazing the flat green fields beyond the trees. Sometimes there was a tree or two, similar to the ones I had drawn in kindergarten, with thick brown trunks and big, round green tops, standing out like islands in the wide fields.

Not long after we stopped for lunch, I saw a sign for Al-abama. Dad said we were only a hundred miles away from it. It seemed unnatural for me to look forward to being far away from home. Wasn't home the place that you wanted to come back to? I got on my knees and looked out the rearview window as Dad played his Cambodian cassette. All I saw were gray roads that stretched off to the horizon. I felt as if the world were not round but flat, and my past had just fallen off somewhere along the way.

"Sit right, Amy. I don't want to get a ticket."

"We're actually leaving St. Pete." I said it more to myself than to him. There was a hollow in my stomach, and suddenly I wanted to tell him to go back to St. Petersburg because this trip without Mom was all wrong. I wanted to go back to my house. Back to a place that I knew, a place that knew me.

"Good," Dad said simply. "I knew the trip would be easy."

I sat back down and looked at him, waiting for him to turn to me for at least half a second so that I could look into his eyes. But he kept them steady on the road. The hollow within me grew larger as I realized that even he wasn't sure about this journey.

●

Four days later we still hadn't reached California. I was dirty, sour-smelling, and itchy from layers of unwashed sweat. More than anything, I wanted to take a shower and wash myself all over with soap. Or soak myself in a big tub of ice cubes. Everything about the trip had been hot; the only relief we ever got was at night, when we rolled down the windows to let the soft wind brush the sides of our faces. The days felt as if we were in a rice cooker. Heat came from every direction. Rolling the windows down during the day meant feeling the sun slowly cooking our faces, necks, arms, and legs. But with the windows up, it meant we were cooking from the inside, ready to explode at any moment.

"Dad, please let me turn on the AC," I would beg.

"You go ahead and turn it on if you don't care about the car breaking down *again*," he would answer.

Several times the Olds started overheating when the AC was on, and at one time we had to pull over to the shoulder. That wasn't pleasant, either. While the car cooled down, we waited outside, watching the other cars whiz by and breathing their exhaust. After that Dad told me I couldn't turn on the AC anymore; so we rode on quietly, certain that every spoken word or gentle movement only made the unbearable even more so.

The best parts of the ride were when we stopped for gas. I would go directly to the bathroom, praying that no one was in line. If there were people, I would let them go ahead of me. Some, mainly mothers with babies on their hips, thanked me, praising how wonderful and thoughtful I was. They didn't know that I had my own reason for doing what I did.

Once in the air-conditioned bathroom, I would flush the toilet twice, place three layers of paper towel all around the seat, and sit down. The coolness around my neck and my bottom felt delicious, like sucking on a lemon-flavored ice cube that never lost its taste. If I could, I would have closed my eyes and slept. I thought to myself that if I could sleep for just one hour, stretched out on any soft, flat surface and without having to wake up every five minutes because of the torturing heat, I would be happy.

Since we'd left Florida, we'd slept in a motel off the highway only on the first night. Because the floor was grimy and there was no toilet paper, Dad didn't think it was worth the money. So for the second and third nights, we slept in the car, which he said was safe since we parked in well-lit gas stations. While Dad snored, I woke up every time a semi roared down the highway, sure that one was going to hit us.

Now, with only one day to go, I looked at the car clock every five minutes. When the sun finally reached its highest intensity, Dad exited and pulled into a gas station. I left the car and took the money he handed me to give to the cashier. "Don't take too long," I heard him say as I ran for the cool air.

"For number four." I gave the man the money and pointed to our car outside.

I walked to the bathroom in the back of the store. As my body began to relax on the toilet, I realized that soon we would be in California. Once we got there, we'd never go back. We knew no one there. . . . What if we needed help?

"Amy?" It was Dad knocking on the bathroom door.

"I'm coming."

"Are you okay?"

"Yeah."

"Hurry up. I want to reach Las Vegas before it gets dark." He was eating a hot dog when I opened the door. The sight of it made me sick. We'd been eating hot dogs and burgers ever since we finished the beef jerky and pickled vegetables. The smell of ketchup and mustard was beginning to nauseate me.

"Are you sure you're okay? You've been spending a lot of time in the bathroom lately." I nodded. "Don't you want something to eat?"

"No," I mumbled, and headed back to the Olds.

As Dad drove, I looked at our map. "Didn't you say that we're going to San Diego?" I asked. He nodded. "Then why are we going to Las Vegas?" He stared straight ahead and didn't answer me. "Dad, why are we going to Las Vegas?"

"Amy, I don't have to answer you."

I thought his answer sounded like something Mr. Yen would say. On an ordinary day I wouldn't have dared to talk back, but on that day I couldn't help it. Maybe it was the heat. "Las Vegas is out of the way. I want to go to our new house. I want to sleep on a real bed and I want to take a shower. And I'm hungry." I didn't know why, but I just wanted to cry and pound my fists on something. Even more, I wanted to roll down my window, stick my head out, and yell.

Dad turned on the radio.

"I'm hungry," I said again, under my breath.

"I asked if you wanted something to eat." This time it wasn't what he said but how he said it. And I knew not to complain anymore.

In a softer tone, Dad suggested that I read my new book. "I paid full price for it," he said. He hadn't; we had found it on the hood of our car when we left the motel. I knew he was trying to be funny, but I didn't find it amusing. I had taken out *Where the Red Fern Grows* several times during the trip, running my hand over the new cover. It was a brand-new book, something I'd never owned before. Initially I was eager to start on it, but as the ride grew to be endless, I no longer cared about it. And by the time Dad had made his joke, all I wanted to do was yell, or cry, or both.

●

Just as Dad wanted, we arrived in Las Vegas before the sun set. The city was nothing like St. Pete. In every direction bright lights were blinking, infusing the air around us with an urgency to move on, go forward, don't look back. The people crossing the streets didn't even bother to look both ways for cars.

"Look at everyone, Dad. Is today a holiday?"

"Nope, it's always like this in Las Vegas."

"You've been here before?"

"A long time ago on a trip . . . before you were born."

Traffic was horrible, some cars turning on red lights, others stopping in intersections, and pedestrians crossing the streets when there were DON'T WALK signs blinking. But it was exciting, too. As the evening grew darker, lights on buildings and poles burned more brightly, as if each of them had just been polished.

We stopped at a red light. "Do you want to stay here tonight?" Dad asked me.

"Are you joking?" I turned away from the window and the people to look at him. He wasn't joking, and I jumped up and down in my seat. "Can we afford to stay in Las Vegas, though?"

"I think so. We deserve something for sleeping in the car for two nights, don't you think?"

"Yes!" I clapped my hands. He looked at me with a huge smile and pinched my cheek. For sure, California wasn't a bad idea after all.

We drove to the Red Falcon. The hotel was packed even though it was only Wednesday. It was big and grand, like something I would see on TV. Some visitors had bellmen rolling their luggage in, and the workers wore suits with either a matching tie or scarf.

While we waited in line to check in, Dad pulled me close to him. "You're happy?" he asked. I nodded with big eyes and gave him a quick kiss. It was good to see him relaxed. "Amy, that over there is a casino," he said, pointing to an area with machines that people sat at, "and casinos have one bad thing in them. If you learn only one thing from me, learn that gambling is a bad, bad thing." I asked him what people did at casinos.

"They play cards for money, which is really bad." I didn't understand what the big deal was. Back at home, Dad and his friends sometimes played cards for money. He himself had even told me that in Cambodia it was a tradition for people, including kids, to play games for money on special holidays.

"Okay," I said.

"I mean it. You learned in school that drinking is bad, right?" I nodded again. "Well, gambling is ten times worse."

I knew I had to say something worthwhile so that he would stop talking about it. "I promise to never gamble, Dad," I said, even though I still didn't really know what the word meant.

When Dad signed for our room, the lady at the counter asked if he wanted coupons for the dinner buffet. Dad purchased two of them, and we walked to the elevators.

We waited to get in the one that had glass on three sides. As we walked in, more people joined us. They briefly looked at me and turned the other way. I wondered if we smelled.

Our room had two queen-size beds and comforters with maroon and purple flowers. I immediately ran to the one closer to the window and rolled on it.

"Look at how new everything is. Even the furniture is glossy," I said to Dad, who took off his shoes and stretched out on his bed. He combed his fingers through his hair and yawned.

I left him alone and headed for the bathroom. On the way I ran my hand along the shiny wood dresser and looked at the tips of my fingers. Not a speck of dust.

The bathroom, too, was clean, with white tiles and white towels. Next to the sink was a small basket of lotion bottles. It was difficult for me to decide what to do first: sleep or shower? But I remembered my mom telling me that it was always important, especially for girls, to go to bed clean, so I opted for a cool shower while Dad chose to nap.

I washed myself everywhere, including under my nails, behind my ears, and in all of my private places. I couldn't believe how many pounds of dirt and sweat I washed off. When I got out of the shower it was as if the whole world were just a little bit lighter. I wrapped an oversized towel around my body and began to comb my hair. Since Mom had left, I had not gotten a haircut. Looking into the fogged-up wall-size mirror, I saw that my hair hung thickly past my shoulders, almost like Mom's. I would have to get it cut soon, I thought. I wiped the steam off the mirror and studied myself closely, not sure whether I liked what I saw. How I was cute to some people, I didn't know. Maybe they were actually expressing sympathy and I mistook it as a compliment.

To get to dinner, Dad and I walked through rows and rows of card tables and slot machines that rang loudly and shone brightly with pictures of cherries and flying monkeys. Once, we saw a man jump up from his seat. The red light-bulb on top of his machine went off like a siren. Dad said he had just won a lot of money. Many people came over to the man and congratulated him. A couple of times Dad stood in the aisle watching card players until I nudged him to keep moving. At the center of the hotel was an indoor garden of red pepper plants, violets, small rose trees, and white gardenias. I wanted to pick a flower and keep it as a souvenir, but Dad said that if I did we would get kicked out. I believed him and took his hand as we strolled over to the other end of the garden, where the restaurant was, and waited in line for a table.

At first the wait wasn't so bad as I took in every magnificent sight. Huge paintings of flowers in gold frames hung on the walls, and chandeliers with glass pieces resembling diamonds hung from the ceiling. The heavy braided-metal chairs and the large cream and coral tiles that covered the floor were also impressive. Each table was occupied, some people eating and some getting up and sitting down every five minutes with a new plate. As we waited in line for our turn, my stomach growled, and I would have paid anything to be in those people's shoes.

At last the hostess took us to our table. Dad and I didn't bother to sit down but walked right to the buffet, which overwhelmed me. I thought that if we didn't hurry I wouldn't have enough time to eat everything or that someone might eat it all. I hadn't eaten a good hot meal since we left home.

The spread of this buffet was about a hundred times bigger than the ones I'd been to in St. Petersburg. There were burgers, spaghetti, ham, salad, and even a small Chinese food area. I decided that I wanted a little bit of everything. On the initial trip, Dad helped me pile my plate with mashed potatoes and corn, roast beef, noodles, and a taco. But he took his time, looking over the different dishes when all I wanted was for him to give me what he was looking at. My legs itched to go ahead on my own. It was my dumb luck that I needed his help to scoop up the food.

To my great relief, Dad and I finally sat down with our plates and drinks. As I began eating, I noticed that the food was not as delicious as I had anticipated. I couldn't believe that a taco with extra sour cream and guacamole could be so tasteless.

"You have to eat more." Dad pointed to the leftovers in front of me.

"It's not good."

"Well, you shouldn't have asked me to get you all that." I knew he was right, but how could I have known that I wouldn't like it? After a while of watching me try to finish the food, he finally told me I could get some dessert.

When I came back, Dad said, "I'm taking you upstairs after dinner."

"Why? I thought we were going to walk around." I had brought a slice of carrot cake and a slice of chocolate cake with me; I had planned to give Dad one but changed my mind. He would have to get his own. He said again that I shouldn't be so careless about taking food and not finishing it.

"Dad, if I had known it wasn't good I wouldn't have taken it in the first place."

"Don't be disrespectful, Amy." Lately, when I offered him explanations, he took them as a sign of disrespect. And when I tried to explain that I wasn't disrespectful, he said I was talking back. I gave up and asked him again about walking outside.

"We'll do that tomorrow before we leave. I have something I need to do tonight."

"What?" A bite of the carrot cake was stuck to the roof of my mouth, and I was trying to scrape it off with my finger.

"Nothing." His eyes glistened, and I heard an urgency in his voice. I knew something was wrong.

"Is everything okay?" I asked. I was prepared for him to tell me that we had another problem. The car had been stolen, he had lost his money, or we had to be on the road for another four days. He nodded, but I was still uncertain. I figured that we'd come too far together for him to leave me out of the plan now.

"I'm going to play some cards." He didn't look at me but at the family seated at the table across from us. It was a family of four, and the mother was wiping her son's face.

I thought about what he had told me earlier in the hotel lobby. "You're going gambling?"

"Yep."

"But you told me that's bad."

"It is," he said, "but not always."

"Can I come, then?"

"No."

"Why?"

"Because it's not good for you. Plus, you're too young. The hotel won't let you come with me."

I hadn't thought about being left by myself, and the idea of it frightened me a little. I was in a new place in a new town. What would I do if I needed help? "Aren't you going to get in trouble for leaving me alone?"

"Amy, the hotel will only know if we tell them." He said it as if I should have known.

I was silent for a while, still not comfortable. Florida had been our home, so we could do whatever we wanted. But here, couldn't the hotel call the police and put Dad away if they found out? I had learned in school that a kid had to be twelve to stay home alone. If people saw him leave me in the room alone, what would happen to me, to us?

"I won't be gone for long . . . one hour at the most," he

said, and pinched my nose. The touch of his fingers made me giggle.

Before Dad left me that night, he showed me how to change the television channels and then kissed me all over my face for luck, stopping only after I begged for mercy. He gave me his wallet to hold and made me promise not to give it back until we left Las Vegas. "Don't you want to take it with you?" I asked.

"No, and remember, if I ask for it, you are not to give it to me, for any reason." It was a strange instruction, but I didn't think too much of it. "We're going to be rich, Amy. Get ready for it because I feel lucky," he said, rubbing his palms together.

When Dad was gone the room was quiet, except for the air conditioner and the quick footsteps out in the hall. The drapes were dark and heavy-looking, like something out of a scary movie. I waited for something to crawl out from under the bed or out of the drawers. Although everything in the room was much more expensive than what we had owned in St. Petersburg, it was nothing like home. At that moment, I wouldn't have minded listening to Janet's bossing me around or to Mr. Yen's making fun of us.

I grabbed the remote control and turned up the volume to relieve the silence. I couldn't believe how many channels there were, and each was so clear. Cartoons, news, sports, and a couple of channels that said *For Adults Only*. But my mind was easily made up once I landed on MTV. We didn't have cable at home, so I'd only watched MTV at Janet's. When her parents weren't around, she would stand in front of the TV and try to dance like the girls in the videos, shaking her hips and moving her hands up and down the sides of her body. She'd ask me to dance with her, but I would always say no, choosing to slouch on the couch. In front of other people, I never trusted my body to move the way it was supposed to.

Like Janet, I liked dancing, but only when I was alone. About a year before Mom left, I was in my parents' room and turned on their radio. I took Mom's hairbrush and sang into it as if it were a microphone. Not knowing all the words to the song, I mumbled a lot. As the song continued, I jumped on their bed and pretended that I was onstage, performing for the entire world to see. Later that evening during dinner, Mom cleared her throat and announced to Dad that if he didn't watch me closely, I would turn into a no-good, nonsense girl. I didn't know what she was talking about until Dad prohibited me from singing and dancing, and for a short time he even didn't let me listen to American music. I wasn't sure how Mom had found out about my performance, but I wasn't mad at her, thinking that she was right for saying what she had said. At the time I was certain that a mother couldn't be wrong.

I wondered if Mom would let me watch MTV now if she were with me. But I realized that I wouldn't be watching it in the first place if she were with me because I would be back home. I turned up the volume even more and lay on my stomach on the bed. Everything about the video was in sync, pretty words with pretty girls in pretty scenes. I wished that at the snap of my fingers I could be one of them.

I got off the bed and tried to move around like the girls on TV. The steps were too fast, so I could only handle the arm movements. While my arms whirled around my head I heard the loud bang at the door. *It must be the hotel people,* I thought. I cursed myself for having the television on so loud. I ran to the TV and turned it down, but the banging didn't subside.

"Amy!" It was Dad's voice, loud and piercing. But why wasn't he using his key? I couldn't figure it out, so I didn't answer the door.

"Amy!" He sounded angrier, and I didn't understand why he should. Wouldn't he be happy, bringing back a lot of money? I rushed to the door, ready for him to pick me up and swing me around the room. As I unlocked the door, he pushed it open.

"Where's the wallet?" he screamed in Cambodian. Not waiting for me to answer, he began to search the room, pulling our clothes out of the luggage and throwing down bathroom towels. I was stunned.

"Amy!" Dad's lips were white and his jaw was clenched. "Where is the wallet?" I reasoned with myself: Dad was trying to trick me. Of course he was. He had specifically told me not to give him the wallet, and now he was testing me to see if I would listen.

"I'm not giving it to you, Dad," I said with a smile. But he didn't smile back. Then I tried to joke with him. "I don't know what you're talking about," I said. But he didn't get the joke.

"Give me the wallet." He stuck out his hand. Not knowing what else to do, I took it from under the pillow and gave it to him.

He walked to the door and left me. It was as if he had never been there at all. The room was quiet once more, but this time there was a buzzing that didn't go away. I couldn't understand how things were good one minute and turned bad the next. And I wondered if my life would be like this forever. I climbed into bed without bothering to double-lock the door. I was no longer scared about the hotel people coming and taking Dad to jail and me to an orphanage. In fact, he deserved to be sent to jail. Both he and Mom.

When Dad didn't come back by midnight, however, I began to count the minutes. There were fewer footsteps out in the hallway. The buzzing finally went away, but the room was still heavy with quietness that seemed to hang in large blocks around my head. At one o'clock in the morning, I got worried. *What if he doesn't come back?* I wondered. What if he decided to leave me? He might have figured that since I was under a roof and was clean and fed, I was safe until the police came to get me. As angry as I was with him, I didn't want the police to come.

I must have fallen asleep because when I opened my eyes it was eight o'clock in the morning. I listened for Dad but didn't hear him. Then I looked at his bed and noticed that it remained untouched. I tried to go back to sleep, hoping that the next time I opened my eyes I would see him. But I couldn't fall asleep. I prepared myself for the worst. I decided that whatever happened to me, I would never see Dad again, either because he had been sent to jail or because he had left me.

Just as I was telling myself to be strong, Dad walked in. "Amy!" he said in a high-pitched voice, walking to my bed and kneeling beside it. "Get up and get ready." He had a huge grin on his face and stank like cigarettes. I ignored him and shut my eyes.

"Come on, let's go explore this city." I turned my body away from him. "Are you mad at me?" He put his hand on my head. I didn't answer him. "Look, I won a lot of money." I didn't bother to look.

"Amy, we can go shopping."

"I don't want to," I said.

"Why?"

His simple question only made me feel worse. How

could he not know why? Was I communicating with a wall? I sat up, and I was ready to give it to him, to lay everything on the line. But as I started my voice quavered and the tears came. "You were mean to me. You left me here all alone. And you weren't even worried," I said between sobs. I didn't want to cry—I had been forcing myself to hold back the tears since that night. Now that they were out, I didn't care anymore, and I didn't care that my voice got louder. I didn't even care that I might get another beating.

He opened his arms to me. He seemed surprised I didn't crawl into them. "Don't be silly. I'm here now. So get dressed and we'll have breakfast."

"I don't want any."

"Fine, you stay here while I go eat breakfast by myself."

He left. I went to wash my face and came back to bed to watch more MTV. Once I knew that Dad hadn't left me, a huge weight was lifted off my shoulders. But I still planned on not talking to him forever, making him pay for leaving me alone and not caring about my safety.

It wasn't much later when Dad returned with a couple of bags. He pushed a small table to my bed and set out what smelled like pancakes and sausages. However, I focused on the television set, pretending that I was enjoying myself when all along my mouth was watering. Then he sat on my bed, pulled back the covers, and began tickling me.

"Stop!" I screamed.

"Not until you eat." He continued the tickling, giving me only enough time to catch my breath. "Are you going to eat?"

"No."

"Then back to the tickling . . ." I felt his strong fingers under my arms and on the bottom of my feet. I tried to tickle him back but couldn't reach him.

I yelled for mercy. "Okay, I'll eat." He laid out pancakes, sausages, and a fruit bowl and opened an orange juice carton. Then he pulled me close to him.

"I need to brush my teeth first, Dad."

"Why? You're going to eat anyway."

"Because, don't I have to?"

"That was when your mom was around."

It was odd that we were changing a lot of the things that we'd been doing. Before that morning I had never even considered eating or doing anything without brushing my teeth first.

"These Americans are disgusting for eating with dirty teeth," Mom would have said. She was right, though. My lips felt sticky, and I could taste my breath while chewing the pancake.

"Aren't you going to eat?" I asked Dad.

"I'm full." He rubbed his stomach. Then he rubbed my head and asked if I was still mad. I nodded.

"Sorry about last night." There was no laughing as he said it. Of course, it was in English, but I knew he meant it.

"I don't understand why you did something that you told me not to do," I said.

He remained quiet for a long time. "Gambling is bad, just like I told you," he said. "I shouldn't have done it. But when you're a parent, you want so much for your kids. And sometimes you get desperate and do things that you know aren't right. You understand?"

I didn't understand, but I didn't need to. He was my dad, and I believed him.

Dad told me that he had won more money than I'd ever seen. We would have enough for new school clothes, and a hotel until we found a house to rent in San Diego. We could get the AC fixed. "We even have a little bit to put into savings, Amy," he said.

"You look very happy, Dad."

"I am."

I fed him a piece of cantaloupe, and juice squirted from his mouth. I was beginning to feel that we'd do okay in California.

7

DAD WAS ANXIOUS to leave Las Vegas after his big win. "This place is dangerous, Amy, very dangerous. . . . You stay too long and you'll drown," he said. So while I finished the breakfast he had brought me, he wasted no time resting from his all-nighter and headed for the shower. When he stepped out, I almost forgot where we were. Seeing how handsome he was took me back to the not-so-long-ago days when Mom would tell him to shower, shave, and wear something nice for a special occasion. His face was so clean and smooth, like the tiles downstairs at the buffet. I rushed to him, and when he bent down, I ran both hands down his cheeks. It wasn't the cleanness of his face that thrilled me but the idea that things were finally getting back to normal.

Even though the day was very hot, the Strip was crowded with people. The air around us was filled with laughter, and I felt as if we were walking on air. When I told Dad this he said, "Money can make you feel that way." I was sure he was right, but I preferred to think that happiness could, too.

Dad kept his promise and took me shopping, real shopping, the kind where I was allowed to touch and try on clothes and know that there was a great possibility of our buying them. At a small shop with stands of sunglasses, goofy-looking hats, and stickers, Dad found a cap with I WAS A BIG WINNER IN LAS VEGAS written across the front. I chose a cheap T-shirt that had a picture of two dice. As I held the two small bags while we walked from store to store, I remembered the first day of third grade, when the teacher had made us introduce ourselves and tell what we liked to do for fun.

Because I was in the first seat in the first row, I introduced myself first. I knew what I was going to say, and wasn't I lucky to be the first to say it? Surely some girl would think my answer was cool. And if I was even luckier, she would repeat it and the other kids would think she was just copying me. The teacher nodded at me, so I sat up and turned toward the class and with a big grin said, "Hi, my name is Amy, and I like shopping."

Of course, what I said was not original—and not even true since we didn't have money to *go* shopping—but I wasn't after something original. I was after something more important, something that would get me friends, more friends than just Janet and Melissa. The teacher gave me her dutiful grin, and I gave her my genuine one. As I turned back in my seat, I heard someone say, "Yeah, window-shopping." The soft snickers that followed were hot enough to singe my ears and neck. And I hated knowing that Janet and Melissa had heard the laughter because I knew *they* knew what I was after and how badly I had failed.

On the Strip there were several big expensive-looking stores with expensive-looking ladies going in and coming out. The walkways leading to them were free of litter, and along the edges grew blue and purple pansies. Some stores were adorned with animal-shaped hedges, like elephants and turtles. And some had archways painted in gold. We found Little Princesses by accident. The sun had beaten down on us until our legs no longer wanted to move, so we decided to rest on one of the benches of a grand hotel beside some water fountains. Behind one of the fountains was a little store flanked by pink rosebushes and a couple of blue birdbaths.

We walked inside, and I lost my breath. There were stars on the ceiling and soft pink painted walls. From the center of the ceiling hung sheer pink sheets that fluttered to the ground. I could tell that there were five saleswomen because they all wore pink dresses with small straw hats that had pink satin bows tied around them. The store smelled of roses. I had to be in a fairyland, and I knew right away that Little Princesses was only for window-shopping.

"Is this your only princess, sir?" We hadn't noticed that a lady in pink had come to greet us until she spoke. I couldn't take my eyes off her long red hair, which she wore straight down the front of her right shoulder, and her glued-on smile flashing white teeth. She waited for Dad's response with big fluttering eyes. He and I looked at each other, he moving his eyebrows in a "Huh?" Then, for a brief moment, she put a cold hand on my shoulder.

"Uh, yes, Amy is my only princess," Dad said a couple of seconds later, sounding unsure. The word, no matter how much it reminded me of Cinderella, was just . . . weird . . . because he had never called me that before. I thought only American girls were princesses.

Dad, whose neck stiffened and whose feet started turning toward the front door, avoided looking at the pretty lady, who was still standing in front of us with her hands folded on the front of her dress. Dad glanced around the store, and I knew he was trying to find a way out.

"Well, isn't this nice. D-day." She must have seen the even more puzzled look on our faces because she quickly added, "Dad and Daughter Day."

She introduced herself as Missy and shook Dad's hand. I could tell that he had begun to relax—dropping his shoulders and holding her hand a bit too long. He smiled at her so big I didn't think he could contain himself. I didn't like that Missy was able to change him so quickly.

I told Dad that we should leave, pulling him toward the door. But Missy grabbed my hand, placing her fingers around the tips of mine. Then she said, "Well, honey, you go and look all you want. If you want to try on anything, let me know."

I didn't want to look around and I didn't want to try on her clothes, but when I looked up at Dad, his nod told me to go. I was still hesitant. I didn't want to leave the two of them alone and risk having him smile at her again the way he used to smile when Mom was around.

"It's okay, honey, your dad will be fine here. I'm just going to get him a chair."

"My name's Amy." I stared at her.

"I'm sorry, Amy. Take your time and see if you like anything." She still wore her smile.

When I didn't start looking, Missy left and returned a few minutes later with a chair with a pink cushion. Following her was another lady, who gave Dad a cup of coffee.

Missy took my hand again. "Amy, go and have fun. I'll be here," Dad said, waving me off.

Missy walked me farther into the store. The inside wasn't large, probably only twice the size of our hotel room. But it was beautiful. There weren't racks of clothes like in other stores. Instead, the blouses, skirts, and other apparel filled wood cabinets, trunks, and tall chests that were painted with rosebuds and bushes. There was even a small couch with pink hearts to rest on. When I saw a couple of girls sitting on it Missy told me they were having tea.

"What are you looking for?" she asked. Her eyes twinkled at me, and now that it was just the two of us I thought that maybe she wasn't so bad after all. I shrugged and told her that I wasn't sure.

"Well, every little girl deserves a new dress once in a while, don't you think?"

"I guess," I said, and giggled.

She took me to the dress section, and after looking at the price of one I knew that we would never be able to afford it. Missy put a purple sundress up against me and said how perfect it was. Then I couldn't help liking her. Until her, no salesperson had ever paid that much attention to me. But I was afraid she would get mad once she learned that Dad would never buy anything there, no matter how much he seemed to like her.

"I think I should go back," I said.

"Why so soon? You didn't even find anything you want yet."

I knew Dad said that he had won a lot of money, but that didn't mean he was going to go crazy and buy me everything. I decided to tell her the truth. "This costs too much," I said, pointing to the dress she had picked out for me. She turned quiet for an extraordinarily long time. I grew nervous and didn't want to disappoint her, so I offered an explanation, "Dad has a lot of money . . . but we need it all for California."

Missy then spoke up, "Well then, a dad who has a lot of money can afford at least one pretty dress for his pretty daughter." She clapped her hands and laughed, and this made me laugh, too. After all . . . she was right.

I chose a yellow dress with a satin bow over the purple one Missy had shown me. But it was too much fun to stop there. "And this"—she held up a jumper—"you can wear on the first day of school. All the girls in California will be so jealous." She scrunched her nose, and I could hear more excitement in her voice. Then we chose a denim miniskirt and a pink shirt that tied in the back. Unfortunately, I had to face reality again: Dad could never afford all these things.

"I don't think Dad will go for all this," I told Missy.

"Well, you just smile your big smile and tell him how happy it will make you. He would be crazy not to buy them for you then." She sounded so reassuring.

Missy took me back to Dad, who was sitting in a corner with a couple of other adults. He watched us walk over to him, looking back and forth from Missy to me. But when he saw all the items we were carrying, he seemed to forget about her. He began to shake his head, but she quickly told him how wonderful it would be for a young lady to start a new school in a new state with new pretty outfits. He slowly nodded a couple of times, even rocking his body back and forth.

After she left us, Dad leaned in and whispered, "Do you need the dress?" I told him that I did, just in case we went to a party. "And the skirt?" I told him I would pick out a longer one if he wanted me to.

In the end, I didn't pick out another skirt because he didn't give me time to. He quickly paid for everything and left the store, leaving me to carry my two pink Little Princesses bags. It was awkward to walk with them, and they were pretty heavy in the heat. But I guess even a princess had to do some work.

We left Las Vegas after a late lunch. "We have to eat at McDonald's since you spent all the money," Dad had said, but the grin on his face told me that he didn't mind.

"By this time tomorrow, we'll be in a new place," he said in the car.

The trip from Las Vegas and the one from St. Petersburg were so different. Yes, the dominating sun remained excruciating, especially through the deserts of Nevada. But it didn't bother me. Too many good things had already happened to us, and I knew that there would be more.

"So, we're going to see a lot of movie stars when we get there, huh?" I asked.

"You're thinking of Los Angeles. Remember, we're going to San Diego."

"Can we go to Los Angeles, then?"

"No, I don't think so."

"Why?"

"Because we don't know anyone there."

I was confused. I thought we didn't know anyone at all in California. "So we know someone in San Diego?"

"No. Amy, you're asking too many questions again, and I can't concentrate on the driving." But he quickly added, "And we don't have to tell people we meet everything that has happened, okay?" I knew his friends had disappointed him when he had opened up to them. But what did he mean by "everything"?

"Then what *do* I say if someone asks us?"

"They won't," he said. Was he joking? Of course they

would, if they were Cambodians. Was he expecting us not to talk to any Cambodians? One part of me was excited at that possibility. But the other part, the one that knew not to talk back to teachers, not to cuss, and not to hate my parents for even just a second, told me that if I got rid of everything Cambodian about myself, I would be lost.

8

AFTER WE LEFT Las Vegas we had to stop several times to let the car cool down, so we didn't reach San Diego until around midnight. I had fallen asleep and Dad woke me up to the sound of crashing waves. For a second, as I was trying to come out of my sleep, I forgot where we were. I thought we were back at a beach in Florida and almost asked for Mom. "Come and see a California beach, Amy," he whispered in my ear. I couldn't find any energy to get myself up. I couldn't feel my arms or legs, just my heavy head attached to my little body. He picked me up and carried me until he said that we were standing on a cliff in La Jolla. "Can you smell it?" he asked. I didn't know what he was talking about and didn't really care. For that moment the only thing that mattered was that my father was carrying me in his arms, something I wished he would do forever.

Dad was still snoring when I woke up the next morning to the roaring air conditioner in another dark, small motel room. I crept out of bed quickly so as not to wake him. Immediately I felt the sticky carpet. Ugh. I tiptoed to the small bathroom and got into the shower, closing my eyes to the mold and mildew. When I came back out Dad was up and stretching. He gave a big yawn and a shake of his head.

"We have a lot to do today," he said. "Don't you start school in a week or so?" I shrugged, but I knew it had to be soon because it was close to the end of August. "I have to find a job," he added before heading for the bathroom. A few minutes later he screamed that the water was too cold, and I couldn't help laughing.

"California looks a lot like Florida, doesn't it?" I said when we were in the car looking for breakfast. Both places were warm and sunny, except that it was hotter and stickier in Florida. Even most of the homes and lawns weren't that different. But San Diego had mountains, which were both fascinating and intimidating. They looked like something I could build out of clay, yet they were so huge, almost threatening to collapse over me.

"I guess so," he answered absentmindedly. Even though he didn't talk much, I could tell that he was enjoying himself. He even rolled down his window and turned up the radio, tapping his fingers on the steering wheel. I decided to be quiet and let him enjoy whatever he was thinking about.

But I couldn't stay quiet when I saw Asian Mall. "Oh, my gosh!" I screamed.

"What, what?" Dad hit the brakes.

"Look, look at the big Asian store," I said, pointing to the left.

Dad turned his head, but he wasn't impressed. Instead, he told me I shouldn't scream like that again; he could get into an accident. At the next light he made a U-turn and pulled into the mall's parking lot.

Eating up everything in sight, I soon forgot my hunger. I

couldn't believe what I saw. It was truly a mall with jewelry, flower and video stores; small restaurants; clothes boutiques; and a grocery store the size of Publix or Winn-Dixie. And everything was Asian, from lucky bamboo to Chinese movies to taro, a creamy purplish and grayish white root.

But what really amazed me was that most, if not all, of the shoppers were Asians. I instantly felt a connection with the people; their hair was black like mine . . . and they didn't look too different from me. They were me, and I was them, and because of that, we didn't have anything to hide from one another. But that realization also brought me fear—because if we didn't have anything to hide, we would have to tell them what happened to Mom.

We walked to the back of the grocery store where all the fresh seafood was. The stench of it was overpowering, but instead of blocking my nose I found myself sniffing for it. There were so many shoppers, some pushing each other to get around and others putting in requests for their fish. Three-way cut, in which the fish was cut into three pieces; head and tail on; or deep-fried. There was a fish tank with live shrimp and another with live eel, creatures that I found to be as ugly as alligators and snakes.

In the produce section Dad bought a bag of sugary-sweet orange-colored persimmons to eat outside. After the mall we drove to a nearby playground with picnic benches. When Dad unfolded the *San Diego Union-Tribune* I took off my shoes and walked on the grass, which was soft and moist. It was almost like squishing my feet in mud.

"What job are you looking for?" I asked.

"I don't know, probably something with cars again."

I knew it was important for him to find a job, but I was getting bored. "Can I go on the swings?"

"Yeah, but nowhere else."

A couple of kids much younger than I were on the jungle gym, climbing and swinging and looking like white monkeys. All three swings were available. I wanted to grab one, run forward with it, and then jump onto it for a big push, but I was afraid of missing it and falling down. So instead, I just plopped into one and immediately felt the burning seat scorching the back of my thighs.

When Dad called for me to come back, I turned around and ran to him.

"Where are we going?" I asked.

"To these jobs." He pointed to some ads he had circled in the newspaper. "It's Friday, maybe I'll get something."

"Then can we look for a new place?"

"It's a deal."

We drove past all the big streets and gas stations and fast-food restaurants into an area with old-looking houses. We were searching for José's Garage.

"I hope we don't live in a place like this, Dad."

"We won't if I get a job soon."

Soon we reached José's Garage. It was literally a garage attached to a house. A wire fence encircled the property, and in the yard there were three old cars. Near the mailbox was a tire in which pink flowers grew. The garage door was rolled up, and we could see a man in a jumpsuit walking around inside.

"Hi, I'm here for the job," Dad said, extending his hand to the man. The man introduced himself as José and shook Dad's hand.

Dad and José began talking. I knew José was a Spanish name since I had known a couple of Latinos at Jefferson, but this José didn't look Spanish at all. He was a small man, even shorter than Dad was, with light skin, brown hair, and the type of mustache that looked like a frown.

"What about your daughter?" José asked Dad.

Dad put his arm around me. "Amy, she can go to her babysitter after school." Sure, I thought. I had never been to a babysitter's, and I knew I wouldn't be going to one anytime soon. But I knew better than to ask Dad what he was talking about.

"Good," José continued, "because evenings are busy here. You won't be getting off until seven or so."

"That won't be a problem," Dad replied.

"Okay. Well, before I give you the job, why don't you see what you can do with that car." José pointed to a white car with its hood open. But Dad was hesitant. "And I'll give you forty dollars for it," José added. Dad headed straight for the car.

While Dad worked, I sat in a corner of the garage, watching a television hung from a corner of the ceiling and listening to José answering the phone. "No, the car won't be ready until tomorrow. I know. . . . I know. But I'm short here. An employee called in sick," I heard him say. He hung up and cursed.

"Sorry," he said to me. And I smiled, a big smile, at him. No adult had ever apologized to me for saying a bad word.

"It's okay," I said.

Then he walked over and gave me the remote control. "Now, don't lose it. I don't let just anyone hold this. Okay?"

"Okay."

"So, your dad told me you two drove here from Las Vegas." I nodded. So far, I liked José, but his questions were beginning to make me uneasy. *Save them for Dad*, I said to myself. But he didn't ask me anything else; instead, he told me that we would like San Diego much better. Pointing outside, he said something I would hear a million times: "You can't find better weather."

It was almost dark by the time Dad had finished. José went to check the car, and a couple of minutes later he returned and told Dad that he could start the next day. Dad broke into a big smile and picked me up.

"Thanks, José, but I need time to find an apartment for us." Dad looked a little nervous when his new boss didn't say anything. "It's just that we got here last night, and I wanted to find a job first, and I promised Amy we would get a place soon . . ."

José nodded really fast, "Sure, man, just call me as soon as you can start. I can't go without someone here much longer, though, so don't take too long." Dad told him that it shouldn't take more than a couple of days. They shook hands once more and I waved to José before we left.

We woke up early the next morning, determined to find a permanent place. First, though, Dad wanted to go back to the beach in La Jolla, a suburb of San Diego. We drove up a small hill with grassy fields on both sides and parked near the cliffs. When we got out of the car he started telling me how beautiful the ocean was, but my mind was elsewhere.

"Am I really going to get my own room?" I asked as we walked to the edge of a cliff.

"I told you that you would," he said. "Now look out there, Amy."

I had to adjust my eyes to see through the fog to where he was pointing. The sky and the ocean looked like a piece of light blue paper that was folded in half and opened to let one side stick up. The morning clouds hung low and loose.

"I bet it would be so soft to be in the clouds," I said,

reaching out my hands to touch the clouds that sifted right through my fingers.

"You are in them," Dad said, and took several big breaths. I did the same.

We stood there for a long time and only turned to leave when we realized how cold it was standing over the ocean. "It doesn't get cold like this in Florida," I said.

Dad nodded in confirmation. Then, as if he were talking to himself, he said, "It doesn't. The ocean here is more powerful."

Dad wanted to live near the cliffs, but the apartments there were too expensive for us; plus, there were waiting lists. "We can call you, sir, when one becomes available" was a typical response. As we drove from place to place, Dad grew less talkative and more tense. At the last place he yelled at the leasing officer.

He raised a hand into the air. "It's okay," he said to the lady helping us, "your place is actually way out of our budget. Is everything in San Diego this much?" He sounded like a mean man on a TV show. The woman didn't answer right away, and Dad slowly began to explain that we needed a place.

She was kind, though, in her answer. "No, I understand. Things are more expensive in University Towne Center because it's near La Jolla and the ocean." Then, in a quieter voice, she added, "If you go inland, prices are better." She wrote down the number of a friend who had a place for rent. Dad thanked her, and we left.

In the car Dad was in a better mood, but I didn't talk to him. I knew he had apologized for being rude to the lady, but I still didn't like how he had spoken to her. I wanted so much to tell him to leave that side of him, the Mr. Yen side, back in Florida, but I didn't dare to. When he stopped at a gas station to make the call and asked if I wanted anything to drink, I just shook my head and looked out the window.

Dad was even happier when he returned. "Amy, this might be the place. I have a good feeling," he said, and started the car.

We drove to a neighborhood with small, pretty houses with manicured gardens. The lawns were emerald green and each flower bed contained brilliant flowers like orange marigolds or my new favorite, light blue lilies. The lilies grew on swanlike green stems. At the top of each, the lilies burst into blooms like firecrackers.

Dad pointed to a duplex. "That's it—155 Magnolia Place." It was mustard colored with a brown roof and a low black railing. I loved it immediately and got out of the car. It looked like a real home.

I turned in a circle and screamed, "This is perfect!"

"The landlord will be here soon to meet us." His voice was calm, but I could tell that he was as eager as I was to call it ours. "We have to see if everything works out first."

See what? I thought. *Is it not available? Isn't that why we're here in the first place? Oh, God, please give me this house, please, please, please.*

"When is he supposed to come?" I asked.

"Right now." But it wasn't Dad's voice.

I turned around to see an old man and an old woman come out of the house next to the one we were looking at. They introduced themselves as Mr. and Mrs. Jackson and took us inside the small house, which had only one bedroom . . . my bedroom. It was in the back of the house, across from the bathroom. There was a small hallway with closets on either side. The walls were clean of fingerprints, and the carpet, grayish blue, was brand-new, we were told. I stepped out of my shoes and walked on it, and it wasn't sticky at all.

We walked back outside because the house, since it was now getting late, was growing dark. A few people were walking as their little kids rode their tricycles. Down the street I saw a couple of girls jumping rope and faintly heard the rhymes they were jumping to. Mr. Jackson and Dad began talking immediately. Mr. Jackson wanted to know where we had come from, how many people were going to live there, and about Dad's credit check and references. I didn't like how the conversation was going; there were too many questions, and Dad didn't answer them readily. I thought that I would die if the old people turned us away.

Dad spoke gently. "Sir, we need a place soon. I have a new job I'm supposed to start in two days."

Mr. Jackson was equally soft in his tone. "I know, but what happens to me if something happens to my property?"

"My daughter likes it here," Dad said.

The old man thanked me and smiled. Both he and his wife had warm smiles, the same as Mrs. Yen's.

With reluctance Dad said, "I'll give you three months' rent up front."

The couple looked at each other, and I looked at them. *Look at me,* I begged silently. *Look into my eyes and see that we're good people . . . even though Mom didn't think so. . . . Help us.* Finally, Mrs. Jackson said that two months would be sufficient. I ran to her and hugged her and felt how fragile she was as her bony arms pressed around me.

Then they invited us into their place for a cold drink. The house was decorated with a lot of silk flowers on the walls, on a corner stand, and on the coffee table. I could smell a faint scent of potpourri. Against one wall stood a tall book-

case. I immediately walked over to it and studied their col-
lection. The books were all thick, the kind only adults would
read. I was running my hand along the bindings when Mrs.
Jackson came to stand beside me. "You like reading?" she
asked. I nodded, still taking in the titles. A lot of them had to
do with history and geography, subjects I wasn't crazy about;
nevertheless, they all looked good standing side by side on
the shelves. "I have a box of books you might like," she said.
"They were my daughter's, but I guess she doesn't need them
now." I looked up at her and smiled.

It felt nice to be inside a home again. We spent a lot of
time talking about how pretty San Diego was. "You can't find
better weather," Mr. Jackson said to Dad when his wife
brought me a couple of freshly baked cookies. I waited a couple of minutes before biting into one.

"So why did you move here?"

It was just like that that the question came out, almost
like a snap of the fingers. I was surprised to hear it from Mrs.
Jackson. She wasn't a nosy Cambodian. And I was equally
surprised that the question didn't sound intrusive at all. It
was simply a question . . . why we had moved. And the answer should have been simple, too. But I still didn't want to
give it, and turned to Dad. I remembered him telling me not
to tell people *everything*. But he had never given me a clear
answer as to how I should respond, so I waited.

"Amy's mother died."

My chest collapsed. I knew Dad wanted a new start, but
did he have to kill my mother to get one?

I heard Mrs. Jackson say how sorry she was for us. I
didn't look at her because I knew my eyes would only betray
my father.

Before I fell asleep for the last time in a motel room, Dad

told me that we had been lucky the past couple of days and that we should go to temple the next day before we moved into 155 Magnolia Place. I didn't say anything and pretended that I had fallen asleep.

The St. Petersburg temple had been converted from a three-bedroom house and didn't have enough parking spaces for visitors. There wasn't even enough room for all the people who wanted to attend service. But in San Diego, the temple, which was in a residential area with a twenty-four-hour Laundromat, a gas station, a video store, two restaurants, and a couple of convenient stores, was large. It had a parking lot and a lawn big enough for two picnic tables, with plenty of room left for small kids to run around. A tall eucalyptus tree stood in one corner of the yard. The exterior of the temple was painted a bright orange, and hanging from the eaves all around the building were blue, red, and white miniature flags of Cambodia. Dad and I climbed three steps that took us to the front porch, where shoes were laid out in two neat rows, and took off ours.

On each wall of the service area were life-size pictures of the Buddha, some of him standing on a crown of pink water lilies and some of him sitting and meditating under a Bodhi tree. He was not the Buddha with the jolly, chubby face and fat stomach that people rubbed for luck. This Buddha, the real Buddha, dressed in a saffron robe, had a young face with long ears, and wore his black hair on top of his head in a bun. In the front of the room was an altar with burning candles and sticks of incense that perfumed the entire area, and bowls of oranges and bananas that served as offerings to our ancestors. Dad put down a bag of fruits we had bought earlier at a nearby grocery store.

Following Dad, I knelt at the foot of the altar, bowed three times, and lit three sticks of incense.

Because it wasn't a special Cambodian holiday, not many people came for service that day, only the usual old people and a couple of younger ones who, I assumed, volunteered at the temple. I sat on the floor near a wall, and even with my head bowed, I could feel eyes on us already.

After Dad took the bag of fruits into the kitchen and sat down beside me, an old woman in a simple white shirt and a black silk sarong turned to him. She called him son in Cambodian. *"Kohn,"* she said, "we have not seen you here before."

"No, *Ohm,*" he said. "My family and I just moved here . . . only a couple of days ago."

"Just you and your daughter?" someone else asked.

I kept my head down, playing with my fingers. Dad was on his own. There were more questions, but the monks, who shaved their heads and dressed like Buddha, were ready for the prayer session, which included a lot of chanting.

Because the chants were in an old language—Pali—I didn't understand a word. I just kept my hands folded under my chin and tried to think of only good things: a new school year, our new home, and the nice Jacksons; but the idea that Dad had "killed" Mom hurt like a bad tooth.

Late-morning service in Florida had usually ended with food for everyone—served first to the monks and then to the visitors after the monks had retired to their chambers—and it was no different at the temple in San Diego. After the chanting the couple of young people who helped at the temple brought food from the kitchen and laid it in front of the monks. There were plates of stir-fries, dried fish, and fresh mangoes. I noticed that the persimmons and nectarines that we had brought were also laid out for the monks to eat. The room wasn't quiet, but there wasn't much talking while the monks ate their lunch.

Afterward, a young monk stayed to talk before retiring

with the others. He welcomed us. "Come often to visit," he said. "There is always room for new people." Dad thanked him.

When the young monk left, everyone's attention turned back to us. One question led to another. "Oh, how long was the drive?" "Where do you live now?" "How much is the rent?" "Does your new job pay well?" "My son's car isn't running well, maybe you can look at it someday." A couple of times, someone tried to talk to me, but I kept my head down.

"She must be shy," someone said. I wasn't sure if that meant I was also impolite. Not only did I not talk to them, but I also hadn't greeted them. It occurred to me that it was rude not to have *chumreab suor*ed everyone, but it was too late for me to do anything now.

As the talking continued, I grew angrier at Dad. And I was determined to do something about it. Finally, the moment I was waiting for: "What happened to her mom?" It came from somewhere in the back of the room.

I didn't give Dad time to answer. I raised my head and saw the Buddha, with the sun behind his head, on the wall. I looked at Dad and then at everyone else. "She left us," I said, "and that's why we moved here." As I expected, I heard a lot of "Oh"s.

"That is terrible," an old woman said, "a grown woman leaving her family."

A couple of minutes passed before Dad stood up. Everyone invited us to join them for lunch, but he said we had to move into our new house.

Dad didn't talk to me in the car, and when we got to the motel he slammed the door. I had just started to pack when he told me to sit.

"You forget who you are sometimes, Amy. You are a

daughter," he began in Cambodian, pointing his finger at me. I was going to say yes but decided to keep my mouth shut. "You shouldn't be talking in an adult conversation. You are a kid. You don't know anything."

"Sometimes you don't—" I started to say, but stopped when he yelled, "Silence!"

He continued, "Next time you are not to say anything." What did he mean? Was I supposed to look dumb when people asked about our past?

The room was dark; neither of us had bothered to open the curtains. "You can't make her dead," I said quietly.

"She is. She left us, you ignorant girl." I did not like being considered dumb, and for him to call me ignorant hurt my feelings. I got up from the bed and balled my hands into fists against my thighs.

"She might be dead to you," I said, "but she isn't to me. She is still my mom." I expected him to shut me up again, but he didn't. "Why do you have to lie to people about what happened?" He still didn't say anything, only looked at me with eyes so big I saw the whites in them glow, but I wasn't afraid. "I don't want to tell these people anything, either. But I want you to tell them the truth, so that I can."

"Quiet!" he finally screamed at me.

"No!" I screamed back. I thought he was going to grab me or hit me, but he just sat down on his bed. My head hurt from so much yelling. Seeing him sit at the edge of the bed so helpless made me ache for him. But I didn't apologize that day because I was not sorry.

NORTH PARK ELEMENTARY was only two blocks from Magnolia Place, and it took me only ten minutes to walk there. In the mornings after Dad left for work, I would lock the front door with the silver key I wore on a chain around my neck, wave good-bye to Mr. Jackson, who sat on his porch swing sipping coffee, and walk to Hasting Street. There I turned left and continued until I reached Cherry Blossom Place, which I crossed to get to North Park.

At the corner of Cherry Blossom and Hasting stood the biggest magnolia tree in the entire neighborhood. The tree was expansive, with powerful branches growing high and low and wide, and unlike the other trees in San Diego, it blossomed year-round.

On the first day of school I stopped under this magnolia tree to admire its glory. It was beautiful, majestic, and motherly, with thick, swinging branches so low they seemed about to scoop me up and hug me. The scent, soft and sweet, dazzled me. It was as if someone had dropped rose petals and gardenias in a bowl and mixed them up with lemon juice.

And the magnolias themselves, shaped like shallow dishes, had creamy, velvety petals. They blossomed randomly in the tree, some new ones about to open, some in their best days with the firmest and most even coat of French vanilla, and some slowly browning away. Surely it was a good omen for the days to come, I thought as I dropped my backpack and pressed my face into a flower. When I couldn't get enough of the fragrance, I began breaking it off the branch.

"Young lady," I heard someone say. I turned in a full circle but couldn't see anything until I found my way out from under the tree. "Young lady," I heard again, "what do you think you're doing?" I looked across the street and saw a fat lady wearing a housedress. She stood at the top of her steps with her hands on her hips. "You heard me, what do you think you're doing?" She tightened her red lips.

I stammered, "I—I was trying to pick a flower."

"I see. And why would you do a foolish thing like that? Those flowers are fine where they are. They belong in the tree. They got here that way, and don't you think that they should stay that way?" I thought she was crazy and wondered how many others like her lived in the neighborhood. Nevertheless, she was older and deserved my respect. When I didn't answer, she asked, "You have problems hearing or something?" I had just opened my mouth to apologize when a small Asian girl walked up.

"Mrs. Cupelli," she hollered, "I think she's new."

Mrs. Cupelli didn't look satisfied and muttered, "You better tell her to read the sign." Then she turned to go back in the house.

"How did you know I'm new?" I asked the small girl. She shrugged off my question.

I couldn't tell if she was Thai, Laotian, or even Hawaiian.

She wore her thick black hair in two long pigtails with red ribbons that matched her jumper, which was similar to mine. I was about to start my first day as a fifth grader, and I considered running home to change because I didn't want to wear something a little kid had on. Even with her thick glasses I could tell that she had a mole under the corner of her right eye. She would later tell me that the mole was really a beauty mark, and she was right because whenever she smiled the beauty mark made her milk-chocolate-colored face even more pretty to look at. She handed me my backpack, and we headed for school.

"Are you Khmer?" she asked. I almost jumped at hearing a kid use the word *Khmer*, which sounded so old to me; I had always preferred the word *Cambodian*. The two words meant the same thing, but *Khmer* was ancient and personal, and only Cambodians themselves used it.

"Yes," I told her, "but how did you know that?"

"Because we're sisters." For a brief second my throat tightened and didn't release until she explained, "I mean because I'm Cambodian, too."

"Sure," I said, although I would have never considered her to be so. I could tell already that she was gutsy, defending me to Mrs. Cupelli and coming right up to talk to me when she didn't know me. I couldn't remember any Cambodian girl doing that before. "What's your name?"

"Sopiep."

"Do you have an American name?"

She said, "Yeah, but I like my Cambodian one better, so that's the one I use. What's yours?"

"Amy."

"Do you have a Cambodian name?"

"No," I said. For such a simple answer, it left me with an

emptiness that I couldn't figure out. Why hadn't my parents given me a Cambodian name, too?

North Park Elementary was a box-shaped, two-story building painted a deep red. A couple of school buses had already pulled into the front circle, and some parents and smaller kids were crossing the street. It reminded me a lot of Jefferson, except that it was newer-looking.

"Come on, I'll show you around," Sopiep said, and pulled me. I had already seen the school when Dad brought me for registration, but I didn't want to hurt her feelings.

We pushed our way through the mass of students, parents, and teachers to get inside the building. I noticed that there were other Asians—probably Vietnamese and Laotian.

Sopiep wanted to go check the class roster and see if we would be in the same class when I stopped her. "I'm in the fifth grade," I said.

"So am I." She giggled as she cocked her head to the left and tugged at her pigtails. "I know. My mom says I'm too old to wear pigtails, and my brothers think I only wear them to get attention. And I get made fun of all the time. But I don't care, I like them."

She didn't even wait for my response, just hooked her left arm around my right as we climbed the stairs to the second floor. A couple of American girls walked by, and Sopiep said hi. They gave us small waves, but I wasn't sure if they knew her. Kids were already entering their classes, so we almost ran down the hall to room 206, Mrs. Ortiz's class. We found my name but not hers.

"That stinks," she said, and frowned. "I'll be across the hall from you. We'll only see each other for PE and lunch, if you want to eat with me." Of course I did. I was so stunned that I didn't know what to say at first.

Finally I said, "Yeah, will you save me a seat?"

"Sure."

Mrs. Ortiz was a young teacher whose smile looked borrowed. She was never happy with us that year, always yelling and criticizing us for one thing or another. But through all of her lectures about what terrible children we were, she wore the pasted-on smile. When I first entered her classroom she stood against the wall with her shoulders very square, almost like the school itself. She shook my hand with a firm grip and gave me a name tag with a yellow smiley face on it. There were pictures of happy faces all around the walls. Even the ceramic sun that sat on her desk was smiling.

There were seven tables with four chairs each in her classroom. Most of the seats were already taken, so I walked to the far side of the room and pulled out a chair at a back table. The kids seemed to know each other and were talking away about summer camps and vacations. My table with two other girls and a boy was the quietest.

"Good morning, boys and girls," Mrs. Ortiz said, and we all said "Good morning" in unison. Her voice was strong and crisp, demanding a quick response from us. "I am your homeroom teacher, and I will teach you math, science, and social studies in the morning." She held up three fingers. "Then you will go to PE. And then you will go to lunch." Like a flight attendant I had seen on TV, she pointed across the hall. "After lunch you will go to Mr. Summers for reading and writing."

After spending most of the morning signing out books and teaching us the school and classroom rules, Mrs. Ortiz asked us to take out paper and pencil. A couple of moans soon followed. She scanned the room like a curious hawk and eyed us individually, never forgetting to form her smile, and said, "One thing you'll learn in here is that there will be no complaining, understand?" There was a heavy silence in the room. "On your paper I want you to write about your summer."

A hand went up at my table, and all eyes fell on the boy. "Yes, Anthony?" Mrs. Ortiz said.

"I thought this was math class." Giggles arose from the other side of the class.

"It is."

"Then why are we writing?"

"Because I am asking you to," she said in a firm yet quiet voice, signaling that no question like that should be asked again.

A couple of snickers started once more at the opposite side of the room but stopped when Mrs. Ortiz turned to the four girls. I noticed that two of them, Kelly and Belle, were the ones Sopiep had tried talking to earlier in the morning. I wasn't sure if Kelly was pretty—but there was something very special about her.

I didn't know what to write about. A lot had happened, but it was nothing for me to share with people I didn't even know. So I had only written *This summer* when Mrs. Ortiz told us to finish it for homework because it was time for PE.

The two coaches with their visors and whistles made our class stand in a straight line beside Sopiep's class on the basketball court. Sopiep's eyes and mine fell on each other and she gently pulled at her pigtails, bringing a smile to my face.

Coach T arranged the equipment while Coach Williams did most of the talking. "Always put the balls back in the crates," she said, "and, girls, after you finish jumping rope, make sure you wind up the ropes neatly." Coach T grabbed a rope and entangled himself in it, and we all laughed when

Coach Williams shook her finger at him. "Kelly, please come here and show everyone what I mean," she said.

Kelly left our line and, with her back erect, walked to the front of the court. All of the kids, myself included, paid close attention to her. She took the jump rope and neatly wound it up until it was about a foot long. Coach Williams told her that she had done a good job, and we all clapped before she got back in line and stood in front of Belle. Had I been the one to be called on, I thought, those claps would have been for me.

Finally we were allowed to sit and talk. Several of us moved around to find our friends. The idea of having one made me delirious. But the coaches stopped us. "Stay in your lines," Coach Williams said, and we all shuffled to our original positions.

"Hey," someone said. I turned around. It was Anthony, the kid who'd been dumb enough to ask a question in class on the first day.

"Hi," I said quietly. He was a tall kid with tanned skin, blue eyes, and thick wavy black hair.

"You're new?" he asked. He also had two big front teeth that made him look like a rabbit. He wasn't going to have many friends and the year was going to be tough for him, I thought, almost sad for him.

"Yeah. Are you?"

"No," he said. I turned back around. "You know anyone here?"

I answered over my shoulder, "Yeah, Sopiep."

"Oh, that crybaby?" he asked, and from the corner of my eye I saw him pointing at her and laughing. I turned to see his body rocking and rolled my eyes at him.

"She's not crying, and she's not a baby," I said.

"She is too. I mean, who still wears pigtails in the fifth

grade? Pigtails, pigtails," he began singing. Several kids around us stopped talking and laughed at what he was doing. Their laughter was a bell urging one of us to say something more clever and insulting. I waited to hear from Sopiep, but she stayed busy scraping old pink polish off her fingernails.

As I scanned the court I saw that no one else in the two classes looked like us; I was sure that their still faces were already judging what we were: different. We didn't have small, pointy noses or orange freckles, and we probably didn't even smell like them. No one would stand up for Sopiep except me. I pressed my palms into the gritty cement, letting the heat of it burn them and making them itch. Then I stared at Anthony. We were two boxers fighting in the last round, and only one of us would be the winner.

"Shut up, Rabbit Face!" I said, looking directly into his eyes. It was a knockout.

Choking at my comeback, he blinked in such slow motion I almost counted every one of his long, dark eyelashes. And when he did open his eyes, there was a glaze over them that I hadn't seen earlier.

"Young lady!" Coach Williams said. "Come here." The tone of her voice stunned me. I got up and walked to her. "I know you're new here, but we don't cut each other down. Do we, boys and girls?" I heard everyone say no. Weren't these the same kids who had congratulated me only a minute before? "Would you like to tell me what the two of you were talking about that you felt the need to make fun of someone?" Of course I would, but how could I? Repeating what Anthony had said would only give him the last laugh, so I shook my head. "If that's the case, you need to apologize." I began to walk back to apologize. "No, you can do it from here," she said and pulled me back.

"Sorry," I told Anthony.

In a serious voice that got the kids chuckling again, he said, "I accept your apology." He got the last laugh after all.

The lunchroom was set up with six long tables with metal chairs and a small stage at the front where a couple of teachers sat. Since we shared the lunchtime with the third and fourth graders, we got the two middle tables. Mrs. Ortiz told us that as long as we stayed at those two tables, we were allowed to sit with anyone we wanted. While the rest of the kids jumped up and down at this, I felt an ache. After PE, no one had talked to me, and I was unsure if Sopiep still liked me. Another rotten school year had begun.

But true to her word, Sopiep did save me a seat at lunch and even waited until I got my food and joined her at the table before she started eating.

"Sorry about what happened," I told her.

"Why?" she asked. I looked at her in surprise. "No one has ever stuck up for me. Thank you." She bit into her sandwich.

I was about to ask her if she had any more friends who were going to eat with us when Anthony sat down across from us.

"What are you doing?" I asked him.

"What are you doing?" he repeated.

I turned to Sopiep. "Is he always this annoying?"

She shrugged. "I don't know him. Aren't you new?" she asked him. I glared at Anthony, astonished that I had believed his lie so easily.

"You're so annoying, Anthony."

He put his hands to his heart. "Oh, you just hurt my feelings," he said.

Sopiep started giggling, but I didn't think he was so funny. I ate my lunch of fish patty and Tater Tots quietly while she continued to laugh at his not-so-funny jokes. Didn't she remember what had happened out there? Didn't it matter to her *at all* that he had made fun of her?

After lunch I stopped by the bathroom and walked into Mr. Summers's class late. There were two sections of desks, both facing the center of the classroom. Again, all of the seats were taken. "Amy." I could tell it was Anthony, but I was determined not to talk to him and get in trouble again. "Amy, I saved you a seat," he said, loud enough to get everyone's attention. I scanned the messy classroom, whose walls weren't decorated with anything but a crooked metal clock. It was disappointing to find my favorite class—language arts—to be so yucky-looking.

"Amy!" he screamed.

With only one seat left, I was forced to sit right next to Anthony. "*Anthony and Amy sittin' in a tree . . . ,*" someone started singing before a couple of more kids joined in. The heat in my face slowly climbed to a boiling point. Certain that I would explode from embarrassment, I quickly walked to the crummy seat and hid my face behind my hair. The room had to be hotter than the car ride from St. Pete to Las Vegas as I sat there listening to Mr. Summers talk all afternoon.

The dismissal bell interrupted my planning the perfect murder of Anthony. As I was packing up he told me to wait for him, but I pretended not to hear him and ran out the door to meet Sopiep at the flagpole. As soon as we crossed North Park Place I could see the magnolia tree and remembered how one nasty encounter with Mrs. Cupelli made the day so horrible.

"Why is that old lady so mean?" I asked Sopiep.

"Oh, she's not really. She's just lived here forever."

"And what's the big deal with that tree?"

"Her name is Maggie."

"You're joking," I said. A tree with a name?

"I think that it has something to do with how old she is."

"I know about Maggie." The voice was familiar and didn't sound too far behind us. "I'll tell you if you want to know."

I ignored Anthony again, but Sopiep took him up on his offer. He squeezed himself between the two of us, almost knocking me over. With each step his arm brushed mine. The hair on his cool and sticky arm was like the fuzz of a peach. Touching him was so awkward that I chose to walk behind them. I was surprised that Sopiep, a Cambodian girl also, was comfortable with his walking right beside her.

"Okay, girls." He cleared his throat and started.

"A man named Landon, or was it Langston? Anyway, he planted Maggie about twenty-five years ago on his land somewhere on Magnolia Place, hence the tree's name. But Maggie didn't make it there. She drooped over to one side and lost all of her leaves. So one day the man moved her to his friend Joshua's place on the next street—Cherry Blossom. With more room in Joshua's corner lot, Maggie grew twice as big as she had been, and had flowers for the first time. People started standing around every day just to look at her. Some even drove across the county just to see her. This made the people in the neighborhood really proud.

"The Landon man and his friend Joshua started having problems because Joshua's neighbors wanted to have their street name changed to Magnolia Place. It was only right, they said, since theirs was the one that Maggie made her home. Landon and the other people on Magnolia Place were mad! They said that they would never, not in a million years, turn over their street name. So a neighborhood war between the two streets began. But it didn't last long. Since the neighborhood was small at the time, there weren't enough people who cared enough to sign a petition to have the two streets switch their names.

"But a bunch of years later there was another problem. Maggie had grown so big that her roots were breaking Joshua's house in two. He had to do something or he would be homeless in less than a month. It was either him or her, so Joshua hired a company to chop down the tree. But the company never did because, to his surprise, his own neighbors had a petition sent around against him, and this time there *were* enough people to sign it. They said that the tree was now a historical site, so Maggie would stay and Joshua's home had to be torn down.

"After Joshua moved in with Mr. Landon—I forgot the reason why Mr. Landon took him in—and his house was crushed to the ground, the people on Cherry Blossom, who weren't rich at all, raised money to build a park in honor of Maggie. They had a white fence built around her so that she would always have enough room. They also put two benches inside the lot and nailed a plaque to her, which says something about how beautiful she is and her immortality. And that's the story."

"Mr. Landon still took Joshua in after he had been so mean to him?" Sopiep asked.

"I guess so," Anthony answered.

I thought his story was ridiculous. "How do you *know* all of this, Anthony?"

"My grandma. She's been living here for a long time, so

she knows everything and she tells the story to me almost *every* night." Sopiep wanted to know who his grandma was. "Phyllis Cupelli. She lives there," he said, and pointed to the house across the street. So the two people responsible for my horrible day were related!

I was unlocking my front door when Mrs. Jackson stuck her head out her door and asked if I wanted to come over for cookies. The smell of chocolate wafted out of her house. After that first time we met, I had never had the guts to talk to her again, fearing that one day my eyes would expose the lie Dad had told about Mom. So I said, "No, thank you," and tried not to think about mouthwatering cookies or the lunch that hadn't filled me up.

As soon as I closed the front door, an awful smell hit me. I dropped my backpack immediately and went into the kitchen. The dishes hadn't been washed since yesterday. Surprisingly, Dad hadn't even scolded me this morning for not having touched them. I could see the bloated cooked rice floating like maggots on the dishes from where I stood. Crumbs of dried rice lay on the countertop, and a splatter of soy sauce and wilted iceberg lettuce were waiting to be cleaned up. But they weren't the cause of the smell. Something was more pungent and rancid, grabbing my stomach. I moved the dishes around and sniffed down the sink. I looked around the refrigerator and microwave. My nose next led me into the cabinets and the oven. And upon opening the oven door, I ran to the living room window, opened it, and gasped for fresh air. We had forgotten to throw away the leftover chicken Dad had baked two days before.

I stuck my nose underneath my T-shirt and returned to the kitchen in search of a trash bag. Not finding any, I used a grocery bag and dumped the chicken and the pan in there, hoping Dad wouldn't miss the pan. I wanted so much to open the front door and air out the place, but I knew the Jacksons would be outside by now, eating their cookies and drinking iced tea and watching the neighborhood kids play, and I didn't want to risk having them look in and see the mess we had turned their house into.

I decided to spend the rest of the afternoon cleaning up. I started on the dishes, making sure to wash the glasses first, then the plates, bowls, and pans. Then I straightened the living room. Along with the gray and white striped sofa Dad had bought, he had also purchased a twenty-seven-inch color TV and a VCR from Sears and a small coffee table from a garage sale. I folded Dad's blanket and sheet and adjusted the sofa cushions that he had been sleeping on. Underneath one cushion I found a pair of dirty socks with holes in the big toes.

Since we had moved in it seemed that Dad just let himself go. A couple of mornings he didn't even bother to brush his hair for work. Once when I asked if he had taken a shower he told me to shut up and quit telling him what to do.

He hadn't gotten over what had happened at temple or our fight at the motel. A couple of days after that I had tried to explain why I had said what I had, but he wouldn't listen. He was sure that the *people* would now disrespect him, for having his wife walk out on him. "If I wanted to have people talk behind my back, I would have stayed in St. Pete," he yelled at me. "I wouldn't have driven all this way for a fresh start for you." He pointed his finger at me and then looked the other way.

Since then Dad's anger toward me hadn't subsided.

When I finished cleaning I opened one of the books Mrs. Jackson had given me. Not long after we'd moved in,

Mr. Jackson had brought over a box of their daughter's books. As I sat on the couch reading *Blubber* I looked at the wall clock every ten minutes, waiting for Dad to get home. I dreaded seeing him because I didn't know what mood he would be in. He would either not talk to me or yell at me. Both hurt me. But that night, I couldn't wait to see him and tell him about my first day of school.

Dad got home around seven-thirty, and I was ready for us to eat. He left the door open, and the evening breeze slowly flew in. Outside, night bugs sang to one another.

"Hi, Dad," I said, and got up to greet him.

He didn't take off his shoes like he was supposed to but walked to the couch and picked up the remote control, flipping the channels back and forth between *Jeopardy!* and the evening news. A few times when I asked him a question, I didn't get a response. I wasn't sure if he hadn't heard me or if he just didn't want to answer.

"Dad," I said, "how was your day?" I stood against the couch and watched him stare blankly at the newsman. "I made a friend today, and she's Cambodian." I thought he would brighten up if he knew that a Cambodian family lived just on the next street.

"Amy, I'm tired. And what's that smell?" He looked at the kitchen.

I moved to sit next to him. "Should I cook some rice?"

"If you want," he said. I didn't even see his lips move as he said those words.

I went into the kitchen and washed three cups of rice. Then I cleaned four eggs and gently pushed them into the bed of rice before placing the pot in the rice cooker.

When I came back to tell Dad dinner was cooking, he had already fallen asleep. Crusts of dirt stuck to his hair and the grooves around his eyes and mouth. His arms, stretched out on the couch, were dirty all the way to his fingertips. I wasn't sure whether he had taken a shower since the morning before. I shut the front door and tiptoed to my room.

The headboard of my bed was of an ugly brown wood with a crack down the middle. The week before Dad had woken me. "Up, let's go get your bed things today." Relieved, and certain that he was no longer mad at me, I jumped out of bed and got dressed for another D-Day.

We drove on the busy highway again, and I noticed that we were heading toward La Jolla and the beaches. "Let's go see the ocean. Let's swim!" I said. Dad shook his head as he exited at Miramar Road. There was an air base on the left and a strip of furniture stores on the right.

Ever since Las Vegas I had dreamed of getting a white canopy bed with pink ruffles, and I was sure that we would find my dream in one of those stores. I turned on the radio to find music to go along with the special day, but Dad quickly turned it off. Disappointment filled my chest each time Dad turned me away like that. I knew that he knew I was sitting next to him, but I was unsure if he wanted me there at all. I pressed my face against the window. *Cars go really fast.* And the thought crept into my head: What if the car door opened? No, I wouldn't open it . . . but what if it just opened by accident? If I fell out would he try to catch me? And if he couldn't and I was taken to the hospital, would he cry and feel terrible for ignoring me? What about my mom? Would she find out and come to my bedside?

We visited three big furniture stores. At each one a man in a business suit came to greet us. Dad waved all of them off, leaving us to walk like robots straight down each aisle by ourselves.

When I finally saw the white canopy at Luther's Furniture Store, I stopped suddenly.

"This is perfect," I said.

A salesman snuck up on us and complimented me on my great taste. He left when Dad didn't even give him a hello. When Dad flipped the price tag over I was sure he would buy it, especially since it wasn't as expensive as the other pieces we had seen. However, he shook his head and walked out of the store without saying a word.

We got back into the car and, in silence, drove to a used furniture store a couple of miles down the strip. I knew what was coming and felt the heaviness of it in my heart. I knew we weren't rich even with the money Dad had won; he never failed to remind me of that when he did talk to me. I knew we had never owned new furniture. But I had found the perfect bed to go in my perfect room. If I hadn't seen it, then it wouldn't have mattered as much because I wouldn't even have thought there was a possibility of my wish coming true. And if Dad wasn't going to buy me something I wanted, why did he bother letting me see it in the first place?

After less than five minutes in the store Dad told the owner he would purchase the twin-size bed in the corner and also a dresser, if he had one to sell. The two of them then disassembled the old wood bed. Driving home with the mattress on top of the car and the rest of the furniture in the backseat and trunk, I knew I should be grateful for what I was given.

Now in my bedroom as I waited for the rice to cook, I turned on the radio we had picked up at a garage sale and opened the bottom drawer of the dresser to pull out the only picture I had of Mrs. Yen and Janet. I had found it with the money she tucked in my pocket. We'd only spoken to her once since we'd moved into the new place. Life back in St. Petersburg seemed so long ago, yet it was less than a month since I had left there. The last couple of weeks we had spent there hadn't been so bad; it had been Dad and me against everyone. Now it was just me. Or was it Dad against me?

"*Ohm,*" I said, tracing her face with my finger, "things aren't going so well. He's mad all the time." It might have been the sad songs on the radio that made me want to cry. Or it might have been Dad sleeping in the living room with his dirty shoes still on. Or it might even have been the crickets that chirped outside my window. Whatever it was, my vision began to blur with tears.

I wiped off the tear that fell on the picture and kissed it before putting it back under my clothes in the drawer. Drawing my hands back out from under them, I felt the envelope containing my mom's lock of hair at the bottom and went back into the drawer to search for the one picture I had left of her.

One day back in Florida when I had taken out the photo album to look at our photographs, I noticed there were many empty spaces where pictures used to be. As I looked at the photos that were left, I realized that Mom wasn't in any of them. "Dad," I asked later that evening, "where are all the pictures of Mom?"

Without looking at me, he had said, "You're crazy. They're there."

I had taken the album back to my bed and didn't see a single picture of Mom until the last page. I knew I wasn't crazy, but I also knew I couldn't talk to Dad about the missing photos.

The picture I had of Mom was of a day we had spent at the beach. I was standing on top of the car hood trying to smile for Dad as Mom held me tightly to her. "You're hurting me," I had said. "I don't want you to fall, Amy-a," she had replied, and kissed me. The wind had been strong that day, blowing her long hair in such disarray that it looked like legs of a spider. Looking at the picture now, I could hardly see her face; it was almost as if she had never been there. But she had been . . . because her voice still danced in my head every night.

The rice cooker clicked, telling me our dinner was ready. I quickly tucked everything away and returned to the kitchen. With a big spoon I took out the four eggs and held them under cold water as I peeled off the shells. Next I poured soy sauce into a bowl and placed all the eggs in it.

I woke Dad. "It's cooked," I said. He didn't budge. "Dad, dinner is ready. I cooked some eggs."

Without opening his eyes he said, "Move. Go away. You think those stupid eggs are going to fill me up."

I went back to the kitchen and ate an egg at the counter. I didn't want to cry, and I forced myself not to, tensing the muscles in my neck to hold back any sadness. I wanted to count all the good things in my life: my new friend and my own room. But these things, I realized, meant nothing when your mom was gone and your dad was on his way.

10

THE NEXT MORNING I waited to hear Dad locking the front door before I got up and dressed for school. He hadn't woken up for dinner the previous night until sometime past midnight. Hearing the television on, I had gotten out of bed and walked into the living room. Still in his dirty work clothes, he was munching peanuts on the sofa, and on the coffee table was a beer can. I could see peanut hulls sticking to his chin. The light from the television made his face glow strangely, and I was almost afraid to look at him.

"Dad," I whispered. He neither looked at me nor said anything. As I called for him I wasn't sure what I wanted, but I needed something . . . maybe for him to just see me or smile at me. "Dad," I whispered again, a bit louder.

He wiped his mouth, and with the same hand he brushed me off. "Go to bed."

I did as he had said, but I couldn't fall asleep. I wondered what had happened to my father, the one who used to kiss me and make me laugh. I wondered if I had already lost him, along with my mother. I hadn't shut my eyes until many hours later when he turned the TV off.

That morning as I turned at the corner of Magnolia Place, I saw Sopiep and Anthony waiting for me under the tree. From where I was Sopiep looked even smaller than she had the day before. And for the first time since I could remember I felt big. The feeling was good—as if power stardust had been sprinkled over me. I made a small jump before taking bigger strides.

I had expected to see Sopiep, but not Rabbit Face. "Why are you here?" I asked Anthony when I met up with them. I should have guessed that he would show me his teeth. The morning sun glinted off them as if they were pearls.

"Why are you so mean? I'm here to walk you two to school." He stuck out his arm like a maître d' and bowed. I took Sopiep's arm and pushed past him.

"He likes you," she whispered to me. I told her she was crazy and she should never say that again.

As I was heading to my table in class, I heard my name and turned around. To my amazement, Kelly pointed to a chair, and I quickly walked up to her. Up close I could see that she had a dimple in her right cheek. I looked at her friend Belle, who was as beautiful as her name. She had a soft beige face with a perfect nose that complemented her Barbie-doll lips.

"Sit here," Kelly said, and pulled out the chair next to her.

"Hi, Amy." Belle waved at me, her fingers fluttering.

The two girls smiled at each other and then at me. I didn't know why they wanted me to sit with them, but I didn't care.

We were talking about cafeteria food when Mrs. Ortiz started class. "Amy," she said, "that was not the seat you chose yesterday. Someone sits there. You can't just take any seat you want." She talked to me as if I were a regular troublemaker, and her tight lips told me there would be no use explaining anything to her.

Back at my original table, Anthony couldn't shut his mouth, and the sight of his teeth made me just want to yank them out. "I'm a cooler person for you to sit with, anyway," he whispered, and winked at me. He had to be joking! I had had the chance to sit with the two most popular girls in the fifth grade, but because of him I couldn't.

"Leave me alone," I growled under my breath.

Kelly and Belle surprised me even more that morning when they waited for me to walk to PE.

"Anthony is so cute. Are you good friends with him?" Belle asked me as we left the building.

I started laughing. "No. I can't stand him."

"You're just saying that," she said.

"No way, José, I'm not joking. Anthony is annoying," I reassured them.

Kelly stopped both of us with her right hand held out. "I don't think he is. And I think you like him," she said. Her voice was friendly enough, but her eyes were needles trying to prick me. I had to look away so that she would put her hand down and let us go.

I adjusted my eyes to the sunlight. It was a big PE area. In the center was the basketball court where we had sat the previous day and to the left was a playground. Near that was a cluster of tall trees and a couple of picnic tables. Kids were spread out doing different things. Sopiep waved to me from the court with a jump rope in her hand.

"Come on," I said excitedly to Kelly and Belle, "Sopiep has a jump rope." They told me that they'd see me later. "It will be fun," I insisted. But they were already running off to the big tree down near the playground.

"If you want you can come play with us," Belle called back.

They met up with some other kids and began playing tag. There was a boy, probably in Sopiep's class, who all of them were running from. As I continued to look I realized that the girls weren't really running away from him; instead, it seemed that they wanted him to tag them. I heard their shrieks and laughter from where I stood. Every ounce of hot blood in my body urged me to go, but I joined Sopiep on the court, where it was just the two of us jumping rope.

At lunch, Kelly and Belle saved me a seat, and I completely forgot about Sopiep when I joined them. They wanted to talk more about Anthony: which house he lived in, did he talk about them at my table, did he have a girlfriend. I tried explaining that I didn't know him and didn't want anything to do with him. They giggled, thinking I was joking. Toward the end of the lunch period, I saw Sopiep sitting with Anthony at the opposite table. She had turned to look at me, and I waved at her. She waved back, but it was only a small wave.

Later in Mr. Summers's class, Anthony wanted to know why I hadn't eaten with him and Sopiep. "We saved you a seat, you know," he said. I didn't know why he thought I would want to eat with *him*.

"Well, I was at the other table," I said.

"You want to be their friend, don't you?" He nodded at Kelly and Belle, who were staring straight at us. I didn't know what to say. Of course that was what I wanted, but I didn't know why I just couldn't tell him. I mean, there was nothing wrong with eating with people you want as friends. "They're not very nice," he said several seconds later.

"For the thousandth time, leave me alone, Anthony. You don't even know them. Remember, you're *new* here."

Sopiep and Anthony waited for me at the flagpole after school. I didn't know how he had gotten out of class so quickly but didn't care enough to ask. I walked behind them again, all the while wishing Anthony would just leave so that Sopiep and I would have time alone to talk. From their conversation I learned that he liked painting and corn dogs and she had three brothers.

Before Sopiep turned at her street she asked if I could come out to play later.

"I think so," I said.

"Can you ask? I'll meet you here." Sopiep had both of her parents and three older brothers, so someone would be home for her to ask if she could go out and play. I didn't have anyone to ask. I didn't know why, but I almost stuck out my tongue at her and told her to leave me alone. The urge to do so disappeared when she cocked her head slightly to one side and smiled, not at Anthony or the things around us, but at me.

"Okay, I'll ask my dad," I lied.

"I'll come out, too," Anthony yelled before crossing the street.

I almost skipped the rest of the way home. I had friends, and two of them were the most popular girls in the fifth grade. Maybe the school year wouldn't be so bad after all.

About an hour later I walked back to Maggie's corner. Anthony was pacing back and forth with a long twig in his hand. "Where have you been? We've been waiting for you," he said. Sopiep was playing with grass blades.

"Sorry. What are you guys doing?" I asked.

"Let's go in the park and play tag. Maggie will be home base," Sopiep said, and got up.

Anthony was It first, and he had a hard time tagging us. Each time he was close, Sopiep and I held hands and one of us would touch Maggie's trunk.

"You're It," he said to Sopiep.

"I am not," she argued.

"Why not? I just tagged you."

She and I giggled and tumbled to the ground. "Yeah, but I'm touching Amy, and she's touching Maggie, so both of us are safe." Her body shook with the laughter. Whereas my laughs were loud, hers were quiet and were shown in happy tears.

"That's a stupid rule," he grumbled, but I knew from the expression on his face that he was impressed with us for having implemented the *stupid* rule first in this game.

We took a break and sat down to rest against Maggie's trunk, wishing we had something cold to drink. I would have asked them back to my house, but there wasn't anything in the refrigerator. A few minutes later Anthony crawled onto his stomach and lay with his arms and legs stretched out. I was envious of him. The grass was as thick and soft as a comforter, but I wouldn't dare to lie around like that in public, especially with a boy nearby. As a boy, he could do almost anything he wanted.

"Do you like living with your grandma?" Sopiep asked Anthony. He turned onto his back and stared at the blue sky before nodding. I wanted to know about his parents but knew not to ask.

"Hey, Sopiep," I said, "where's the sign that Anthony told us about in his story?"

She and I stood up and walked around Maggie until we found it. It was much smaller than I had imagined, and the words were barely legible.

"What's *immortality*?" I asked.

Anthony got up, too, and walked over to the plaque. "I think my grandma said something about living forever and ever. And you're It." He hit me on the back.

I was chasing Sopiep when Kelly walked by. "Hi, Amy. Hi, Tony," she said.

"Anthony," he corrected her.

"You want to play?" I asked.

Kelly walked around the fence and volunteered to be It, which I thought was really nice of her. The three of us spread out, teasing her to catch us. And when she took a step, we ran away and screamed as if someone were coming after us with a whip. But she soon stopped chasing Sopiep and me, leaving the two of us to stand and watch her run after Anthony.

●

About a week later during PE I went to the trees near the playground with Kelly and Belle. I intended to invite Sopiep to join us, but Belle stopped me. "Don't ask her," she said.

"Why?"

"She's weird," Kelly answered. I didn't understand why Sopiep was weird, but I also didn't want to question Kelly. As I followed her and Belle my stomach felt the same way it had when I had ridden a roller coaster once back in St. Pete.

As I started walking with the two girls, another girl with swinging pigtails waved to me from the court, and I told myself that she wasn't Sopiep. When we reached the other side of the basketball court we slowed down because Kelly and Belle wanted me to ask Anthony to play. I called him over, but when he saw them he screamed, "No."

"If you want, Tony, we'll watch you shoot baskets," Kelly called out. He shook his head. "He is so cute," she cooed.

I didn't understand these girls—or, in fact, many of the girls. Lots of them liked Anthony, wanting to be his partner in music class, or sharing a palette with him in art class, or offering him their snacks at lunch. It wasn't unusual for him to find a note with a big heart drawn in red on his desk. Even Mrs. Ortiz was nicer to him than to the rest of the boys.

For the next two weeks I spent almost all of my time at school with Kelly and Belle. It was hard not to play with them or eat with them at lunch because I would have had to be crazy to turn their friendship down: during PE, they wanted me, of all the girls who yearned to be part of their group, on their team or in their game of tag. Each time I played with them and as I ran away from the boy who reached his hand out to tag me, I told myself that Sopiep did have other friends . . . what would she have done if I didn't attend North Park? At lunch, I sat in the important seat next to Kelly and Belle. They trusted me with their stories and jokes, especially when they were about someone else. Sometimes they even asked me for my opinion of someone. And when I said something funny about another girl needing to brush her hair or her teeth, the three of us would huddle and break into a long laugh, one that others wished they could join in.

One day when I left school I didn't see Sopiep or Anthony. I waited for Sopiep near the flagpole, but she never showed up. So I walked home alone.

"Hey, Amy!" Anthony called from his grandma's porch.

"Where were you guys?" I asked.

"Sopiep didn't want to wait anymore." He crossed the street to where I was.

"Why?"

"She said you don't like her."

"That's not true."

"She said you don't talk to her and you act like you don't know her."

"I do too talk to her."

"Yeah, but only after school," he said, and went back home. I wanted him to come back so I could prove I had been nice to her and hadn't ignored her, but I changed my mind. *Sopiep's just jealous,* I said to myself. *She's jealous that I've become popular, and she's mad because I have more friends than she does.*

Dad was on the sofa when I got home. As soon as I saw him I almost walked out, thinking that I had unlocked the wrong door. It wasn't right that he was home in the middle of the day; he was supposed to be at work. It occurred to me that maybe he had lost his job, and the fear of it weakened my legs.

I could hear my voice cracking as I said hi. He nodded without taking his eyes off the TV. A beer can was in one hand and a cigarette in the other. It vaguely reminded me of the night when Mr. Yen had been at our house bad-mouthing women. I walked into the kitchen for a glass of water and saw a couple of empty cans on the table and a couple of new ones in the fridge. I was now certain that he had lost his job. And I began to think how unfair it would be for me to have to move again and to make new friends.

"Where were you?" he asked.

"School," I said before drinking the water.

"Don't get smart. I asked you where you were."

I put the glass in the sink and tiptoed back to where he was. It amazed me that he always thought I was trying to get *smart* with him.

"After school, I walked home."

He finally turned away from the screen and to me. His eyes landed on mine and challenged them to relent. I looked down at the carpet, at his feet, at his work shirt, at his chin, anywhere but his eyes. As I waited for him to speak my heart beat in my ears. "I know everything," he finally said. "Who were you talking to after school?"

Relief washed over me as I realized he was just talking about Anthony. "Oh, he's a boy from school," I said.

Dad slowly lifted the can to his lips and drank from it. "Is he your *boyfriend*?" He huffed at the end of the question.

"No," I said, and laughed lightly to show him it wasn't what he was thinking. "Dad, he's just a kid from my class."

He rambled on. "Kids *here* have boyfriends. I mean, how absurd is that?"

"Dad . . . ," I started to explain, but he told me in Cambodian to be quiet.

"When they're just two years old, their parents think it's cute that they have boyfriends. Teasing them about it. It's the parents that make a child turn bad. Setting bad example. Ha!" In a louder voice he said, "I will not have you turn out like your mom. If you ever think of becoming like her, I'll chain you up." He shook a finger at me. "Do you understand me?"

I told him that I did understand him . . . though I really didn't. What did Mom and a two-year-old have in common? And why was he acting crazier than ever? Nevertheless, it comforted me to know that he hadn't lost his job and that we wouldn't have to move.

●

One morning as soon as I walked into class Kelly handed me a note. When I lifted off the top flap she grabbed it back. "It's not for you," she said. "It's for Tony—I mean Anthony."

"Why are you giving it to me?"

"I want you to give it to him." She explained that every

note she'd given him he had thrown away. So my job was to hand-deliver it. "Make sure he gets it, and make sure he reads it and answers it *today*," she said. I didn't want to do it, but she told me I was one of her best friends. And best friends did things like this.

I sat at my table and waited for Anthony, hoping Mrs. Ortiz wouldn't return anytime soon. *Keep her at the door*, I prayed. As soon as Anthony sat down I slid the note to him. He looked at me and opened it immediately.

I read the note with him. *I like you. Do you like me? Yes or no. Love, Kelly*. I couldn't believe a girl would write something like that. If Dad or Mom ever caught me writing those words, they would kill me. "Good Cambodian girls don't go after boys," she would have told me. I raised my head and turned toward Kelly and Belle, who were looking back at us. Belle was fidgeting in her seat, and Kelly sat as still as a tree on a windless day.

The bell was going to ring in a couple of minutes and Anthony didn't look as if he was going to do anything. "Answer it before Mrs. Ortiz comes in," I ordered.

He rolled his eyes and lazily dug into his backpack and took out a red marker. It was the color of love; everyone knew that. I was so grateful that Anthony was going to say he liked her back. I had succeeded in being her best friend. I gave Kelly a thumbs-up, at which she just nodded.

"Circle *yes* fast," I urged him when Mrs. Ortiz walked in. He held the marker clumsily and slowly circled *no* instead, and drew a picture of a devil's head on the entire paper. I had forgotten that red was also the color of blood.

Mrs. Ortiz heard the other two girls at our table snicker and walked by. I quickly yanked the paper from Anthony and put it inside my math book.

At PE I gave Kelly the note and waited with Belle for her to read it even though I already knew what it said. As a best friend, I would stand by her side. Kelly balled it up and threw it in a nearby trash can. "Come on, Belle," she said, and pulled her away.

I ran to catch up with them. Kelly turned around, and with a tightened-up face, she pointed her finger at the court. "Amy, you can go back and play with them."

"Why?" I asked. She didn't bother to answer as they walked away. Something told me there would be no use going after them. I had lost them forever.

I went to the playground anyway, but not near the tree. I sat on a swing and shoved my feet under the sand. I wondered if all American girls were that mean and selfish. If they were friends with you only when they wanted something from you. And I wondered why they acted as if they were better than me. I looked up and scanned the playground. I didn't see anyone who looked like me or Sopiep. It was me, alone now, against all the light-skinned people. Thinking about Sopiep, I kicked my feet into the sand a couple of more times.

"Told you they're not nice," Anthony said. I hadn't noticed he was standing in front of me.

"You're so mean," I said to him with a sneer.

"Why? Because I don't like her back?"

"All they wanted was to be your friend."

"They weren't very nice to you," he said again.

"I don't care."

"I do." He sat on the swing next to me.

I looked hard at him, still not understanding why he wouldn't leave me alone. I was about to tell him what the girls thought of him when I changed my mind, not wanting his head to get any bigger.

"Is Sopiep still mad at me?" I asked.

"I don't know. But I'll save you a seat at lunch and you can ask her."

Sopiep didn't talk to me at lunch, though. And deep inside, I didn't blame her. I was grateful to Anthony for trying to help, but I knew I needed to fix things on my own.

Five minutes before school ended I told Mr. Summers I had to go to the office. I took my backpack and slowly walked down the hall, waiting for the bell to ring. When it finally did, I ran outside and waited at the flagpole for Sopiep. I saw her and Anthony walking toward me and felt the thumping in my heart swell into my head.

"Hi," I said. Anthony ran off, leaving the two of us to walk the rest of the way alone. "I'm sorry for being so mean to you," I said. She didn't say anything. "You were so nice to me, and I wasn't nice back. Please don't stay mad at me." I waited for her to say something. Except for a dog barking down the street, the world stopped turning as I waited for her answer.

"It's okay," she said, but something—the perkiness, maybe—was missing in her voice.

At Maggie's corner, she turned onto her street. I knew if I didn't fix everything with her then, we would never be friends again.

"It's not okay," I said, and held her arm.

"You only want to be my friend now because they turned on you," she cried. Her pigtails swung from side to side.

I couldn't blame her for thinking that. "No." I shook my head. "That's not true."

Her face was so sad that it pained me to look at her. Memories of Janet and Melissa and all those mean kids back in St. Petersburg flooded my mind and heart. How could I not have seen that I had turned into one of them?

"You were the only person who really liked me . . . and," I said, beginning to hiccup, "and . . . and cared about me . . . and I treated you . . . like . . . like you didn't matter."

She shuffled her feet, but I was ready to hold her down if she made a move to leave. I would do anything to make her not be angry anymore, anything. "Please believe me," I begged.

Neither of us said a word for a long time. Then she jumped on me and wrapped her arms around my neck. Surprised at her affection, I fell to the ground and took her with me. With our arms still encircling each other, we rolled around, letting Maggie's low branches gently brush us.

We finally stopped and lay still, looking up at the gorgeous tree. "We'll be friends forever and ever," Sopiep said.

And I knew we would. "Because we're sisters," I said.

●

I had been sleeping when the bedroom door was kicked open. The sound jolted me up in bed. It was late and silence surrounded me, but my head continued to pound from the surprise. Sure that a burglar had gotten into the house, I screamed for my dad.

"Quiet!" the man said in Cambodian. I had come to hate the word. Even if it was said at a softer volume, it didn't carry the same meaning it did in English. In Cambodian it meant something more like *Shut up!* "It's me," he said. Yes, the voice was Dad's, but it was unusually raspy. I blinked a couple of times to make out the figure at the door. "Where are my keys?" Dad asked.

I was dumbfounded and had to think over his words before answering. "I don't know."

"Yes, you do." He said each word slowly, as if he'd forgotten the sound of them.

Although the hall light silhouetted only his slumped body, I knew that he was ugly and drunk. I wanted him to shut the door and pretend that he hadn't allowed me to see him this way. I knew that he had changed a lot since we moved, but I was willing to forget his sloppiness, his rude comments, and even his drinking if he would just leave and pretend he wasn't drunk. But he didn't leave and instead yelled again, "Where are my keys!"

"I don't know."

"Come here." His voice turned eerily soft. I tried to move, but my legs anchored my body to the bed.

"Are you *dumb*?" Dad's body twitched and his teeth, pointy little razors, shone in two rows. "I said come here."

I knew that I couldn't just refuse to do what he had ordered, so I forced my legs and body out of bed and deliberately walked to him. I saw his strong hand reach out and lock around my arm, his grip penetrating to my bone as he pulled me into the living room. All the lights were on and the TV was blasting; it was odd that I hadn't heard it earlier. Beer cans were scattered around the room and a couple of bottles lay empty on the kitchen table. Even though the sight shocked me, all that ran through my mind was how grateful I was that the Jacksons weren't home. They had told me earlier that day that they would be out of town for the weekend. I wouldn't have known what to say if they had knocked on our door that night.

With a hand around each of my arms, Dad picked me up and dropped me on the sofa. His sour breath exploded in my nostrils even as he walked away.

"Where are my keys?" he asked me again from the kitchen.

Suddenly I turned cold and began to shiver. I looked at

him and shook my head. "I don't know, Dad." His body was limp against a kitchen chair and his eyes were glazed over. Embarrassed for him, I quickly turned away.

"Liar!" he screamed back.

I jumped at the sound of his hand hitting the table. What should I do if he hurt me? I could run to my room and lock the door or I could run to the bathroom and lock that door. But he might break it down, and that would create more problems when the Jacksons found out. The safest way out would be through the front door . . . but I could never do that. I couldn't just run down the block and scream out that my dad was drunk and crazy. What would we do if someone called the police? No matter what he did, he was still my dad, and I couldn't let anyone, myself included, shame him.

Surprisingly, Dad's rage subsided. The TV was still on, but the silence between us was so thick that I didn't hear anything at all. For the first time that night my body started to relax. I began to hope for a better morning, although I would never be able to erase the sight of my drunken father. My eyes grew tired, and my body yearned for sleep. As I got up, though, Dad began hollering.

"Call the police," he said. I sat back down and ignored him. "Didn't you hear me? I said call . . . the . . . police." I glanced at him briefly, and he chuckled. "All you girls, you give no man respect." He began to hit his chest. "I brought her here!" He pointed to his right, as if that were where Mom was standing. I wished she were. Then maybe I wouldn't have had to see him this way. And as suddenly as he had started yelling, he turned quiet once more.

I counted the minutes that passed: one, two, ten, and sixteen. Positive that I had waited long enough this time to show no disrespect, I stood up and headed back for my room.

"Where are you going?" he asked. "Come here."

I walked over to the table but distanced myself from him. "Call the police." He pointed to the phone resting on the wall beside me. "Call the police and tell them how terrible I am. Tell them to take me away. You want me to go to jail? Well, call the police." His eyes were red and small and seemed to be dancing in their sockets.

Could he have heard my thoughts back in Las Vegas? But that was so long ago. "I never said I wanted you to go to jail," I said quietly.

He smirked and brushed a hand through his hair. "We are Cambodians! And I am your father! I will do whatever I want. I'm not scared of the police! So call them!"

Yes, we are Cambodians, I thought. I didn't need him to tell me that again and again. What did that have to do with the police or Mom? My head tightened.

I rubbed my temples in a circular motion with my fingers to relieve the pressure, something I had seen adults do. And it did alleviate some of the pain. As the tension continued to lessen with my massage, a sense of lightness and freedom came over me. *Who does Dad think he is? Yelling and getting mad at me whenever he feels like it. If he's mad at Mom, that's one thing, but he shouldn't get mad at me!* And just like that, any fear I had of him was replaced by contempt. Even if Dad was a big and mighty mountain, I was a more powerful force. With a single puff of my breath, he would fall!

"Okay!" I screamed back.

I took the two short steps as if I were a giant and picked up the phone. When I began punching 911 he dove onto the table and knocked over the empty bottles. They shattered as they hit the floor. He yanked the phone out of my hand and knocked me onto the floor in the process.

A stinging radiated through my left arm as I lay there amid the broken glass. Dad loomed over me, his eyes so big they had stopped dancing and were ready to pop out.

"Give me the phone!" I yelled at him.

He shook his head slowly as I continued my demand for it. I didn't know what he was going to do next. Not wanting to lose the fight, I kicked my legs against the floor, feeling a sharp pain each time.

"Don't," he said, "don't."

"I want the phone," I screamed, hearing my own shrieks as though they came from someone else.

He moved forward, and I braced myself by covering my face with my hands. He put his arms around me, and I fought to push him away. But he didn't do anything more than hold me against his chest. I felt his heart beat loudly.

"Oh, Amy, oh, Amy," Dad cried into my neck.

I didn't know when he would explode next, so I continued yelling for the phone. "Give me the phone. I *will* call them. You are not my dad!"

His tears and saliva wet my neck and cheek; the sliminess disgusted me. He lifted me off the floor and set me on the counter near the sink. As he walked away, I screamed after him still. When I looked down at the floor I saw a small puddle of blood and droplets that led to the sink. Thinking it was Dad's blood, the sight of them thrilled me. But I still felt that he deserved so much more punishment than a little bit of bleeding. I rubbed my stinging arm with my right hand and felt an unusual warmth and stickiness.

Dad came back with a wet towel and cleaned the cuts on my arm and feet. There wasn't much blood, but that didn't matter. What mattered now was that he was drunk and that I had almost called the police on him. Wasn't it true that I used to climb on his back and ride on his shoulders? Didn't he used to bring me cherry lollipops? Didn't he used to call me his little girl? I couldn't have imagined all those things. And now, why did he yell and threaten me almost every day, and worse, why was I yelling at him? I hated to think that our house now was filled with only shameful things.

"Do you hurt anywhere else?" Dad asked. I ignored him. "Do you want ice?" He didn't wait for my answer as he walked to the refrigerator.

When he opened the door, his keys jingled before landing with a thump on the floor. We didn't even bother to look at each other and pretend that there was no humiliation in what had just happened. Under different circumstances we both would have laughed about it, but not that night.

11

IN THE DAYS that followed Dad tried to act as if the incident hadn't happened. Before leaving for work he woke me up in the mornings to say breakfast was waiting for me. He called after school to check up on me. And when he returned home in the evening he went directly to the kitchen to cook dinner. But I made sure he didn't forget about that night. I did my best not to let the two-inch superficial cut on my arm heal by picking at it just to let it bleed some more. And I made sure he was never far from his keys. When he was at home I set them on the TV so that they would stare at him when he fell asleep and when he woke up. I couldn't let that night go as I had let the others. If he felt the need to remind me of who he was, then he, too, would have to remember who he was, no matter the time or day.

I knew Dad was trying to be a better father, but I still felt uneasy around him. To me, he was not *my* dad. Whenever I was with him and my heart beat fast, I waited for the moment he would blow up. I couldn't look at him without being embarrassed for him. Seeing his face meant more than seeing the eyes, the nose, and the lips . . . it meant seeing him drunk on that night over and over. So I spent most of my time either in my room or with Sopiep and her family.

It had gone well the first time I'd met Sopiep's family and stayed over for dinner. When Mrs. Sok asked about my parents, the table turned quiet. Even her three sons respectfully stopped talking. I moved the rice on my plate around with my fork as I considered how Sopiep's house was so perfect: a loving mom, a hardworking dad, and three caring brothers. Because I had none of that, I was scared that my answer would make Mrs. Sok look down on me. What if she turned mean like Melissa's mother had? What if she took the plate of food away from me and sent me home?

But I didn't want to lie. Besides, I had already told the people at temple; since she was Cambodian, I wouldn't have been surprised if she already knew. "My mom doesn't live with us, *Meing*," I told her. Figuring a long discussion about my parents was going to follow, I put down my fork. I glanced at her and then at her husband before looking back down at the table.

"And how is your dad?" Mrs. Sok asked while spooning more rice onto Sopiep's plate. My hand trembled as I picked up my fork again. I was prepared for many things, but not for her not to care about my past.

She probably hadn't heard me right, I thought. I cleared my throat and said, "My mom left us." My eyes felt wet, but I didn't want to cry in front of these people and ruin their dinner. I scrunched up my forehead to hold back the tears.

"I'm sorry," she said softly, "but I'm glad you're here. Sopiep told us that you're her best friend."

Sopiep, sitting next to me, nudged me with her shoulder and I couldn't help giggling. Telling someone about Mom and not feeling bad about it was like dropping an unwanted bag of secrets.

●

It was a cool Sunday morning in early October when Dad knocked on my door. "Someone's on the phone for you," he said. He was already dressed and shaved, but that no longer mattered to me.

"Amy, it's me, Sopiep." She had never called me before, so it took me a moment to clear my head. "We're going to the beach. Do you want to come?" she asked.

"Yeah, but I have to ask my dad first," I said.

"My parents wondered if he wants to go, too."

"Really?" I thought it was the greatest idea for Dad to meet Mr. Sok. Maybe he would see how a *real* father was supposed to be and act like one. "Wait while I ask." I put down the handset and walked to the couch.

When I asked Dad, he didn't answer immediately. I begged him to go, telling him how great Mr. Sok was. But he didn't agree. "Do you think they're better than me?" he asked.

I didn't answer him, and I didn't want to stay home with him. When I asked again if I could go, he looked disappointed. "Sunday is my only day off—don't you want to spend it with me?"

I quietly stared at the carpet, satisfied that I was answering his question. The clock ticked as he waited for me to say how much I would rather stay home with him, but I didn't change my mind. *How do you feel now? How do you feel about not being wanted?* I wanted to ask him.

"Fine, you can go," he finally said, and turned the TV on again.

I went back to the phone and told Sopiep that Dad was tired.

With my towel in my backpack, I opened the front door every few minutes. "Shut the door," Dad almost growled. "You act like you've never been anywhere before. If they're picking you up, they'll come to the door."

I didn't want them to come to the door and meet Dad in a bad mood. So when I heard the station wagon pull up, I ignored him and ran out with my backpack. I knew I would get in trouble for what I had just done, but I would deal with that later.

Except for the nearby noisy highway, Mission Beach was beautiful. There weren't many trees, but the water was greenish blue and the sand was toasty white. Many people had already found themselves picnic shelters and grills, piling their tables with coolers, bags of food, and beach towels. Others played Frisbee, and even though the day was chilly, some people strolled down the nearby sidewalk in shorts and women even wore bikini tops. In the distance, sailboats decorated the ocean with colorful sails. The entire scene, with babies wailing and little kids arguing with each other and mothers telling their children to put on sunscreen, was a duplicate of a day at St. Pete Beach.

"Let me see your bathing suit," Sopiep said when we got out of the station wagon. I told her I had left it on my bed. The truth was that I had outgrown the one I had brought from St. Pete.

"You forgot it? How can you forget it when we're coming to the beach?" She put her hands to her head in fake disbelief. "It's okay. I won't wear mine today, then."

As we walked to a picnic shelter, I held her back. "Who are those people?" I asked.

"They're my parents' friends. They're nice, you'll like them."

I wasn't as sure as she was. One of them was bound to ask questions about me and my parents. I didn't have trouble with telling the truth, but I still had a problem with people asking me questions I didn't think they should ask in the first place.

"What's wrong?" Sopiep asked. I just shook my head. No matter how I felt about her, I knew that she would never understand. And for a brief moment, I felt a familiar loneliness.

I stood back as her family greeted their friends. Everyone was very well dressed. They almost looked American in their tailored shorts and shirts, especially the woman who rested her sunglasses atop her head to hold back her hair. There were also other children, but they were either older than Sopiep and me or much younger than we were.

Sopiep *chumreab suor*ed the adults. Afterward, each of them pulled her into their arms, telling her how much she'd grown. Big grins fell over her parents' faces. With the rest of us watching, the last man tickled her and pretended not to let her go. "Let me go, please," she squealed.

"Only if you tell us who your friend is," he said, and for the first time that day they turned their attention to me.

Sopiep's mom gently pulled me to her and put her arms around me. It was comforting to have the warmth of her body on my back; I could almost feel her soft skin through our layers of clothes. That day, Sopiep could have everyone else's attention just as long as I could have her mom's.

"I will, I will . . . if you stop first," Sopiep begged the man.

"It's a deal."

She came over to where her mom and I stood and put a

hand on my shoulder. "This is my best friend, Amy," she announced.

Remembering my manners, I also *chumreab suor*ed the adults.

"Where are your parents?" one lady asked.

"My dad is sick," I lied. In the car, I had told Mr. and Mrs. Sok that Dad had caught a cold.

"What about your mom?" I was about to answer when Sopiep's mom told them that it was just me and my dad.

"Well, next time you have to make sure your dad comes so that we can meet him," the lady said. And that was the end of the interrogation. Wow, I thought. I wondered if the Cambodians in San Diego ate a different sort of rice from the ones in St. Petersburg.

"Let's get back to the game," the man who had tickled Sopiep said.

Three other people, including Sopiep's dad, walked with him to a nearby volleyball net. Sopiep and I stayed at the picnic table with the others and watched the four of them play a game that looked a lot like volleyball. Instead of using a big leather ball, though, they used a hollow wooden one the size of a softball.

"Why do they have towels around their heads?" I asked Sopiep.

"For protection. One time my dad got a cut when the ball hit him on the forehead, and it bled."

"Really?"

"Yep. There's still a scar from it."

A little bit later Sopiep's mom and a couple of younger guys started grilling beef shish kebabs and chicken wings while two ladies stayed at the picnic table to fix the vegetables. I liked the sound of the chicken fat sizzling on the grill, and the smell of meat was mouthwatering. One lady, with a cleaver in her hand, shredded a large green mango into a big bowl. As the knife cut into the hard fruit, bits of the light green flesh splattered onto her hands. I hadn't eaten tart green mango for so long that my stomach growled.

"If you girls are hungry, have some potato chips," she said, and handed us the bag.

"Thanks," Sopiep said.

Embarrassed, I looked away and wondered if she had also noticed that I was eyeing the cooking meats. Sopiep offered me some chips, but I told her in a loud voice that I wasn't hungry.

We didn't start eating until the players stopped their game. Two men carried plates of beef and chicken from the grill to the table while the women waited for them. I had never seen a Cambodian man serve his wife or children before.

Even though there was a lot of food, my eyes were larger than my stomach. I waited patiently as my hands itched to grab some kebabs and wings, and I even panicked when the big kids came back from wherever they had been. *What if we don't have enough?* I thought.

"Help me with the towel," Sopiep said from a tree about fifteen feet away. She wanted the two of us to have our own picnic area. I was more interested in getting our share of the wings and green mango, so the towel would have to wait.

"Come here," the lady who had shredded the mango said to me. I watched her long dark fingers work her chopsticks to load two plates with shish kebabs, six wings, rice, and a nice helping of shredded mango—leaving almost nothing for the rest of them.

"Thank you," I said, and took them to where Sopiep was.

"Let me know if you need more," she said. With big pores and frizzy hair, she wasn't very pretty. But her smile was.

Sopiep turned up her nose when I brought her the food. "What?" I asked.

"Ugh. That smells." She pointed to the green mango, which was seasoned with fish sauce and scallions. "You can have mine." That was fine with me.

"She gave us a lot of food," I told her, and pointed to the lady.

"Yeah, Auntie Sarah is nice. We've known her forever."

"Why don't you call her *Meing* like I call your mom?" I asked.

She thought for a moment before answering. "I don't know. I guess it's because she's not like the other ladies. Just wait and you'll see what I mean."

As we made ourselves comfortable, Sopiep's oldest brother came by and took a wing off her plate. "It's mine," she whined, and hit his hand. She talked in a different voice, a softer, more babyish one, from the one she used at school. Then he took one of mine, too, before walking away to his friends. I didn't want to hit him, though. It was actually kind of thoughtful of him to take food from me, too.

"How old is he?" I asked.

"Twenty-two."

"Wow."

"I was a mistake." I choked on my drink. "Seriously, my parents didn't plan on another kid, especially when they thought they were going to have a fourth boy."

"So what happened?"

"I overheard my brothers talking. They said that after

they came to America, my parents did it, and my mom got pregnant."

"Did it?" I asked.

"Yeah, *did it*. You know what I mean, right?" She looked intently at me.

"Yeah!" I said, and rolled my eyes at her. And we burst out laughing. I knew what she meant, but it wasn't something that I could imagine her parents, or mine, doing.

Sopiep licked her fingers, and I licked mine. The chicken, marinated in oyster sauce, was delicious.

"Did you ever have a boyfriend?" she asked.

"No!" I screamed. "What about you?"

"Shh . . ." She put a finger to her lips and covered my mouth with her salty hand. "No, but I liked someone." She said that if I promised not to tell anyone, she would tell me the kid's name. It turned out to be the same boy who played tag regularly with Kelly and Belle. She had stopped liking him when she found out he was dumb and didn't know half of his spelling words. At least she was smarter than Janet and didn't like a boy just because she thought he was cute, whatever that meant. "Do you like anyone?"

"No way," I said. I didn't want to talk about boys anymore. It made me feel that Dad was watching me or listening in on our conversation. And, I didn't want to think about him.

When the sun was at its highest point, Sopiep and I lay on our backs, trying to brown our already dark skin. She talked about how bossy her brothers were, but I didn't really listen. My stomach was full, and although there were many people around us, it was quiet and peaceful. Her voice grew fainter and fainter as I let my body melt into the tranquility around us.

We must have been sleeping for half an hour when Sopiep's mom woke us up. "Get up," she said. "Sleeping right after a meal makes you lazy."

"Do we have to go now?" Sopiep asked her mom as I stretched.

"No, but don't the two of you want to swim?" I was relieved when Sopiep said no. "Then you can walk with us."

We waited for Sopiep to kiss her dad good-bye before starting on our hike. "Be careful, Daddy," she said to him at the volleyball net.

"I will," he said, and kissed the top of her head.

Mr. Sok was shorter than his wife, but he still looked like a father. He had a receding hairline and a clean face. He spoke kindly to her and the people around him. Actually, when he spoke, people stopped to listen, and they often asked for his advice and opinion. And I never heard him say anything foolish or hurtful, even to Sopiep. I wanted so much to yell to the world that my father, *my father*, was once a gentle man, too.

The legs of the three women ahead of us moved in unison. I felt an unfamiliar pride in walking behind them, wanting to let the people around us know that I was part of this group of beautiful, intelligent Cambodian women. I allowed my laughs to roar loud enough to make themselves heard at Sopiep's silly jokes.

"Amy! Sopiep!" We both looked around to see who was calling us. "Over here." At first I couldn't believe it was Anthony who was running toward us in his swimming trunks.

"It is him, it is him," Sopiep said excitedly, and waved both arms at him.

I watched her take her hair out of the pigtails, then I waved at Anthony, too. I had stopped calling him Rabbit

Face once I decided he wasn't such a bad kid. But at the sight of his almost naked body—nipples and belly button included—I turned my eyes away. "Come over here," he urged, and beckoned us with his hand.

With Sopiep's mom's permission, we went with him to his picnic shelter. It was about twice the size of ours, and little kids were all over the place, some with wet hair and over-sized bathing suits and some with sticky-looking faces and fingers. Most of the women lay on their towels wearing big sunglasses, bright red lipstick, and extra-small bikinis while the men, who had hairy chests, lounged around in shorts. Older men and women sat in a small circle holding babies and talking in an Italian accent.

"You want anything to eat?" Anthony asked. We shook our heads. "Well, then, do you want to play cards?"

Sopiep jumped up and down at the mention of that and pulled me with her as Anthony took us to a grassy area. Several other kids and a man Anthony introduced as his uncle sat in a circle on a blanket. Next to it was a huge watermelon.

"What's that for?" I asked Anthony.

"It's the prize."

"For what?"

"If you get the most watermelon seeds at the end of the game, you win it."

"What game?"

"Blackjack," he said

"I love blackjack," Sopiep squealed, and clapped her hands.

At the sight of us his uncle made the rest of the kids move back to make more room in the circle before explaining the rules of the game. "Every player will get twenty watermelon seeds to start off," he began, and lit a cigarette.

"Here are the basics, for those of you who need reminders." The cigarette seesawed up and down between his lips as he spoke. "You get two cards, and you want them to add up to twenty-one."

"What if they don't?" a kid asked. Anthony's uncle gave her a funny "Don't you know?" look, and the rest of us laughed. "If they don't, you can ask for more cards. But"—he raised a finger—"you don't want to go over twenty-one because if you do, you *lose!*" He took out his cigarette, stuck out his big tongue, and shook his head fast.

"Neil, why are you teaching those kids how to gamble?" It was the same woman who had yelled at me on the first day of school. Mrs. Cupelli wore an apron and was at the grill turning sausages and burgers. Afraid of being sent away, I looked in a different direction so she wouldn't see me.

"It's okay, Ma, we're playing with seeds, for crying out loud . . . it's not like there's money involved." I remembered what Dad had said in Las Vegas. Gambling was gambling, and I didn't want to stay any longer. I stood up. "Where are you going?" Anthony's uncle asked. I told him that I would just like to watch, thank you. "Suit yourself," he said, and went back to distributing the seeds.

I remembered Dad's specific words: "Gambling is a bad, bad thing." But didn't he do it himself? He'd always told me to do this and to do that, be respectful, be thoughtful, be kind, be smart. Well, what about him? Plus, if it was so bad, why was Sopiep playing?

"Place your bet," he told the six kids. Sopiep moved half of her seeds in front of her while the others put out only two or three. "Baby, what are you going to do if you lose it all?" She shrugged off his question but pulled back all of her seeds except for one. He shook his head. "Anthony, help her out.

And, you, you sure you don't want to play? Tell Uncle Neil why you don't want to play." He looked up at me with a deck of cards in his hand. He didn't wait for my answer and shoved me my seeds. Relenting, I sat back down and bet two of them. Uncle Neil dealt the cards.

"Blackjack!" a boy across from us screamed. I looked at his cards and saw a red king and a black ace.

"Good job, Joey." Uncle Neil gave him three seeds even though he had bet only two and took up his two cards.

Anthony, on my right, got eighteen; Sopiep, on my left, got fifteen. I got twenty. Anthony didn't want any more cards, but I asked for another one.

"You sure?" Uncle Neil asked. "I have a nine showing."

"Yeah, you told me to get twenty-one."

"Anthony, explain it to her, will ya?"

Anthony started to open his mouth when I put my hand in his face. "Fine, I won't take one," I told Uncle Neil. Then he went to Sopiep, and she said that she didn't want another card.

"Why not?" he asked.

"I don't want to go over," she said.

"And how do you expect to win with a fifteen when I'm showing a nine?"

"I will," she said adamantly, and he went to the next kid.

Just as she had said, Sopiep won when Uncle Neil exposed his second card, which was a five, and drew another nine to make his three cards equal twenty-three. Only one kid, who had busted with a twenty-five before Uncle Neil drew his cards, lost.

"We won! We won!" Sopiep pulled at my arm, getting Uncle Neil to chuckle.

"Calm down." He winked at her. "That was just luck."

But it wasn't. Sopiep won many hands, although she hardly got anything above a seventeen. But I won even more seeds and was taking more chances, as Anthony said. I learned how to split two cards with the same value and how to double down by betting more seeds on good cards, all of which brought my winnings to more than anyone's, except Joey, who kept getting blackjacks.

About thirty minutes later most of the kids, including Sopiep and Anthony, had lost all their seeds and had to step out of the game, leaving them to watch Joey and me. He continued to have easy wins: twenty, nineteen, and twenty against Uncle Neil's top card showing an eight. I had to work for mine, drawing on a seventeen to beat the eighteen, or splitting two eights when he showed a seven. With Sopiep behind me, massaging my neck, my adrenaline was high and pumping. Soon, some grown-ups even crowded around us.

"These two are good," Uncle Neil told his mother, but she wasn't amused and waved him off before walking away again.

"Two more minutes," she warned him. It was the last bet, and Joey was up by three seeds. He bet four and admiring applause broke out.

"Come on, Amy, you can win," Anthony said.

My two sidekicks were the best, I thought as I bet five seeds. My arms grew numb and my face felt flushed as Uncle Neil dealt the cards. Joey got a pair of queens and gloated. I got a seven and a four. And Uncle Neil showed a red ten. I would only win if I doubled down by betting five more seeds and got a card with a ten value. I didn't really care about the watermelon; it wasn't something I would be proud of when I took it home. In fact, I wouldn't be able to take it home without explaining to Dad how I had won it. But so many people were around us, some of them even chanting my name. I couldn't disappoint them. "Joey, Joey . . ." "Amy, Amy . . ."

"Shush," Uncle Neil said. And all was silent. When I concentrated hard enough, I even heard swimmers splashing each other in the ocean and a siren speeding down the highway.

I counted five seeds and moved them next to the original five. Sopiep dug her nails into my shoulders.

"Ouch," I said.

"One card?" asked Uncle Neil. I nodded. "Are you sure?" I nodded again. "Just one card, right?"

"Yes!" I nervously yelled at him, causing laughs to break out.

"Okay, just checking."

It was a two, followed by a sympathetic "oh" from the spectators. I got a total of thirteen, so my chance of winning was almost zero. Joey was going to win his hand for sure. The crowd chanted "Bust, bust, bust . . . ," as Uncle Neil moved his hand to flip over his second card. Everyone broke out again in hoorays when they saw it was a two; Uncle Neil had a crummy twelve, so he would have to draw another card. By then I had learned that the chance of drawing a ten was very high . . . and if he did, he would bust and Joey and I would win. Because my bet was higher than Joey's I would win the game, including the watermelon. Panic broke out on Joey's face. My heart thumped against my chest and up into my head. "Bust, bust, bust . . ."

Uncle Neil drew a king.

"You win, you win!" Sopiep cried.

She, Anthony, and I got up and hugged one another. I was so happy that I didn't even care when Anthony threw his arms around me.

Uncle Neil offered to carry the twenty-pound watermelon to our shelter, but Anthony said he would take care of it. He encased the humongous fruit in the big blanket that we had sat on and dragged it all the way to our area. It climbed over pebbles and was kicked a couple of times by kids who ran into it, but I didn't care. It was my prize.

"What do you have there?" Sopiep's dad asked her.

"It's a watermelon. Amy won it in a card game." I wished she hadn't said that. With all their eyes on me, I wasn't sure if they were judging me or admiring me.

"Sopiep almost won," I said. I didn't know what I was aiming to do, but I figured that whatever they thought about Sopiep, they could ditto it for me.

I asked Sopiep's mom if I could use the cleaver to cut open the watermelon.

"You should take it home," Mr. Sok said.

"Thank you, *Phou*, but we already have one at home," I lied, again.

For the next half hour all of us, including Anthony, stood around eating the sweet red fruit, letting its juice drip down our chins and between our fingers.

As we drove back home the sun was beginning to set. The station wagon was stuffy, but it felt good to breathe in the salty air that stuck to our clothes, hair, and skin. Sopiep's parents sat up front talking about the high cost of electricity, two of her brothers sat in the back talking about soccer, Sopiep fell asleep on the same brother she had hit earlier, and I watched other cars go by, afraid of leaving this life and going back to my real one.

●

In late October, I found Dad on the couch at home again in the afternoon on a workday, with disheveled hair and wet eyes. The only other day he had left work early was the time he accused me of having a boyfriend. I never knew why he had come home early that day; I only knew he was in a bad mood. And sure that he would be in another bad mood, I wished I had just stayed at Maggie's corner.

Dad's eyes were fixed on the muted television. No light was turned on, so I walked to the window and tied back the curtains. "Don't," he said. I stood at the window and wondered, certain that Sopiep and Anthony would be waiting for me, if I should still go outside and play. On the coffee table I saw a brown paper bag that held a six-pack, and glared at Dad.

Dad remained in the same position in front of the muted television. I picked up my backpack and headed for my room.

"Do you know what today is?" he asked. I walked back to the couch and sat beside him. "It's been one year today that your mom left us. One year." He showed me his index finger.

I did know; I had known about it the week before when Mrs. Yen called. And since then I had been counting the days and hours. I had even woken up that morning with a thick lump in my throat. I knew it was one year, but I didn't want to think about it . . . at least not until later that night, when I would be alone. I figured that I would just cry by myself before falling asleep. That was what I had planned, and to have him bring it up before I was ready agitated me.

"One *year*," he repeated softly, as if he finally understood it. We didn't talk for a long time, just stared at the voiceless cartoons.

"Don't you miss her, Amy?" I told him I did. "I still miss her," he said. And he broke into a cry that I had never heard a man give before, not even on television. As my own had so many times, his body shook and his eyes seeped an endless amount of tears. "I was so sure that she would come back. She's somewhere here in California. . . ."

"What?" I exclaimed. "Mom is in California?"

"I don't know. I think so. That's why we moved here, Amy. I figured it would be easier for her to come back to us if we were nearby."

"Dad, she's either here or she isn't." Astonishingly, I didn't feel mad at him for withholding this information. I wasn't even surprised to hear what he had just said. By then nothing seemed surprising. But I did want to know. "So why do you think she's in California?"

With his face turned up at the ceiling, Dad squeezed his eyes shut and took a deep breath. "Remember that big brown envelope I was carrying when we went to Mr. Yen's house?"

"Yeah," I answered. How could I ever forget that awful night?

"Those were the divorce papers, Amy. Your mom's lawyer's in Los Angeles, and I think she's there, too."

"I thought you said we didn't know anyone there. Why didn't we just go there and look for her?"

"It's not that easy, Amy. We have to do things carefully."

I could feel my heart thumping. "Did you at least try to find her?"

"Yeah, but she doesn't want to talk to me."

"What about me? She'll want to talk to me."

Dad didn't say anything, and started crying again. As much as I wanted to know the answer to my question, I was also afraid. For the next few minutes, I watched him cry. Sometimes his shoulders shook, and sometimes there was complete silence except for his deep breathing. Then he would start up again. I wished he would stop, not because I felt sorry for him, but because he wasn't supposed to cry. That was my job, and *he* was supposed to comfort *me*. I didn't understand this weak man beside me.

Finally he said, "I was sure she would come back."

I didn't want to remind him that she didn't even want to talk to him, so I said the only thing I could think of. "It's okay."

He didn't believe me. I didn't even really believe me. But I thought that if it wasn't okay, then what was? I couldn't imagine Dad and me going on like this and nothing ever being okay. I didn't think God was that cruel.

He shook his head emphatically. "It's not. I miss her." His voice cracked.

I wanted to crack, too, not just my voice, but all over. But I couldn't in front of him, not now. "She's not coming back, Dad."

He squealed in horror as I said these words, and dug his fingers into his head and stomped on the carpet. *What am I supposed to do?* I asked myself. I tried to grab his hands, but he pushed me away.

I had to get out of the house and leave him to deal with his own misery. Without looking back at him, I walked to the front door and said, "Dad, she's not coming back. You've got to let it go." Then I left the house.

"Don't say that," I heard him moan behind me as the door shut.

"Is everything okay?" The voice startled me.

"Yeah, thanks," I said to Mrs. Jackson. She stopped watering our rosebushes and faced me with the running hose still in her hand. Her eyes watched me intently, and I sensed that she was waiting for me to explain why Dad was home so early. "He's not feeling good today," I said, and walked off.

I walked to the end of our street but at the last moment turned in a different direction from Maggie's corner. Sopiep and Anthony would wonder where I was, but I didn't feel like talking to them.

The autumn air was cool and breezy, and in the distance the sky began to turn orange. Except for the couple of streets I used every day, I didn't know the neighborhood well. But I was determined not to return home to Dad's mourning, so I continued to turn onto unfamiliar streets. I was looking for a dark, cold place where I could completely fall apart. I wanted a place that was sticky with dried-up tears.

Like Dad, I had prayed for Mom's return. Secretly, I dreamed that Mrs. Yen would call us one day and tell me that my mom was looking for us. "She misses the two of you," Mrs. Yen would say. Or else I would go home and see our belongings in a U-Haul truck. Dad would surprise me by saying, "We're going back home. Your mom's waiting for us." Although Sopiep, Anthony, and I had become good friends, I would have given them up easily just to have her back. Now that she hadn't come back, I guessed her decision to leave us was final. But that realization didn't make me cry—no matter how hard I tried to.

I turned onto a street where a couple of young men with long hair were standing in front of a car drinking and smoking. One of them said hi to me and asked why I was out so late. The sight of them made me notice the gray sky. I turned back around, racing to get back home before night fell, and heard them laughing behind me. With each big step, I strained my ears for following footsteps. Houses and corners looked alike, and street names sounded similar. I started to think that I would never get home. When I did find Magnolia Place I ran the rest of the way to our house.

Fearing Dad would go into another rage after the way I had left the house, I reluctantly unlocked the door and walked in.

"Come and eat dinner," I heard him call from the kitchen.

I cautiously walked in and found a meal set on the table. Dad was already seated, and he motioned for me to take a seat. He had washed his hair and put on clean clothes and cologne. And I realized that the kitchen had been cleaned, the carpet had been vacuumed—I could still see fresh marks on it—and his blankets had been folded. He scooped some rice onto my plate and told me that he had cooked his favorite dish of beef, tomato, and pineapple.

"Before I got married, I cooked this almost every night. My mom used to make it for me when I was little."

I wondered if he had forgotten what had happened before I left the house. I even wondered if he had forgotten who he was, or if he had more than one personality.

Halfway through dinner he said he wanted to talk and I was allowed to say anything I wanted. "Things will be different from now on," he began. I didn't mean to, but I jerked my hand away when he laid his on top of it. If I hurt his feelings, though, he didn't show it. "For one," he continued, "you will be inside when it gets dark. There are crazy people out there. And two, when I am at work you are to call me every hour." I thought calling him every hour was a little too much but didn't think it was the right time to say so.

"Amy, listen to me." I laid down my spoon. His tone was soft and kind, but I still didn't trust him. "I know that things have been bad here." There was a begging in his eyes that asked for my understanding. "You are my only child. I love you."

At those words, the lump in my throat opened like the gate to a dam. He put a napkin to my nose and told me to blow. I grabbed his hand and felt the roughness of his palm. I covered my face with it, holding his fingers, and cried into it. I didn't cry because my mother hadn't come back, but because he had told me he loved me and because something deep within my heart reassured me that Dad was going to change . . . and I was, too. We, the two of us, would be okay. For the first time in a year, I tasted happy tears.

12

Dad parked our Oldsmobile under a tree across the street from Del Mar Beach. It was still early on a Sunday morning, so the area didn't have many visitors except for us and a young couple in purple running suits jogging by with a golden retriever on a leash. Dad and I didn't say anything to each other as we got out of the car and crossed the street.

Even though the fog hadn't lifted I could see waves rolling in, leaving white foam to melt in the sand. The breeze whipped strands of hair in my face, and I shivered just thinking how cold the water must be.

"Where do you want to go?" Dad asked.

A car flew by behind us, and I turned to see that it was a yellow Ferrari. "Anywhere you want," I said.

With no destination in mind, Dad and I took slow steps toward a small grassy cliff, where he spread an old bedsheet for us to sit on.

I looked over at the quaint white Del Mar Hotel and down the street at the homes with huge rocks edging plants and flower gardens. And just up the street were the post office, Starbucks, and other small businesses we had driven past. I knew the world would turn big and busy that morning just as it always did, but it would be big and busy elsewhere, with no regard for us.

Dad and I looked out at the water, and there really wasn't anything about it that I hadn't seen before. It was blue just as beach water should be, just as the sun was yellow and the clouds were white. Just as the two people had run with their dog earlier, and just as Sopiep was home with her parents, everything but Dad and me was as it should have been.

For the past two weeks Dad and I'd been doing better. He yelled at me less. And I slowly began to see him as the father I had once known. Each morning I went to school and he went to work, and in the evening we ate dinner and watched TV together until we fell asleep, only to start over again the next day. We were together, but whatever we did we were loners, standing side by side but not complete, like a stool with a missing leg. After seeing Sopiep's parents and their friends, I wanted us to be with the world, to move with it, to be with people. But Dad didn't think we needed to. I told him over and over how much the Soks wanted to meet him, and he refused each time.

From the cliff Dad pointed to a dark blue spot in the sky. "See there, Amy."

I looked up from the beach, squinted, and focused on that dot until I realized it was an airplane. "I don't understand how it stays up." I turned to him for the answer, but he was gazing out at something else . . . something that wasn't even there.

"You know, I looked out the airport windows when your mom's plane was landing. I couldn't wait to see her. I thought

I was the luckiest man in the world." His voice sounded far away, even though he was sitting right next to me.

I had a feeling his story about Mom was going to be about how awful she was, and I didn't want to listen to it. It would have made me feel as though I was the one saying those mean things about her. What would I do if I ever, ever saw her again? But I wanted to be polite to him, so I said, "Yeah."

"And when she came, I tried to be the best husband and father. I should have believed everyone when they told me not to do it, not to marry her. . . ."

"But, Dad." I cut him off. He held up a hand for me not to talk.

"Now they're all laughing at me. Every single Cambodian is laughing at me."

"No, they're not, Dad."

"Amy, you're too young to know."

"But if you hadn't married her, I wouldn't be here." I tried my best not to sound hurt. If Sopiep was special, wasn't I? Shouldn't I be at least special enough for him to be thankful that he had married Mom, whether or not she had left us?

He didn't hear me. "Look," he said, "another one." The planes turned out to be fighter jets from the nearby air base. "Why didn't I know better? When I was in Cambodia I saw many young men go to her cart to buy food. They stayed longer than they should have, and she laughed louder than she should have. I should have known that something wasn't right. But I believed her when she said she loved me. I will not let you grow up to be anything like her. I will die before I let that happen!" He pulled me close to him, and I could feel his body shiver. He was right; I was too young to understand. I was certain that no matter how I grew up, I would be something like Mom. Wasn't she part of who I was already, just as he was?

Dad was combing his hair in the bathroom before work when I said, "They really want to meet you."

He ignored me and looked at my hair. "It's so much like your mom's."

"Thanks," I said. It was the first time in a long time that he had said anything nice about her.

"Don't thank me." He grimaced. "She's not a good woman. You shouldn't want anything to do with her."

I didn't say another word.

Dad bent down and pointed to a gray hair on his head. I wrapped the silver strand that stuck out like a sewing needle around my finger and yanked it out of his scalp.

"So, do you think you can visit Sopiep's parents this weekend? They're having one last barbecue before winter, and they want to meet you," I said.

"I don't need to know anyone who thinks he's better than me." He huffed, the horse sound coming out his nostrils.

"They're nice, not like people in St. Pete."

He shook his head and walked out of the bathroom. "You don't know anything, Amy." But I did.

I followed him. "Dad, I thought you said things would be different around here?" From behind, his shoulders curved forward a little, and he seemed to be shorter than before. He didn't bother to answer me as he continued to get ready for work. "How can it be better around here if you don't want to meet anyone, and want to be alone all the time? You used to have so many friends."

He took his shoes out of the closet and sat with them on

the couch. He looked at me for a long time. "When you're older, you'll know more about self-respect and pride. When you're a kid, these things don't matter. You have a fight with a friend one day, and the next day you're back to being best friends. Self-respect is about who you are, who your family is. If you don't respect yourself, then your family doesn't respect you, and outsiders don't respect you. Do you understand?"

I wasn't sure he wanted me to answer, so I looked down at my feet. I understood, though. I understood that he was a man, and that his wife and daughter were his pride. So without his wife, he was only half a man. I had never felt more sorry for him. "Dad," I said. He glanced up from his shoes. There was a pause before I continued. "I don't love anyone more than you. And . . ." I couldn't remember what else I had wanted to say.

He smiled at me, took his keys off the TV, and left. I wanted to run after him because there was so much more I wanted to say but couldn't. The words were swimming in my heart, but they couldn't find their way up and out of my mouth. I wanted to tell him that I wanted to be no one's daughter but his. That I would be an important person someday so that I could make a lot of money and take care of him, and never leave him. That we were not separate loners or two legs of a collapsed stool but two wheels of a bicycle.

●

A couple of weeks later Dad came home earlier than usual and full of energy. "Let's go for a walk," he said as soon as he shut the front door. He didn't wait for me to say anything as he walked straight to the bathroom. I could hear water running and him splashing some on his face. "Are you ready?" he called out. I put on my tennis shoes and tied a sweatshirt around my waist.

It was just beginning to turn dark, as if a kid had colored the sky and air around us with a gray Crayola, and the cool air nibbled my nose and cheeks. Dad and I didn't talk; we just walked side by side on the empty sidewalk, letting the legs of our jeans rub briefly against each other. I could almost feel the heat of his body warming me.

We pointed to pretty lawns and peered in at the houses that had lights on inside. I wasn't sure what he was thinking, but those homes made me think about the people who lived inside. I wondered if they were happy . . . or sad . . . and if their lives were anything like ours.

Leaves on the few maple trees had changed to fall colors—pumpkin, rustic apple, and Indian corn—and I pointed to them in amazement. "Nature is pretty, isn't it, Amy?" Dad said and took my hand in his. It was . . . but it was prettier that I heard the words come from him.

We walked to a corner house that had two maple trees in its front yard and stopped to pick up some of the leaves that had fallen to the ground. Some of them had turned brown and were glued to the wet sidewalk from the rain earlier; others had been broken into pieces. I got on my knees and felt the wetness of the sidewalk seep through my jeans. I looked over at Dad, who had already begun a pile of leaves for me. I loved that he got on his knees with me to search for the most brilliant and perfect leaves and didn't rush me to go. If I had it my way, we would be on our knees on that December night fishing for leaves forever.

"Do you want a piggyback ride?" he asked when we finally started back home.

"I'm too big now," I said, and took his hand while holding

my treasures in the other. His hand was rough but warm, reminding me of a hard-baked bread that was hot and soft in the center.

"You are, aren't you?" he said softly. There was a glint of happiness in his sad eyes that I had never seen before. When he caught me looking at him he said, "Your birthday is soon, isn't it. Do you want a party? It would be a good time to have Sopiep's family over."

"Yes! Yes!" I couldn't believe he had said it—he finally wanted to meet the Soks. I ran ahead of Dad and skipped the rest of the way home.

When my birthday got closer I asked Dad how many people I could invite to the party. "Amy, I'm not made of money. You can ask your friend Sopiep, and I'll call her mom and dad," he said. I was grateful that I would have a party and that Sopiep was coming, but what about Anthony? I couldn't leave him out.

"Well, she and I have another good friend," I said at the front table, pretending to look at a math problem. I smelled coffee in the mug he was holding.

"Who?"

"Ah, you know that dumb boy who bothers us all the time?"

"What? If he bothers you, then why are you friends with him?" I almost hit myself for not thinking ahead.

"I mean, he's nice, too." I glanced at him.

"No, no boys." He raised an eyebrow at me, as if what I had said was absurd. "You want a boyfriend or something?" I then regretted that I had opened my mouth. I didn't understand why Sopiep's parents didn't care that she had a boy for a friend but my dad did. He sat back against the couch. "You know, your mom was probably like you—not *liking* boys when she was your age. But . . ." He shook his head and drank his coffee.

I turned away. I hated that he continued to punish me because he *hated* Mom. I wanted to say something, to tell him that I was not my mom. But my party was coming up soon, and I had already invited Sopiep. I would die before telling her the party was canceled.

"So, what can we have for food?" I asked instead, trying to sound cheerful. The question lightened up his face and loosened his jaw.

"I don't know. What do you want?"

"Pizza with lots of pepperoni." He thought about my answer and shook his head again.

"Didn't you say that your friend has three brothers?" he asked. I nodded. "That will cost too much. I told you, I don't have much money. We're not Americans."

"Hot dogs, then," I said.

"No. Hot dogs alone are too cheap. We need something good, presentable, and easy." He snapped his fingers. "Beef stew."

José picked up the phone when I called Dad the next day to tell him I was home from school. "I hear someone's having a birthday really soon," he said. I liked to hear his Mexican accent.

"Yep, it's me."

"Well, happy birthday, sweetie. Here's your dad."

"I'm home," I said into the phone. I could hear Dad's breathing, but he didn't say anything. "Dad, are you there?"

Finally he said, "Okay. What do you want for your birthday?"

"Really?"

"Yes, really." His voice was friendly and joking. "Or do you not want a present?"

"Of course I do. I want a haircut," I said. I figured that since Dad was meeting the Soks to make me happy, I should do something nice for him. And I couldn't think of anything that would please him more than not to have to look at something that was a reminder of the wife who had left him.

"*Little* girls are supposed to have long hair so they can wear bows. You sure you want to cut it?"

"Yep, I want a haircut," I said again.

"Fine, we'll go today. It's Friday, so they should be open late."

Dad drove me to the Vietnamese salon at Asian Mall. It was a walk-in only. It smelled like a regular salon, clean except for the chemical they squirted on the heads of women who were getting perms. The smell of it stung the inside of my nose when I first walked in. Three people were ahead of me, so I had to wait patiently with Dad, who was dozing off. I tried not to think about my long ponytail that would soon be chopped off. Two ladies, about twenty or so, sat across from us in the small waiting room. When I dared to, I would look at them and turn away right before they caught me staring. They looked like they'd stepped out of a magazine. Their hair flowed in soft big waves down their shoulders, and they wore blue eye shadow with a thin black line drawn right above their eyelashes. I couldn't wait for the day when I would look like them.

An old hairdresser with tight curls and a smooth, round face waved at me to come to her. I walked past the counter with the cash register and a station where a lady was getting her nails done.

The hairdresser spoke to me in Vietnamese and gently

pushed me down into the barber's chair before resting her warm hands on my shoulders. "I don't speak Vietnamese," I said, and smiled at her.

"So what you want today?" she asked in English.

I winced as she took out my ponytail. I wasn't sure if her tone of voice had changed or if she just sounded sweeter in her native language.

In front of me was a wall-size mirror that I tried not to look at. The lady on my left was getting rollers put in her hair, and the man on my right winked at me. I didn't like him or his thin, shiny, dark green pants. I didn't like his snakeskin shoes with pointy tips. And I also didn't like that his hair was high and wavy at the top.

"What you want?" she asked again, and pulled me out of the chair to get a better look at my hair.

"A haircut," I said extra gently.

I didn't realize until then, standing in front of the mirror, that my hair reached the middle of my back. It *was* like looking at my mom's hair. I started to change my mind about cutting it. I wanted to have something of hers, something that said I was her daughter. But Dad . . . Dad would be so much better off if he didn't have to look at my hair every day. Didn't I owe it to him?

"Here?" she asked. I looked at the mirror and saw the side of her hand below my shoulder. I shook my head. Then she moved up her hand a little bit more. I shook my head again. "Where?" There was definitely annoyance in her voice that time. I pointed to my shoulder. "Okay," she said, and combed my hair. "You have a lot of hair." I didn't think she meant it as a good thing.

In a whisper, I asked if she could make my hair look like those girls in the waiting room.

"What?" she asked, not quietly at all.

179

"Can you cut my hair like theirs?" I asked again, softly.

"Those two?" She pointed at them with the comb still in her hand. Her loud voice caught everyone's attention. The young ladies stopped talking and turned toward us. They raised their heads and strained to see past the counter, but I didn't bother to watch for their reaction. The couple of people around me also stopped what they were doing and looked at us. I wondered if Dad was awake and watching, too. "You're too young. Don't try to be old," she scoffed at me. I opened my eyes wide to fight back the tears. Didn't she know that I didn't want to look *old,* just a little pretty and not so plain? "I give you a good haircut, trust me," she said.

I was still standing when she held the cold silver scissors against my shoulder. *Snip.* "Ouch!" I said, and winced. In the mirror I could see a handful of black hair falling like a shovelful of dirt thrown into a grave.

"What? You stupid," the hairdresser said. I didn't know what she was talking about until she said, "Hair doesn't hurt."

The people around us started laughing again. Then she cut off the rest of my hair before pushing me into the chair once more to tidy up the work. A young man came by us with a broom and swept my hair into a dustpan. *It's all wrong,* I thought. *My life does not belong in a trash can.*

"You like it?" Dad asked me in the car. I looked out the window and shook my head. "Yeah, I don't like it, either."

I wasn't mad at his brutal honesty . . . I was used to it. Cambodian parents, unlike American ones (at least the ones on TV), are never sympathetic just to make their kids feel better. But I *was* mad at him. It was because of him that I had ruined my hair.

And I was mad at that Vietnamese lady who had been so

mean to me, probably because I didn't speak her language! And I was mad because even though I'd asked her to cut my hair to my shoulders, she had made me look like a Chinese baby doll with hair that was chopped to above my earlobes and straight bangs that were only halfway to my forehead. She couldn't even cut me pretty bangs! Knowing that she *knew* what a terrible job she had done lit a fire of rage in me that I couldn't extinguish. After she had finished with me she had just left—without telling me I was done or could leave—and gone to the next person. I wasn't sure if she even bothered to charge Dad. I could have run all over that mall spitting fire-balls at her. Was I not cute enough for her to pay attention?

That night I dreamed about Mom. Almost everything in the dream was white. I was alone and lost, walking on the highway in a heavy rain that poured down like sheets of white paper. I couldn't see where to go for shelter. I couldn't move an inch without fearing that a car was going to run over me. Just as I started to call for help I saw the headlights of a car coming toward me.

Amy-a, I heard. *Amy-a, Amy-a,* the voice continued to sing. It was the sound of a mother lulling her sweet baby to sleep.

Mom, I screamed. *Mom, help me, I can't see!*

Amy-a, she called again. In a tunnel of complete white-ness, I ran toward the sound of my mom's voice and the bright headlights. As I got closer, the car seemed to be back-ing away.

Mom, stop, please! I cried. Each word was a jagged rock. I could feel my throat about to tear every time I spoke. When-ever I opened my mouth the rain rushed down my throat and threatened to choke me. I reached out my hand. I saw her dark head in the driver's seat, but I couldn't see her face.

The rain continued to pound on me and the car windshield, covering her up like Wite-Out. *Please stop, Mom,* I said. I ran faster toward the headlights and struggled onto the hood of the car. Parts of her face became visible as I cleared off the rain from the windshield with my hands. But I couldn't do it fast enough. *Mom, it's me,* I said. *Stop the car. Please help me, I'm lost.*

I never got to see her face. With me still on the hood of the car, we drove through the white, endless tunnel. I woke up feeling alone and scared that I would lose her forever to something I couldn't even see or feel.

●

Unlike the party we had had the previous year in St. Pete, Dad did the cooking for my birthday party. The night before he held a large chunk of beef under the faucet. "Fat is good . . . it gives flavor," he said, pointing to the white, oily parts of the red meat. I sat on the kitchen table and laughed at him acting like a chef on a cooking show. "You see, this is how you cut meat." He raised the left corner of his lips, and when he opened his mouth to speak he looked like an Asian Elvis Presley.

"You look funny," I said, and chuckled.

He turned back around and began chopping the meat with the cleaver, his elbow bopping up and down and the cleaver making a sharp clicking sound as it hit the plastic cutting board. "You have to do it fast or . . . or it won't be good. Ta-da!" He moved to the side and showed me his work. We both laughed when I saw that the beef wasn't cut at all.

"Good job, Dad." He bowed to me before bending his head over the chunk of meat and cutting it into big cubes.

Seeing him in such a good mood, I asked, "He probably can't come anyway, but can I just invite Anthony?"

Dad minced garlic and browned it in a frying pan. "I told you, no boys. You shouldn't be playing with boys in the first place." His voice sounded neutral this time.

The garlic sizzled in the oil and permeated the kitchen with its sharp smell. Then he added the beef, soy sauce, and a reddish orange powder from a packet.

"Dad, Sopiep and I think of him as a girl . . . I mean, he can't help that he's a boy. Please, Dad, I can't invite Sopiep and not him."

Next he squirted ketchup from a bottle and stirred everything in the pan. From the table I could see the beef and sauce turning into a delicious deep cranberry color.

He moved around easily, almost tiptoeing from the sink to the refrigerator and back to the stove. "Doesn't he have friends of his own?" But he didn't let me answer. He held the handle of the frying pan with both hands and transferred everything into a big pot before adding a couple of cans of chicken broth and water. "We'll cook this for an hour tonight. But tomorrow we have to cook it for another four hours for the meat to be tender." I could tell he was coming around.

"Yes, he has us. Come on, please," I whined.

"It's too late, anyway." He dipped a spoon in the pot and tasted his masterpiece. "Perr-fect."

"No, it isn't too late. I have his phone number."

"Why do you have a boy's number?"

"Don't worry. I don't like him the way grown-ups like each other. I only have his phone number because I have Sopiep's." When he didn't say anything I took it that he had finally given me permission, so I walked over to the phone and called Anthony.

The next morning I slowly got out of bed and put on my socks. I knew that it was just one day later, but I felt heavier and taller than I had the day before. After fluffing the pillow and pulling and tugging at the sheet and comforter to make sure they hung evenly, I went to the closet, took out the yellow dress Dad had bought me in Las Vegas, and laid it on the bed. I ran my hands over the shimmering fabric to straighten out the wrinkles, although there weren't any because Dad had helped me iron it before I went to bed. I couldn't wait to put it on later.

I grabbed my towel, walked to the bathroom, and caught sight of my new hairstyle in the mirror. I laid the towel down and ran my hand through my hair. Since it was a special day, I did my best at fixing the misery of my haircut. I tried wearing barrettes, but they made the hair stick out like pigtails. I tried wearing a headband, but it wouldn't stay. Nothing worked. I had to wear it straight in the back, on the sides, and in the front. I was even plainer than before. I was certain it was Mom's way of punishing me.

I found Dad in the kitchen tending to his stew, which smelled of ripe tomatoes and soy sauce. "I'm finished with the bathroom," I said. Even with his head bent over the pot, I could see wrinkles around his eyes that only showed when he smiled.

"It looks good," he said cheerfully. "When it starts boiling, turn the stove down to low." He patted my head as he walked away. I wouldn't mind eating stew every day if it made him that happy.

As I straightened the living room and swept the kitchen floor Dad checked on the simmering meat regularly, stirring it, tasting it, and adding more soy sauce and sugar when he thought it needed something.

"Okay, it's almost done. This is going to be the best, Amy," he said as he stirred in a bowl of milky water.

"What's that?" I asked.

"Flour and water; it thickens the gravy. That way you can dip the French bread. Doesn't someone I know like French bread?" he asked, and winked at me.

"I do." I giggled. "You know a lot about cooking."

"You're good at cooking, too. Someday I'll show you all of my recipes."

"Why didn't you cook when Mom was with—" I shut my mouth as soon as I realized what I had just said. "I like your food," I finished.

"Thank you, ma'am." He spoke as if he hadn't heard me mention Mom. I giggled again.

Dad left me at home to watch after the stew while he went to pick up the cake and the bread. "Amy, the meat isn't as tender as it should be, so I turned the stove on higher. Be sure to stir the stew every ten minutes or so or it might burn. I'm not sure how good this pot is." He tapped the pot with the back of his finger before leaving.

"Yes, sir." I saluted him.

It was early still, but I put on my yellow dress anyway. I stood in front of the full-length mirror in the hallway, gazing at myself. It was a little shorter than when I had tried it on at the store. The skirt of the dress came just past my knees and puffed out, showing the lacey hem of the white underskirt. I noticed the cuts and bruises on my legs from running and falling, but I pretended that they weren't there as I paraded around the small house. I liked how the dress rustled slightly as I moved. In front of the TV I saw my dim reflection and curtsied.

The soft hissing from the kitchen reminded me of Dad,

and I walked over to stir the stew. It smelled so good. I stuck a chopstick in the pot and pulled it out so I could taste the thick gravy that coated the end of it. As I put the chopstick in my mouth the heat surprised me and I dropped it on the floor. The red gravy splattered, but I jumped away in time to catch only a speck of it on my leg. I was so thankful it hadn't landed on my dress. The day had almost been ruined.

It seemed to take forever for the clock to read twelve. Dad still hadn't returned when Anthony knocked on the door. He handed me a present with a yellow ribbon on it. "It isn't anything big," he said. I wanted to apologize for inviting him at the last minute, but I knew he didn't care. "What happened to your hair?"

"Haircut." I didn't bother to ask if he liked it. No one in their right mind would.

It was nippy outside and I could tell he was waiting for me to ask him in, but I couldn't. Dad would probably chase him home with the cleaver. "Let's play outside," I said, and shut the door behind us.

"Grandma told me to come early in case you needed help."

"Thanks, but everything's done." His hair was spiked in tiny, even rows. And he had recently gotten glasses that he had to wear all the time. They made him look smart. I began to understand why the girls thought he was cute. "So, you're going to see your parents for Christmas?"

"Yeah, but I don't want to," he said, and started picking the leaves off a bush. I never pushed him to talk about his parents, but sometimes he would start to say something and then stop, and I didn't know if he wanted me to ask questions or not. So I didn't.

We were talking about the upcoming Christmas break

when the Soks walked down the sidewalk. Sopiep saw us and left her family to run up to my house. She hugged me and I breathed in her sweet scent, something she must have stolen from her mom's perfume bottle. Then she looked at Anthony and said, "Hi, Anthony." It seemed as though it took a lifetime for her to just say the one, simple sentence.

She didn't wear her hair in pigtails. She shook her head a bit, and her long hair slightly rippled across her back. I didn't like it that she didn't turn away from him. "Hey," I said, "do you see anything different?"

She finally looked at me again and exclaimed, "Your hair!" She lied and told me how pretty it was.

"Really?" I asked. She nodded, but I still saw sympathy in her eyes.

Her parents walked up holding hands, and her brothers threw a basketball back and forth. It was funny to see the sons towering over their parents. Anthony soon went to join the guys. Sopiep gave me my present, and her mom handed me a card before bending down and hugging me. She, too, smelled the way blue flowers should—clean and pretty. I suddenly wished I had asked Dad for a bottle of perfume instead of a haircut.

"My dad will be here soon. He went to get the cake," I said, and opened the door to let them in.

Sopiep noticed it first. "What's that?" she asked, and wrinkled her nose. We all sniffed and began coughing when the bitter burning smell crept up at us. It suddenly hit me like a blow to the head that I had completely forgotten about the beef stew. I ignored the weakness in my legs, ran into the kitchen, and reached to turn off the stove. All I could think about was Dad and how awful the day was going to be. I saw Dad's face and his murderous eyes. Mr. Sok tried to fan the smell out through the front door with a newspaper, and Mrs. Sok carried the pot of stew out of the house. I followed her, and all of us, including the guys, who didn't know what had happened, gathered around the large pot.

The gravy still looked red and the beef cubes weren't damaged. "It's okay, right?" I said to no one in particular, recognizing that my voice sounded pathetic. I knew it wasn't okay because the entire pot reeked of used coals and ashes, but I had to ask. Maybe God would be good and not ruin my special day, even though it was my fault . . . and I did cut my hair not to look like Mom.

"No, the scorched flour at the bottom of the pot would make everything taste like smoke," Mrs. Sok said, and rubbed my back.

She went inside and brought out our biggest bowl and spoon. Sopiep no longer cared about the stew, our only food for the party, and went to play with her brothers and Anthony.

Dad walked up a couple of minutes later with the cake and bread in his hands, and Sopiep took the cake from him to see what it looked like. She brought it to the steps and tried to show it to me. It annoyed me that she didn't realize there was a problem. In fact, none of the kids, even the older ones, seemed to care. The boys were still in their own world and Sopiep skipped away to hers, one that I wished I could escape to.

Not seeing the pot on the ground, Dad was still in an upbeat mood from earlier and shook Mr. Sok's hand. "Go inside. Why are you out here? It's cold out here. Amy, did you pour *Phou* and *Meing* drinks?"

"It burned," I said meekly, and pointed to the pot.

No one could tell he cared. Except me. For a split second I saw disappointment and panic wash over his face. He had so much wanted to impress them, and I had ruined everything for him.

"I told you to watch it," Dad simply said, and smiled at the last minute, for the guests.

How could I forget to stir the stew? Anthony. Anthony came early and I forgot all about it. How does he always manage to get me in trouble? I will never be friends with him again. I kept my head bowed and wished we hadn't invited anyone over. It was just another day, anyway. From the corner of my eye, I could see Mrs. Sok scooping some of the meat out of the pot.

"I'm sorry."

"We'll call for pizza," he said casually, and shrugged, as if he were brushing a fly off his shoulder, but I wasn't fooled. And he would let me hear it when everyone left. I wished they had already left so I didn't have to wait for my punishment.

"No need to," Mr. Sok said. I forgot that he was standing at the door. There was kindness in his eyes.

"Yes, no need to. I can fix us something here," Mrs. Sok added. But Dad said it would be quicker if he ordered pizza. "Pizzas aren't good." She shook her head. "If it's okay, I can make us fried rice with whatever you have in the refrigerator. And it will be faster, too."

She took the bowl and went back in . . . as if it were her house. I followed her, avoiding Dad's eyes.

Dad showed Mrs. Sok what we had: rice, soy sauce, oyster sauce, fish sauce, eggs, Chinese sausages, half a head of lettuce, and instant noodles. "With just the two of us we don't have much. So I'll order pizzas. What do you want on them, kids?"

"Sausages!" Sopiep screamed from the living room. Her mom told her to hush.

"Go sit down and watch TV," Mrs. Sok told Dad. "The girls and I will have everything cooked in a few minutes." He looked worried, and hesitated to move. I knew he was wondering if he could trust these nice people—would they, too, turn on him and tell others he couldn't afford to buy pizzas for his daughter's birthday? But Mrs. Sok was adamant about cooking and shoved him out of the kitchen. He laughed lightly and sat with Mr. Sok on the sofa.

The two men soon began talking, about what I didn't know. I was too amazed at how wonderful Mrs. Sok was. I wanted so much to hug her. I wished that I could borrow her from Sopiep. I would promise to take care of her, to listen, to bring home all A's, and to be good.

An hour later, Sopiep's brothers and Anthony came in from outside and moved the couch and dinner table back against the walls while Sopiep and I laid newspapers on the floor, from the kitchen to the living room, for all of us to sit down around.

"Sorry that we have such a small home," Dad said as we all gathered around for my birthday lunch.

"A small home is okay, just as long as the heart isn't," Mr. Sok said, and he and Dad clicked their beer cans together in a toast.

It was so different from the Christmas party that we had had the year before in St. Pete. We didn't have much food this time, just a pan of fried rice with eggs and Chinese sausages, jasmine rice, the burned meat that Mrs. Sok had felt too guilty to throw out but that hardly anyone took a bite of, and a store-bought cake. Yet I was full—not with anger and humiliation, but with food spiced with love by a woman I was falling in love with, with my best friends, and with Dad, who was happy and talking more easily than I had seen him do since we moved here. All of us, even with Anthony, looked like a family.

"Anthony, eat the fried rice. You don't have to eat that." Dad pointed to the chunk of beef on his plate.

"I like it, sir." He continued eating it with rice that he had drenched in soy sauce.

"Doesn't it taste like smoke to you?" Sopiep asked.

He shrugged. "That's why I like it." Dad smiled at him and offered him his own burned meat. We laughed so hard that Sopiep's youngest brother snorted.

The day ended too soon. After I had opened my presents and we all had eaten vanilla cake with chocolate icing, Mrs. Sok gathered her purse and jacket. I watched her help Sopiep into her jacket and thanked them for the presents.

"So, do you like San Diego?" Mr. Sok asked Dad as they walked to the front door.

"Oh, yes," Dad said.

"You can't find better weather anywhere." Mr. Sok breathed in the outside air. "You should come over. Come whenever you like. We can introduce you to a lot of people. I'll take you to temple and the New Year's party in April."

Dad nodded and shook Mr. Sok's hand. "That will be great. I heard there are many Cambodians here. I've been working, so I don't have much time to go out."

"Yes, there are some Cambodians here. But more in the Long Beach area. Sometimes there are concerts. We go when we have time. You should go, too."

Dad promised to visit their home soon and to call them if he needed anything; then he gently pushed the front door shut.

After I showered I climbed into bed and looked at my presents lying on the comforter. Twenty dollars from Mr.

and Mrs. Sok. A green sweater with white polka dots from Sopiep. And a yellow diary with a silver clasp from Anthony. I would never tell Dad, but the diary was my favorite present. It was my book of secrets. I walked over to the windowsill and picked up a maple leaf Dad had found. It was the size of his hand and looked almost like a starfish. The center was green, but orange, red, and yellow filled up the rest. I found tape and taped the leaf onto the first page of my diary. And on the second page I wrote: *Today, Daddy was happy.*

"I forgot to give you this." Dad walked into my room, carrying an envelope in his hand. "It came in the mail a couple of days ago." My heart raced at the sight of it. I had wondered about my mom, wondering if she remembered it was my birthday, wondering if I hadn't gotten a present from her because she had sent it to the old address. But I could stop wondering now. "It's from Mrs. Yen," he said.

I felt as though my heart had stopped. Then I was angry at myself for being disappointed. I opened the envelope and took out the card as Dad checked out the green sweater. Money and a photo, probably one of Janet's school pictures, fell out of the card. I reached down to pick them up.

At first I thought Janet had decided to straighten her curls, which made her look older. And it scared me that I still looked like a kid. But I then realized that the picture was from a long time ago. The upper left corner of the photo was torn and the photo itself felt different, like old paper. It was a close-up picture of Mom—probably when she first came to the United States.

"What's that?" Dad asked.

I knew that if he saw it he would only get mad, and something told me he wouldn't give the photo back if I gave it to him. I didn't want to lose it. I wouldn't need to hang up the picture or put it anywhere he would see it. I could just put it with the other picture of her and the lock of hair. I tried to think of a lie, but one didn't come quickly enough. Dad grabbed the photo from me and studied it. It seemed that the earth stopped moving and the clock stopped ticking as I watched him looking at a woman who wasn't looking back at either of us. He sat on the edge of my bed for a long time before finally letting out a deep breath.

"Can I see it again?" I asked, and stuck out my hand. I wanted to know if the face in the photograph was the same one behind the steering wheel in the car that hadn't stopped for me.

Dad got up and left with the picture. My heart sank.

"Dad, can I have it back?" I called after him. "It's mine."

I knew better than to go after him. It was one of those times when I needed to stay quiet, a time when I needed to pretend that I was not alive and that my feelings didn't really count. I didn't understand why he couldn't let go of whatever it was that made him angry. I opened my new diary and crossed out the sentence I had written earlier. And I continued to cross it out until the pen tore the page.

After a few minutes, Dad came back. He dropped a present on my bed and left without saying a word. I didn't bother to thank him; in fact, I didn't bother to touch it. He couldn't just give me something to make up for taking away my mom! Who said he could make me feel bad one minute and good the next? It was not fair. In school I got good grades for doing my homework and studying for tests. And Sopiep was my friend because I was hers. The boys who talked back to Mrs. Ortiz were sent to the principal's office. Those things made sense. Dad didn't. And what he had done to me didn't.

Heat burning my nostrils and ears, I threw the small, flat

box. It hit the wall, and the sound of broken glass made a sharp jingle as it slid down to the floor. I jumped out of bed, completely forgetting about how wrong Dad was, and picked up his stupid present. I could hear glass pieces clinking against one another. I tore open the blue wrapping paper and held it at arm's length as the glass fell out like precious diamonds.

It was the picture of Mom, in a frame.

13

DAD AND MR. Sok began talking regularly on the phone and watching football together on Sunday afternoons. Sometimes Dad walked over to their house and showed Mr. Sok how to fix his car. At home Dad read the newspaper instead of watching the TV. He washed our laundry weekly, clipped his finger- and toenails, did push-ups at night, and even bought cream for his face. Some nights, walking with his shoulders squared and his head up and straight, he stopped looking short.

"I think you grew," I said to him one Saturday evening on our way to Sopiep's house for dinner.

"You're silly," he said. "I'm too old to grow anymore."

"I don't think you're *that* old."

"How old do you think I am?" he asked in Cambodian. He'd also begun speaking more Cambodian since meeting Sopiep's parents.

When Dad spoke our native language he sounded happier and freer, as if a large rock that once had lain on his heart had been lifted. But I found it hard to form the words because I hadn't spoken them very much since Mom had left. Dad said I was leaving out syllables and stammering through some of my sentences, so I stuck to speaking English whenever I could.

"I don't know. But if I do my math right, I think you're in your forties." He looked pleased with my answer and breathed in deeply through his nose. "You're bigger here, too." I pointed to his shoulders. "You even have less gray hair! Oh my gosh, did you dye your hair?" I asked.

He put an arm around me, placed his hand over my mouth, and in a playful voice said, "You say that again and I'll take you back home." I stuck out my tongue and licked his palm until he took it off my mouth. And when he wiped it down the side of his pants I laughed.

We walked in silence for the rest of the way, but I couldn't help looking up at him and smiling, knowing he was having as much fun as I was.

When Mr. Sok opened the door for us I saw Mr. Youv and heard his wife's voice from the kitchen. They were the Soks' good friends. "Peera's here," Mr. Youv said, and held up a glass of wine.

Before I got the chance to *chumreab suor* the two men, Dad handed me the box of cookies we had bought earlier and greeted his friends with handshakes. I stood at the entrance grinning at the three of them until Dad reminded me to take the cookies to Mrs. Sok in the kitchen.

I heard women's voices, running water, and clattering of spoons and plates as I entered the kitchen. Several dishes of stir-fry were taking up all the space on the counter, so I handed the cookies to Mrs. Sok before I *chumreab suor*ed her and Mrs. Youv. "You didn't have to bring these," she said, and pinched my cheek. She always said that, but Dad refused to go over to their house or those of any of his new friends for dinner without bringing our share of the meal. At the get-togethers the other guests would bring plates of homemade food like chicken and ginger or papaya salad, but since we didn't have a woman to do the cooking at home Dad said desserts or drinks would be enough.

Auntie Sarah stood at the stove stirring a large pot of lobster soup. Her face was clearer than I remembered, but she still wore the bright red lipstick that made her whole face stick out like a red apple in a bowl of yellow ones. She put down her ladle and hugged me. Since we had met at the beach I'd seen her so often that she no longer wanted me to *chumreab suor* but to hug her instead. Whereas I had had to be gentle in hugging my mom, Auntie Sarah would spontaneously pull me into her arms and press me so hard against her chest that the baby powder between her breasts whiffed into my nostrils.

She let me go and said, "It's cold out there. Where's your sweater?" I stayed close to her and shrugged, telling her it wasn't that cold.

Mrs. Youv said in Cambodian, "Kids here never get cold. The other day my husband and I were in sweats, and my oldest son was walking around in shorts. I said, 'Oh my God.'" Mrs. Sok, Auntie Sarah, and I laughed because Mrs. Youv had recently come to America and she preferred to speak Cambodian; when she added American words to her stories she always had a look of surprise on her face. Her eyes would pop wide open and dart around the room, as if to say *Did I just say that word right?*

"Can I help with anything?" I asked. Mrs. Sok had usually said no when other adults were with her, and I knew she would say it again that night. But I had to ask anyway because Dad said I needed to be helpful to not wear out my welcome.

"No," she said. "Go play. Sopiep's in her room folding laundry."

I was looking forward to playing the Clue game that Sopiep's brothers had bought her for Christmas. Several times we had taken the game out of the box, placing the cards of murder weapons in a pile and the cards of guests in the other only for her to begin talking about Anthony, her hair, and the contact lenses she would be getting soon. I wouldn't have minded talking about Anthony if it weren't so strange to see her eyes softening just at the sound of his name.

"Okay, take out the box," I said as soon as I pushed her bedroom door open.

Sopiep didn't hear me. She was dancing in her pile of clothes. The new year had changed her more than it had changed Dad, but with her I didn't like the changes. She had completely stopped wearing her hair in pigtails and let it hang down her back, with bangs that softly curled under. She also wore lip gloss and perfume almost every day. Some days she wore tight shirts that showed her developing chest.

"What are you doing?" I asked. She finally stopped moving her butt in a circle and stuck out her hands to show me her newly painted nails. "You're too young to wear red," I said bluntly.

She blinked at me and asked, "What color should I wear, then?" She sounded like a doll might if it could speak, but I didn't like the voice and shrugged.

Instead of taking the nail polish off, she started dancing again. I didn't know why, but I didn't want to let the nail polish go without her doing something about it. "You're going to look funny if you don't take that off. People are going to say you're a kid wanting to be an adult. You want people to talk about you or something?"

"Fine, but first will you help me fold these?" She pointed to the wrinkled clothes and stuck out her tongue at them.

I sat on her bed and started pairing up her socks while she folded her wrinkled jeans and hung up her blouses. We found some of her brothers' socks and threw them into a heap near the door. Soon the pile grew smaller and only panties were left. I picked up a purple one and stared at it.

"This must be your mom's." I showed her the underwear, and she shook her head. *But it must be,* I thought. Why was she wearing soft, shiny-looking adult underwear when I was still wearing ones with tiny yellow flowers and ribbons? I even had one pair with *Tuesday* written in pink all over it. I threw the underwear back into the small pile and stared at her, remembering the red polish that she still hadn't taken off. "You know what, Sopiep?" I said. "I liked your hair better when it was in pigtails. Now all I see is a black mess. It's always in your face."

"Really?" Her voice turned even softer. "Anthony thinks it looks pretty this way." She walked to her door mirror and looked at her hair, combing it straight with her fingers.

Why did she care so much about what a boy thought when I was supposed to be her best friend? "Go ahead and believe him if you want. But don't say I didn't tell you."

She turned around and stared at me with her hands on her hips. "Amy, are you mad at me?" She scrunched her forehead, making her eyebrows arch into the wings of a bird. I shook my head, even though I had meant to tell her the truth.

"Well, good, because I have a secret to tell you." The

brightness in her eyes told me it was going to be a sweet secret, so I no longer cared about what she thought of Anthony.

"Okay," I said, and made room for her to sit on her own bed.

"But you can't tell anyone I told you," she warned. She scooted in closer to me and said, "I think all the grown-ups are going to set up Auntie Sarah with your dad." Her grin was so wide it almost looked painful as she excitedly nodded her head. Maybe I should have tried to look the same way, because she asked, "What's wrong? Isn't this great?"

I pulled back and stared at her. "No," I said, louder than I had thought I would.

She told me, "Shh!" and asked, "Why not?"

"Because."

"Because why?"

"They hardly know each other, for one."

"So?"

"Sopiep, for someone who wants to be such a grown-up, don't you know that you need to know each other before you get married?" She curled her glossy lips into a pout, making me wish I hadn't asked that question so rudely. I knew I had been mean to her all night, but if she thought about it, it wasn't my fault. I wasn't the one who had started caring so much that Anthony liked my hair or wearing fancy underwear. I said, "You know what I mean. A man and a woman can't get married without knowing each other."

"Your parents did," she answered. *Now look who's the mean one,* I thought, but chose to let it go.

"That's different," I said quietly.

"No, it isn't. Plus, it's not a bad idea. Your dad's alone and Auntie Sarah's alone."

She was only half right. My dad was not alone—he had me.

"Sopiep, if this is true, you've got to tell your parents to stop it."

"You know I can't do that. I can't tell my parents what to do." For the first time that night, she was completely right.

"If we were Americans, I bet we could," I said.

During dinner I couldn't get a very good look at Auntie Sarah, but I tried to watch her and Dad as closely as I could without being noticed. She was not quiet like my mom had been . . . she laughed loudly, drank a can of beer with the men, and even talked more than Dad did. So that night was not any different from other nights we had spent together. Dad didn't look at her any longer than usual, nor did he put food on her plate the way Mr. Sok did on his wife's. No one mentioned anything about them falling in love. Satisfied that Sopiep had made a mistake, I moved forward in my chair and ate a serving of everything.

Springtime in San Diego was even more beautiful than summer, fall, and winter. Some nights Dad would let me sleep with my window slightly open so that in the mornings I could wake up to the scent of freshly bloomed flowers. On his days off we would go for drives up the mountains, where we would see pink and purple wildflowers swaying in the wind. I wanted all the things that came with spring to never end.

Even as Anthony and I lazily sat under Maggie's shade, I could smell that her flowers were more lemony than they had been. We unwrapped the Drumsticks we had bought at the corner store and waited for Sopiep, who was redoing her hair before joining us. She had worn it in a long ponytail on one side of her head at school, and Coach T had asked if her neck hurt since the ponytail was tilting her head to one side. When some of the girls giggled Sopiep had grown red in the face and looked down at her shoes. "He didn't mean anything by that," I had said to her as soon as we were alone. "And those girls are just jealous that your hair is so pretty and you're the one Anthony talks to the most." She finally looked up from the ground and at me, her eyes and nose still puffy.

While licking my ice cream I thought about earlier that afternoon when the two fifth-grade classes had walked down to the cafeteria to listen to our guidance counselor speak about middle school. There was so much to remember. Six different classes with six different teachers. Walk from one building to the next. Get to class on time. Honors classes. Health and PE. Must be mature. Big campus. Lost. New friends. Bad friends. Basically, I got the feeling that I would be starting kindergarten all over again.

"Do you think middle school will be that hard?" I asked Anthony. A lady somewhere down the street screamed for her children to come home.

"I'm leaving," he said, and pushed up his glasses.

Until Anthony turned to look at me I had thought it was the lady speaking. "What did you say?" I asked.

"My grandma said my parents want me back," he explained. His voice was low and slow, as if he were speaking each word for the first time.

"When?"

"At the end of the summer." I was dumbfounded. That was only about five months away. And for the first time in a long time my head hurt. Nail by nail, something or someone was hammering up a wall in there, and I winced each time the sharp nail pierced my head.

"Why?"

"Why?" He bit into his ice cream, and bits of peanuts rolled down his chin and onto his shorts. He carefully picked them up one by one and put them in his mouth. "Because they love me. I'm their son," he finally said, but there was uncertainty in his voice. I felt sad that there was doubt in his answer . . . a son shouldn't have to doubt his parents' love for him. I wanted to reach over and touch his hand, to come up with the right words to reassure him that they did love him, that they had to, because they were his parents. Wasn't it only natural? But something I couldn't see or feel warned me that I wasn't the one to tell him.

"I mean, why are you leaving *now*?"

"They worked out their problems, and I guess they're ready for me *now*. I will have been gone for a whole year." I couldn't believe it had been that long. I remembered calling him Rabbit Face because of his two big front teeth. It amazed me now how my eyes had lied to me. He had grown tanner, fuller in the face, and bigger in the shoulders, yet his long black eyelashes still fluttered like butterfly wings.

"Oh," I said. It was the first time he'd ever mentioned that his parents had problems. Of course, I knew something was wrong since he was living with his grandma. But I hadn't ever thought that they might be having problems, problems that were probably similar to my parents'. "What kind of problems?"

He pushed up his glasses and licked the vanilla ice cream until it turned into a perfect snowball on top of his sugar cone. "I don't know. They always argued, even throwing things sometimes. My dad went drinking a lot after work. One night my mom let the air out of his tires so he couldn't go out. After he showered and was ready to leave, he saw the flats and he and Mom started fighting right in the front yard—the neighbors saw the whole thing. Someone called the cops. And a couple of days later they put me on the bus to my grandma's."

"Wow."

He looked out at the small park and popped the rest of his cone into his mouth before stretching out on the grass. I hadn't known that he had it so bad. At least at my house, no cops came.

As I thought about Anthony leaving I found it difficult to finish the rest of my ice cream; I let it melt down my hand. Anthony had become part of me, as had Sopiep, and I couldn't see how we would remain the same without him.

He was rolling around on the grass when Sopiep finally came, fanning herself with a paper fan.

"What's with that?" I asked.

"It's too hot out here." She brushed her hair back and fanned her neck.

"Did Anthony tell you he's leaving?"

"Yeah." She took off her sandals and neatly placed them right across from us. And holding her skirt down with both hands, she glided down like a ballerina and sat her shins directly on her shoes. "Anthony, you won't go to middle school with us." She spoke in her soft, baby voice, drawing out the words as if they were lyrics. I couldn't tell if she was asking him or telling him. It bothered me that I didn't understand this new secret language that lay in her voice. But it bothered me more that she had known about Anthony's leaving before I did.

Sopiep's smile and eyes lingered on him as she changed position on the grass, this time extending her long skinny legs and crossing her ankles. "Oh, Anthony, it won't be the same without you," she said before fanning herself again.

"Do you really have to go?" *Does he really have to go . . . does he have a choice?* Was she always that dumb? I couldn't sit around listening to her any longer. I stood up and brushed the dirt off my shorts.

"Where are you going?" she asked.

"Home. I have homework."

"You do not . . . none of us do," I heard her say behind me as I walked out of the small gated park. When I was about a block down the road, I turned around, wanting to see if Anthony had followed me. He hadn't . . . and I was both disappointed and mad. For a very short moment I was glad he would be moving.

Dad was vacuuming my room as I was dusting the dresser. I had moved my basket of cheap jewelry and rubber bands, stickers from school, broken pencils, and the picture frame of my mom to my bed before spraying Formula 409 on the dresser. As I ran the paper towel back and forth, dust balls formed and flew down to the carpet.

"Amy," Dad said over the running vacuum, "I just vacuumed there." I gave him an apologetic look as he moved the vacuum back to my area.

While he waited for me to finish wiping the dresser, he picked up Mom's picture. There was gentleness in his hand as he held the cheap gold frame. Just as easily as he had picked it up, though, he put it back down, shook his head, and left, without vacuuming anymore. I put down the dirtied paper towel and looked at my mom, who lay speechless on my bed. Some mornings I woke up to her watching me, and I wasn't sure if she liked what she saw. I would wrap myself in the blankets for warmth before I got out of bed.

Later that night I heard Dad talking and laughing as I stepped out of the shower. *He must be speaking to Mrs. Yen,* I thought.

I tiptoed to the kitchen in my towel. He was sitting back in one of the chairs, resting his long hairless legs on the table. His face was bright, and his eyes were watery. He wasn't speaking into the phone, but his lips were turned up in a perfect statuesque grin. When he saw me the corners of his grin came down like red stage curtains after the last scene of a play.

He didn't speak to me. I stood there, though, resting behind another chair, and waited for him as he said "Aha . . . aha" with the same smile lighting his face. He didn't look at me anymore, only glanced up once in a while to see if I was still there. When I held his glance for more than a second I asked, "Can I talk to Mrs. Yen, too?" He shook his head, and I gave him a puzzled look.

Finally he said in Cambodian into the phone, "Yes, yes, I have to go."

"Why couldn't I speak to Mrs. Yen?" I asked as soon as he hung up. He pretended not to hear me and went to pour himself a glass of water. "Dad, why didn't you let me talk to Mrs. Yen?" The smile was still on his face when he finally turned to me, and I could clearly see that he hadn't heard a single word of my question. "Dad," I said a little more loudly, "why couldn't I talk to Mrs. Yen?"

He finished his water and tilted his head to one side. "Oh, that wasn't Mrs. Yen."

"Who was it, then?"

"Ah, no one." He rinsed his glass and walked to the sofa, unfolding the newspaper. Still wet in my towel, I followed him, studying his unusual smile.

"I heard you laughing. What was so funny?"

He put the paper down and said in Cambodian, "Amy, this is none of your concern. Go comb your hair and put on some clothes. You got the carpet wet." He pointed at where I stood and returned to his reading.

I did as he said, but I was still not satisfied. What was the big deal . . . and why couldn't he just tell me who he was talking to? Besides, what was so funny? I walked back to the living room in a T-shirt and shorts and sat beside Dad, listening to him humming as he flipped the pages of the newspaper. My wet hair was soaking my T-shirt, and I could feel my back and arms getting cold, but I didn't want to go dry it until he answered me.

"Dad?"

"Hmmm?"

"Why can't you tell me who you were talking to?" He put down the paper and turned the TV on. "Dad?"

"Amy, you're too young."

"So? All I want to know is who was making you laugh so hard."

He ran his hand through my hair and said, "I was talking to *Meing* Sarah. Now go dry your hair before you get a cold." He was looking at my face, yet I got the feeling he wasn't seeing me.

"She called you?" I asked.

He turned back to the TV, slowly shaking his head. "No."

He was my dad, so I needed more from him than what he had just given me. I wanted to know why he was calling her. How many times he had called her. If she ever called here when I wasn't around. And what she said to him to make him look as if he had sucked in happy gas. But when he turned back to the TV, I knew that that was the end of the discussion.

Later, in bed, I turned over and looked at the picture of

Mom. The light was off, so I couldn't see her. But oddly, I felt her—not that she was in the room with me but that she was again watching me with bright glowing eyes, watching to see if I would do the right things. I remembered the last morning I had seen her. Even in my dark room I vividly saw her turning around in our car and telling me she would pick me up after school. Her face . . . there had been something different about her face that morning that I hadn't remembered until now. No, it wasn't her face but her hair. She hadn't worn it in a ponytail the way she usually did on workdays. Instead, her hair was freshly washed and blown dry. The washing and blow-drying would take her a full hour to complete, so she would only do it when she had someplace special to go. I wondered if she was at that special place now.

In the past couple of months things had been so good, but it was not fair that everyone around me was changing when I wasn't ready for them to. Soon Anthony would be going to a new place. Sopiep, with all of her new hairstyles, red nail polish, and tight shirts, seemed to be going somewhere, too. And maybe Dad had a place he wanted to go, also. If they all started without me, when would I be able to catch up with them?

14

A FEW NIGHTS later, as soon as Dad came home from work he quickly showered and put on his new shirt so we could go with the Soks to celebrate the Cambodian New Year, which was both a sacred and secular holiday in April. To Mom the Cambodian New Year had represented a time to put all bad things in the past and bring good things forward. She made sure we all wore new outfits on that special day to ring in the new year. In St. Pete the three of us, like all the Cambodians in the city, would go to a rented hall decorated with stat-uettes and pictures brought from the temple for morning service. There we prayed, burned sticks of incense, and shared food. At night most grandparents would stay home to watch their grandchildren while their grown-up children re-turned to the hall for loud music and dancing.

"They're here," I said when I heard the Soks' station wagon pull to a stop in front of our house. Dad grabbed his suit jacket from the closet and hurried to the door. "Whew." I pinched my nose shut.

"Too much cologne?"

"Yeah, but we can drive with the window down," I said. He patted me on the head. "Smarty." I didn't want to share him and wanted to suggest that we—he in his new clothes and I in my new pink dress—stay home and watch TV together. "Let's go. They're waiting," he said, and grabbed his keys.

I didn't know why it surprised me to see Anthony standing with Sopiep beside the station wagon, but it did. When I thought about it later, it was only natural that he came with us that night—just as he had done the many other occasions when he joined our families for dinner or birthday parties. He must have said something nice to Sopiep because she didn't take her eyes off him. She held her little black sequined purse in front of her black and white dress with its white puffy skirt. They continued laughing about whatever was so funny and didn't even see me until Dad and I walked down the steps. Bitterness crawled up my throat.

"My dad thought that we could ride with you, *Phou*," Sopiep said to Dad. "It's kind of full in there." She pointed to her big brothers in the backseat and to her parents, who waved to us.

Anthony rode in the front with Dad so that I could sit in the back with Sopiep. She crossed her legs so that her puffy skirt ballooned around her and tapped her fingers on the door handle to the beat of the song on the radio. She looked so beautiful and special that I was afraid to get near her.

She turned to me and saw me looking at her. With her free hand, she held mine briefly, and I was no longer mad at her. The touch of her hand warmed me from head to toe just as surely as a hot bowl of rice porridge on a chilly night. As the four of us rode in silence, I thought how lucky I was to have a best friend.

We drove to a building with a sign that said ROMANIAN SOCIAL HALL and in smaller figures, CAPACITY 750. Cars were parked in almost every direction. Dad carefully drove to the back of the building and parked near a dumpster. Getting out of the car, I could hear Cambodian music floating through the still night and voices speaking the language my dad called his *home* language. For once it relieved me to know that I was going to be with my people.

"Look how pretty you are," Mr. Sok said to me as we headed for the building.

I thanked him but didn't think I was half as pretty as his daughter or his wife, who walked in front of us. Mrs. Sok wore a long, custom-made Cambodian gown that hugged her body. The glimmering material was a deep green that matched her emerald earrings. As she walked, her hips swayed side to side.

Some young men who hung around the entrance smoking and talking moved to let us through. When we entered the hall we saw a table at one side, and I knew that it was where the donation was taken. Dad handed the old men who sat behind the table a ten-dollar bill and folded his hands in a prayer form to receive blessing. They wrote his name in a ledger and placed the money in a decorative silver bowl. Mrs. Sok followed us and handed them twenty dollars because she had a larger family.

The band at the end of the hall played the same loud music I was familiar with from the parties in St. Pete; the drums pulsed and rang in my ears. People had to almost scream at one another to have a conversation. I never understood why the music was always played at that volume, especially when so many people complained about it.

People sat at endless long tables arranged in rows with

metal chairs and red plastic cups and plates. Little kids ran around chasing their friends; babies cried; men and women from elderly to teenaged talked in groups—all of them looking their best. Men wore their newest outfits of slacks and pressed long-sleeved shirts, and women wore American gowns, Cambodian gowns, or church dresses. Once in a while I would see someone wearing shorts and looking out of place. At one corner was the food station, where cooks sold homemade beef kebabs and green papaya salad.

"There are so many people. Where are we going to sit?" I asked Sopiep.

"What?" she screamed at me.

"I said, where are we going to sit?"

Her dad led us to the opposite side of the hall. Along the way both he and Dad stopped to greet their friends. Compared to the rest of the older men, I thought Dad was the most handsome. His face was freshly shaven, and the new green shirt that I had helped iron made his hair look even darker than usual. Eyes would follow Dad and stop wherever he stood; whenever we met new people I liked to stand next to him so that they knew I was his daughter.

One small group of people made room for us at their table while Sopiep's brothers and Anthony went to get more chairs. Sopiep and I *chumreab suor*ed all the adults. When I saw Auntie Sarah I gave her a small wave but pretended not to see her pull a chair next to her for me to sit in. I knew that Dad had called her a couple more times, and each time he wore the same dazed smile, even after he hung up the phone. Once I had asked him what they were talking about, and he said it was none of my business.

As I grabbed a chair next to Sopiep and Anthony, I noticed that the married women around Auntie Sarah pushed

Dad to sit in the empty chair beside her. I could already tell it was going to be a long night—and wished that Dad, my two friends, and I could have driven in our car forever.

A lady stood on the stage getting ready to sing a famous Cambodian song. She tapped her foot as she held the microphone in one hand, and once she started singing, the applause roared and guys whistled from different directions. The only words I could make out were *sixteen* and *she was turning sixteen*. The music was upbeat and fast, and the people on the dance floor moved to it in the American style, moving their feet and snapping their fingers quickly. But no matter how fast they danced, they still didn't look like Americans, who slid in a way that I thought was so free and easy and natural, like popcorn popping.

"You want to dance?" Sopiep asked. I shrugged. I did want to, but I had never done so in public before. I didn't know if Dad would even let me. Even though he had become less strict and I was allowed to have Anthony as a friend, there were certain things I still couldn't question. I had begun to understand that there were unwritten rules I had been programmed with, and although those rules suffocated me sometimes, I couldn't ignore them. They were permanently inside of me, and without them, I wasn't whole. "Come on, I'll get Anthony to go with us." I immediately shook my head.

The next song was slow, and Sopiep's parents pushed their way to the front, fighting the traffic heading back to the seats. I remembered my mom telling me that slow songs were reserved only for married people, people who loved each other. I closed my eyes and tried to recapture the picture of my parents dancing together but was interrupted every time the band started with a new song.

As the night went on, Dad, too, danced with several women who sat with us at the table. I didn't know why he wasn't dancing with Auntie Sarah, but I was grateful nevertheless. Maybe nothing was going on after all. I noticed he was following the Cambodian custom of asking a lady to dance by *chumreab suor*ing her. Once the lady said yes the two of them would walk up to the dance floor as if they were a couple. He—a grown man with a grown daughter—had never looked more silly to me. Each time Dad would dance, Sopiep would elbow me in the side, and I would ignore her. Once Anthony asked if I was all right, and I ignored him, too.

"Why aren't you guys up there?" Mr. Sok asked us later.

I glanced over at Dad, who pretended not to see me even though he knew what was going on. It was his way of telling me no although he couldn't say so himself. I shook my head at Mr. Sok and put on my shyest smile.

"You want to?" Sopiep asked.

I turned to her to say no, but she wasn't asking me. Without even waiting for me, she and Anthony walked to the dance floor with her parents. The dance was *romvong*, dance circle. The slow, repetitive movement reminded me of a carousel. With the man behind the woman, all the dancers moved in one big circle. Their feet, tapping the floor at a specific beat of the music, moved in unison. The women extended their fingers, allowing only their forefingers and thumbs to meet as they moved their hands slowly up and down.

There must have been close to fifty people on the dance floor. Sopiep's parents didn't really let their daughter and Anthony dance as a *couple*, though. Her mom stayed very close to her and her dad did the same with Anthony, trying to show him what to do with his feet and hands. Each time Sopiep and Anthony came into view, I saw a big grin on her face.

Later that night Dad asked Auntie Sarah to dance, and I noticed that their friends watched to see her response. At first she said she didn't know how and told him to ask someone else. "Please," he insisted, and bowed his head almost like a prince. The sight of his further silliness brought heat to my neck and ears, and I turned away. "It's easy," I heard him tell her. The adults around us clapped and urged her to go with him. I knew he would never ask how I felt about his dancing with women besides Mom, but I waited for him to send me a signal to show he cared. I didn't think it was asking too much for me to be included in his *new* life. Hadn't we come this far together?

"So, what do you think about getting a new mom?" an old woman asked me. I'd met her only a couple of times at Sopiep's house and really didn't dislike her until that night.

Everyone's eyes turned to me, all of them wide and glistening. I tried to search for Mrs. Sok for some support but changed my mind when I realized all of this was her and her husband's doing. They were the ones who had wanted to meet Dad. They were the ones who had had us and Auntie Sarah over at the same time for dinner. I politely smiled at the women and turned around in my seat. I didn't need their help or their joy.

When we left the party I purposely sat in the front seat with Dad. There wasn't anything for me to talk about with Sopiep. It was as if we had gone to two separate parties— one she and Dad had been invited to and one I had watched through a window. I was sure she had a lot to say about her night, but she had Anthony to share it with.

I crouched down in my seat and listened to Dad humming Cambodian tunes and Sopiep giggling softly. "You're so funny," she said in that voice of hers that crawled on my skin like ants. If I could, I would have climbed into the trunk.

●

When June came, I asked Dad again if he was going to our school's awards night. "Yes, and *Meing* Sarah is coming, too." Since the New Year's party he had spoken about Auntie Sarah often, telling me that she cooked well and that she had lived in America for a long time and was still able to retain many Cambodian traditions. "She was about your age when she came here," Dad had said. He spoke in a gentle tone that I would only hear when he talked about her, never about me. And when he spoke about her he always referred to her as *Meing*, not Auntie; I think it was his way of making her more intimate to us.

But I didn't like it. In fact, every time I heard her name from his mouth my body tensed. "Why is she coming?" I felt my face turning ugly with the question.

"She likes you and wants to see you getting all those awards." He smiled at me and playfully waggled his eyebrows.

I knew she liked me, but I doubted she would come just to see *me*. And he should have known that I knew better than to believe him.

"I'm not getting any awards tomorrow night, so you can tell her not to come," I said seriously, not blinking for the entire time he held his gaze on me. He told me not to be crazy and to go to bed.

In bed I took out my diary and pretended I was writing a

letter to Mrs. Yen. *Dear Mrs. Yen,* I wrote. *I like Auntie Sarah but not really. How's Janet? Does she have cones growing out of her chest, too? I don't care if I have any. Anthony is still moving.* I heard Dad's footsteps and quickly put my book away under the bed.

The next evening Sopiep's parents called and said they were running late, so Dad and I walked to school by ourselves. He had asked if I wanted to wait for them, but I told him no. I didn't see why we should wait for them and *Auntie Sarah,* who would be stopping at Sopiep's house first.

With only ten minutes till the start of the awards program, I waved good-bye to Dad at the door of the cafeteria and pushed myself through the many people who were still trying to find seats. I located the students' area, which was set up at the front of the lunchroom, almost right below the stage. I found Anthony and took a seat behind him. As I sat down, Sopiep joined me, breathing loudly.

Anthony turned to us in his seat. "Why are you guys so late?"

"Oh, my gosh," Sopiep said, "Dad got home late from work. And he didn't know if we should drive or walk." She stopped to catch her breath, her chest moving up and down. "So we drove, you know, to save time. But there was no parking. And Mom didn't want to come without him. So we had to drive back home and then walk here. I ran."

He and I looked down at her scuffed white pumps. She rolled her eyes and dramatically brushed her forehead with the back of one hand. When Anthony laughed, I joined him.

The lights dimmed in the cafeteria as our principal, Mr. Stein, walked onstage. My mind wandered as he talked about how our parents should be proud of us, how we were good kids, and how the future held many good things for us.

But when he said "They've come a long way," I really listened, not to his words but to the quiet noises around me: a baby's cry, a sneeze, and a soft weeping from somewhere in the back. Then I listened to my heart beating, the stale air coming out of my nose. I felt the blood pumping down my legs and arms. All of those things reaffirmed for me that a lot had happened, the move from St. Pete and the new life with just Dad and me. At the same time, though, I feared that what I had helped to build for the two of us was getting smaller and smaller and that there wouldn't be room for a third person.

I turned around in my seat and tried to find Dad. He was only a couple of rows behind me, and next to him was Auntie Sarah. Her bare arm and his thick, muscular shoulder almost touched. I searched but couldn't find Sopiep's parents anywhere near them. Seeing Dad sit next to this woman, or any woman, felt so wrong, like two complete puzzles that someone had tried in vain to make into one picture. Auntie Sarah saw me and grinned widely, but I ignored her and quickly turned back around.

A couple of kids around me turned to see why I was moving so much, yet I couldn't sit still. I wanted to take another look; maybe I hadn't seen correctly the first time. But I decided not to. I was sure of what I had seen, and the sight of the two of them sitting side by side, as if they were *parents*, was sharply etched in my mind.

Several teachers walked up onto the stage to help Mr. Stein hand out awards. Mrs. Ortiz held a basket of white carnations and stood at one side of the stage. Earlier that day we had been told that the flowers were for us, "But won't it be great if you give them to your moms," she said. *If you have one*, I wanted to say to her.

The first set of awards was for perfect attendance, and the second was for citizenship. They were given to many students, and I didn't really care about either of them. But when Sopiep's name was called for Citizen of the Year I was truly happy. I knew she wasn't getting any other award that night because of her low grades, and I was afraid her parents had come for nothing.

"Sopiep," Mr. Stein said, "is a wonderful student who cares about her classmates, is polite to her teachers, and is a hard worker." Sopiep walked up the steps to the stage, shook the principal's hand, and accepted her certificate from one teacher and her carnation from Mrs. Ortiz.

The next set of awards was the most special because they were for excellence in academic subjects. Everybody knew you would get one only if you were smart, and I counted on getting at least one so Dad would be proud of me. But I didn't get an award in art or music. I didn't get one in writing, either, which I was not surprised about. When I didn't get the award in social studies and Sopiep squeezed my hand, I looked at her, rolled my eyes, and shrugged. I wondered, though, if she knew that I really did care. What if I went home without anything? What if the night was a total failure? What if Dad was embarrassed by having a stupid daughter? What if I wasn't special at all?

"And the award for excellence in science goes to Anthony Cupelli," Mr. Stein said.

Something heavy dropped in my stomach as I heard his name. Sopiep, however, almost jumped out of her seat. Her eyes shone brightly. I knew her well, but some days I wanted to rip her open just to see if her insides were really made up of jewels.

"The next award is for reading," the principal said. "This

student has read a total of fifteen books this year," he continued. I heard the *Ahhs* from the audience as Sopiep pulled at my arm. She, like me, knew that my name was going to be called.

As I accepted my carnation, Mrs. Ortiz held on to my hand and whispered how much she was going to miss me. The glow on her cheeks told me she was sincere, but I didn't understand why she was holding me up until Mr. Stein called my name again for the math award. Instead of going down the steps and coming back up the ones on the other side of the stage, I turned and walked back to him, causing the audience to laugh and clap.

I looked out into the audience and saw Dad. He stood in the aisle and took pictures of me while Auntie Sarah smiled beside him. I felt guilty for having been rude to her earlier. *I should have at least grinned back,* I thought. After all, she was a nice lady. She probably thought I didn't like her. I told myself I would be friendlier to her from then on.

"You made me happy tonight," Dad said on our walk back home.

"Thank you. But I got only two."

"Two good ones." He waved the two carnations I had given him. "I mean it, though. I was very proud of you." He took a deep breath before speaking again. "A lot has happened to us. But you still worked hard . . . at school. And at home." He put an arm around my shoulders and squeezed me close to him. The squeeze spoke louder than his compliment.

I should have been proud of myself for being a good student. I should have been dancing and singing that night. But I wasn't and didn't. Something was wrong. *Why did Dad choose tonight to tell me all this?* I asked myself. A year and a half had gone by without his saying anything—so why tonight of all nights? Why after the awards night and after having sat with Auntie Sarah? And the answer struck me: he was going to tell me that he and Auntie Sarah were getting married. The thought paralyzed me. Things were moving so fast, and I just wanted them to stop. I wanted our lives to rewind to the days before that night, to before the New Year's party, to before the afternoon Anthony told me he was going to move, and before Sopiep took out her pigtails. I wanted to go back to that short period when it was just Dad and me in our new house. I knew I had wanted him to have friends, but I hadn't expected him to marry one of them.

We walked the rest of the way home in silence.

"Life for us will be okay, huh, Amy," Dad said as we got home. I looked at him briefly before stepping inside. There was absolute certainty in his voice. It was the sound of my opening the bedroom window in the morning to our neighbors' sprinklers and to the blue jays chirping. You couldn't help knowing that the day promised to be a good one.

"Yes," I dutifully confirmed. I wasn't sure of my answer until Dad took the carnations to the kitchen, filled a glass with water, placed the flowers in it, and centered the arrangement on the dinner table. He did everything just right. And I thought, *If Dad is so certain of our future, then shouldn't I trust him, even though Auntie Sarah might be in it? He was the one who had wanted to move, and the move proved to be the right decision, didn't it?*

That night, as I was about to switch off the light in my room, I heard Dad on the phone again. By his gentle tone, I knew it couldn't be anyone but Auntie Sarah that he was speaking to. I no longer wanted to go to bed. I wanted to know what was so important that they had to talk now, since they had just seen each other only thirty minutes before. But remembering to trust Dad, I refrained from going to the living room.

I walked over to my dresser for my diary. The bottom drawer wouldn't open, and as I jiggled it free, my mom's picture frame fell and hit me on my left shoulder. It wasn't the weight of it but the stare of my mom that hurt me. As before, she was looking at me. I should have taken comfort that she and I were seeing each other again. But I didn't. Her stare filled me with guilt and memories of our times together. When we had lain in her bed, she would sometimes whisper how much she loved me. How she would die if anything happened to me. *She would die.* People didn't do that just for anyone, did they? Only a real mother would die for her daughter. How stupid of me to almost forget that and let Auntie Sarah into my life, our lives.

"Sorry," I told my mom, and placed the picture frame back on top of the dresser. More than ever I was certain that she still loved me. Why else would she come to me and remind me not to forget what she and I had? There was no way now that I could let someone into my house to take my mom's place and jeopardize her love for me.

●

I counted every day that passed that summer. In my diary I drew a calendar of June and July. And before I fell asleep each night I crossed off a box with a red marker and counted how many days I had left to spend with Anthony. Soon the two months turned into a quilt where all the patchworks were crosses. Without knowing why, I thought of him often. The fear that one day I wouldn't be able to see him anymore followed me like a shadow. I knew I would always remember him as a kind and loyal friend, but I was unsure if he would do the same of me. So I did my best, even to the very last day, to help him remember me.

One evening, having spent the entire afternoon outside, Sopiep, Anthony, and I headed to her house to cool down. If her brothers were home, then Anthony would be allowed to go inside with us. If they weren't, then he would have to wait outside and we would bring him something cold to drink. Sopiep unlocked her door and yelled for her brothers. There was no answer.

"We'll be right back out," she said to Anthony. "Come on, Amy." She waited for me at her open door. I told her to go ahead and cool down without me. "Why?"

"I'm not that hot," I said. I looked over at Anthony, who was squatting down near a shrub. A trickle of sweat rolled down his forehead and hung over his top lip.

"Well," she said, glancing back and forth at us, "I'll be right out with something to drink."

When the door shut I walked to the shrub and sat next to Anthony. There was so much I wanted to say to him before he left the next day. What, exactly, I didn't know. The words darted around in my head like flies, but no matter how hard I tried I couldn't catch one of them to start a sentence.

I turned my eyes to where he was looking. Across the street a boy, about five years old, climbed onto his bicycle. He seemed to have trouble steering in a straight line as his feet kept falling off the pedals. His mom took small steps beside the bike as he struggled to ride it.

"I used to be that kid," Anthony said.

"Really? I never had a bike."

"No," he said, and shook his head. He scrunched his eyebrows in frustration. "When I first started riding my bike, one of my parents was always nearby." I nodded and looked at him. Freckles dotted his cheeks and the bridge of his nose. "I told them that I could ride by myself, but they never left me. And once, I fell. I remember thinking how much it was going to hurt when I hit the concrete. But my dad was there." He turned to me again. "He caught me, you know?"

"Yes," I said without hesitation. And I *did* know. I knew it from watching Sopiep and her parents and brothers. I knew it when Sopiep's mom stroked her back when we sat outside on their porch eating boiled peanuts. I knew it when her dad told her to be nice to her brothers because they loved her. And I knew it when they were proud of her even though she received only a citizenship award. "Are you still mad at them?" I asked.

He didn't answer for a long time. He smacked a gnat that landed on his face. "I guess so."

"But they want you back."

"My grandma said they sent me away because they love me. But I think that if they really loved me they wouldn't have been able to send me away in the first place." I heard uncertainty in his voice again as he continued to stare across the street. The little boy's mom tried to show him how to pedal, but he pushed her away. "Amy, are you still mad at your mom?" The answer that came into my mind was no, but I decided to tell him the truth.

"Sometimes."

"When?" I thought about the items on my list; all of them raced through my mind as if they were cars out of control.

"Okay, I'm back. Look what I got." Sopiep brought three paper cups and a can of Coke that she delightedly waved at us. "What were you talking about?"

I looked at Anthony.

"Nothing special," he said.

"Well, do you want to walk over to the corner store to get some candy?" She showed us her money.

The corner store was on the other side of North Park Elementary. None of us was ever allowed to walk to it by ourselves. "Bad area," Sopiep's mom said. Even though the houses were the same size as the ones in our neighborhood, they didn't look the same. The walls needed new paint jobs, screen doors needed fixing, and fences needed whitewashing. Mailboxes, caked with bird droppings, were rusting. Dirt patches and weeds took over the grass in the yards. Today, a few girls about our age, who didn't look as if they'd taken baths lately, walked along the sidewalk carrying their baby brothers or sisters on their hips. And the boys, barefooted and shirtless, kicked beer cans into a hole they had dug in the ground. Although I didn't want to think about it, it vaguely reminded me of the place I used to call home.

The store, owned by an old Korean man, was small but carried many different items. There were things we could buy—bananas, notebooks, candy bars, and ice cream—and things we couldn't buy—beer, lottery tickets, and cigarettes. Our favorite place was the section with ten-cent candies.

"Hey," the man mumbled, carrying a stack of blue packages that Mom had once told me were private for women and not to be talked about. I turned away and pretended to peruse the display of candies with Anthony when the man walked by.

Anthony ran his hand down boxes of Red Hots, Airheads, LemonHeads, and giant gumballs. When the owner walked past us, Sopiep giggled. "You know what those are, right?" she whispered in my ear. I inched away from her and

Anthony. Of course I knew what those blue packages were—I'd seen my mom with them and seen them on TV—but there was no need for her to bring it up, especially when a boy was around.

"Come on, Amy, why aren't you helping us?" Anthony signaled for me to move closer as Sopiep continued to laugh. He asked her what was so funny.

"Amy." She pointed at me before clutching her stomach with both hands. "She's embarrassed about maxi pads." I turned my back on them and slowly walked to the door. I couldn't believe what Sopiep had just said. Did she have no shame? "Amy!" she called out.

Too afraid that the skin on my cheeks was going to flame with embarrassment, I didn't turn around. I didn't think I would ever be able to look at Anthony again. My insides felt like hot coals, but still, I hadn't intended to leave my friends. It was not my back I wanted Anthony to remember. Yet I couldn't go back to the store. So I took tiny steps and waited for them at the end of the street.

"Amy!" I heard Sopiep yell. When they finally caught up with me she put an arm around my shoulders, and Anthony walked on my other side. "Sorry. What was the big deal, anyway?" she asked.

"I don't want to talk about it." I pulled her arm off.

"Come on," she said. Anthony kicked a tennis ball he had found along the way and moved several feet ahead of us. I tipped my head forward and motioned my eyes at his back.

"Anthony?" Sopiep said. I told her to hush. But she didn't. "Anthony—you know what maxi pads are?"

He walked backward and blew and popped his gum. "Yeah!"

"You see? It's no big deal." She shrugged and hooked her arm around mine.

It was a big deal, wasn't it? If it wasn't, then why had Mom pushed *her* blue package way back, behind the extra towels and toilet tissue in the closet? And when I asked her about them, why had she told me to *Shhh!*? If Anthony still wanted to know, I was ready to tell him: *It's when something like this comes up that I get mad at her for leaving us.*

We stopped off at Sopiep's house first because she had to complete her chores before her parents came home. Although we'd done it many times before, it was awkward that day, standing there in front of her door. Each of us knew that it was the last time we would be together, and the silence among us in that brief time hung like a heavy weight.

"Well, I have to go," Anthony finally said. Sopiep gave him a quick hug and went inside.

I planned on walking him to his grandmother's, but he said he wasn't ready to go in yet, so he walked me home instead. "Things will be okay," he said.

"I'm sure." I really wasn't, though.

"Yeah, I want to see my parents. I'm ready for a normal life again." I was happy for him. He deserved to have his parents in his life.

"So you're not mad at them anymore?" I asked.

He shrugged. "I don't know. They are my parents, though. I guess I have to forgive them sooner or later."

I had stopped to scratch an ant bite when Anthony grabbed my hand. The touch of his sweaty palm reminded me of a rare pastry my mom used to make for guests. It would take her all morning to knead the flour and steam the dough, so I wasn't allowed to touch or taste them until the guests had visited and left. I pulled my hand from his. "Sorry," I said. But as we continued to walk I rubbed my fingers together, feeling the coolness that his sweat had brought to them.

227

When we reached my house I felt I was competing with time, and I was losing as each minute went by. The sun was already getting ready to rest for the evening. Soon Dad would be home, and I knew that at any minute Anthony would turn around and walk away forever. I thought of what I could say to him to let him know that he was special to me, that I would build a small place within my heart for him just as I had done for Mrs. Yen. And I thought of what I could give him to remind him of who I was. But I couldn't think of anything.

"Can I kiss you?" he asked.

The question sounded like ice cubes hitting the inside of a glass on a hot day. I didn't know where the answer came from, but I said, "Yes." And as soon as I said that simple word, every part of me opened and breathed as if there were windows to my body.

He bent in closer. The warm air from his nostrils tickled my cheek, and I smelled the saltiness of his sweat. And even when he backed away, I still felt the touch of his lips like a magnolia petal I had once rubbed on my face a year earlier.

"I gotta go." He raced down our couple of steps and ran. "Bye, Amy!" But I chose not to say good-bye back.

15

DAD AND I had been invited to people's houses so often that he wanted them to come to ours. I didn't think it was necessary; it was their fault for asking us over in the first place. I had stopped wanting to go with Dad to his friends', but he insisted that I accompany him. "We're father and daughter," he would say. I would then *accompany* him, only to be forgotten later. His friends thought they were so clever in seating him and Auntie Sarah next to each other at the table or on the floor when they played cards for dimes and quarters. Someone might say loudly over dinner: "Peera, Sarah is out of rice." Dad would dutifully reach over for the rice bowl and scoop some onto Auntie Sarah's plate. Another person might say in the living room: "Peera, I want to sit, too." Dad would scoot in closer to Auntie Sarah to make room for the person. Everyone would then laugh in pleasure. I didn't. I had to give myself more rice, and sometimes I had no place to sit. And no one seemed to care.

"Why do you care about having them over?" I asked Dad.

"For a change. Friendship has to go back and forth," he said. He proudly looked around at our place—as if it were a castle. As if he had something to show off to *Auntie Sarah*.

"There's no place for people to sit," I said. I stomped back and forth between the kitchen and the living room. "See? There isn't even enough space for more than two people to walk around comfortably."

"Don't be stupid."

I balled up my hands at my sides and said loudly, "I'm not stupid."

"Amy . . ."

I wanted to say "What?" He hated to hear American kids on TV say that to their parents; he said it was rude—a child speaking to a parent as if the parent were the inferior one. But I knew I was pushing it, so I did the next best thing. I looked back at him looking at me. Until I saw his eyes widening and his chest moving up and down from breathing heavily, trying to control his temper.

"Amy," he said. "You're getting older now. You're not a little kid any longer."

A week later the Soks came. The Youvs came. And a single man who was studying to be a doctor came. From the gossip that I'd heard, he was next in line to be matched up for marriage. Mrs. Sok told me to come sit beside her on the couch. I stayed where I was, near the refrigerator. "There's not enough room in here," I said. Sopiep stared at me from where she sat on the floor with her dad.

Later I came out of the bathroom and saw Auntie Sarah at the front door. "Amy, look who's here," Dad said. He moved a chair to prop open the door so that fresh air could flow in.

"Hi, Amy," Auntie Sarah said. While she bent down to take off her sandals, I headed toward my room.

Dad told me to wait. "Why so fast? Look, *Meing* Sarah brought you a present."

My legs turned into heavy logs. The other adults didn't really care about how I felt; they were talking about the Cambodian government—another election was coming up. But at the same time I could feel them watching me, waiting to see if I would do the right thing.

"Come here and see," Dad ordered.

Auntie Sarah opened her bag and took out two dresses. She showed one to Sopiep and said it was for her. Sopiep jumped up and walked to where I stood. She took her dress and repeatedly thanked Auntie Sarah. Auntie Sarah handed me mine, but I didn't take it. She didn't seem bothered, though. With my arms down at my sides, my body froze as she held the dress against my body. Dad's breathing grew deeper and deeper behind me, reminding me that I needed to thank her. I did want to jump up to hug her, but I couldn't help hating her at the same time. Who did she think she was, buying me clothes and coming into my house as if she belonged here?

"I bought it on sale. Do you like it? I thought you could wear it on your first day of school," she said. I didn't say anything. Sopiep told her how pretty the dresses were, but Auntie Sarah didn't seem to hear her. It seemed she only wanted to hear from me.

"It's too small," I said. "Besides, no one wears dresses on their first day in middle school." I snatched the dress from her hands, put it back into the bag, and dropped it on the carpet before taking the hot road to my room. I was going to pay big-time for what I had just done, and I knew it.

I closed the door behind me and tried to quiet down my breathing so that I could listen to everyone talk about me. There was a silence before Mr. Youv told Dad that it was okay.

"Kids are like that. Sometimes they don't see where they've gone wrong. When they get older, they'll know better."

News flash for Mr. Youv: I already knew where I'd gone wrong. I had been mean and horrible to Auntie Sarah. I had disrespected Dad in front of his friends. I was such an awful Cambodian daughter. But I couldn't help it. I was so angry that no one understood like I did why Auntie Sarah didn't belong with Dad. If only one, just one person understood, then maybe I wouldn't feel so alone.

I could hear someone laying newspaper on the floor and Dad's guests finding cozy spaces around it. Food was being laid out. Ice cubes were being dropped in glasses. Beer and soda cans were being popped. Sopiep was saying she would stop drinking soda from now on—it was nothing but sugar. No one came for me.

It wasn't until half an hour later that Sopiep came to my room. I didn't talk to her at first, pretending to read. When she wasn't looking, I watched her play with my knickknacks. She picked up my mom's picture frame.

"Tell me about your mom," I said. From my bed, I looked back at her in the mirror. She'd finally gotten her contacts, and without her glasses on, I noticed that her eyes looked rounder and her eyelashes longer. She looked older.

She scrunched her dark eyebrows. "What?"

I got up and straightened the bed. "I want to know about your mom."

She picked up my brush and began fluffing her bangs with it. "You know my mom. In fact, you know everyone in my family." She sounded so carefree—as if her gift from God, a wonderful, normal family, was just another item in her life. Watching her and listening to her, I wanted to be carefree, too.

"I want to know how she makes you feel." I stretched out my arms and turned in a circle. I wished I could fly, fly away. Sopiep said I was getting strange and kicked my new backpack under the bed. "Fine, tell me this," I said. "If you had to choose between your mom and dad, who would you choose?"

"I don't know," she said. "Is that why you've been so weird lately?" I rolled my eyes at her. "If that's how you feel . . . you shouldn't."

"Why not?"

She spoke matter-of-factly, as if I were crazy to ask her in the first place. "Because, Amy, your mom isn't here for you to choose."

For a split second my face turned red as I started to explain why my mom wasn't *here*, with me. But I didn't know the answer. I had watched enough sappy television and read enough books to know that it wasn't my fault that she left . . . but then whose was it? There had to be a real reason, even if it was just a speck of light in a big, dark tunnel. It was no longer satisfying to just say that she hadn't been happy.

"She was the best," I said quietly. Sopiep didn't say anything, just looked at me with pity on her face. I didn't know why I never wanted sympathy from her. I walked to a corner and sat down. "You know why I had my hair cut?" I asked.

"Why?"

"Because I didn't want to look like my mom." There was a vague confusion in her eyes. "Don't you see, Sopiep? My hair turned out horrible. It was punishment for having betrayed her. She is my mother—I shouldn't have done what I did." Sopiep didn't seem to understand; she stood before me with parted lips. "Every day, I can feel her around me, watching me. She's warning me not to betray her again." I almost hollered at Sopiep but stopped when the toilet across the hall flushed.

"Amy, for a smart and mature girl, you can be so dumb. You think something bad will happen just because your dad remarries?" I considered telling her about my dream in which I called for my mom but she never answered. But if Sopiep didn't understand the hair, she wouldn't have understood that.

"I don't know. But it doesn't matter. He'll do whatever he wants."

She opened my window and sat at the end of my bed. "Yeah, but he can't be all that happy if you're not," she said. She'd stopped speaking in her singsong voice—maybe it was because Anthony wasn't around anymore. Yet she didn't look sad or lonely without his presence. In a way she was still the same happy and perky Sopiep I had met a year earlier; she just wasn't as young.

I inhaled the warm August air. I remembered having looked out our window many times in Florida after Mom left, watching the other kids running up and down the sidewalk, listening and aching to join them but not doing it because I didn't want Dad to be lonely. "He is happy. Look at him. He walks around like there's no ground," I said.

"That's because he's in love." She smiled at me, and her beauty mark was now dancing beneath her eye. When I didn't return the smile, she continued, "But he's usually gloomy because you are. At least, that's what my mom said."

I hadn't seen that, hadn't even considered it. But it didn't make a difference. The fact remained the same: no one could take my mom's place. I walked over to the window. "It was so bad after my mom left," I said.

As much as I liked Sopiep, I didn't trust her with my

tears. I didn't want to cry in front of anyone who might not understand all the heartache each tear carried. I wouldn't have wanted her to hug me or rub my back and tell me everything would be all right, not unless she knew for certain. So I let my throat tighten as I held back the tears, allowing only a few of them to gather at the corners of my eyes, blurring my vision and my mind. I was so confused.

Sopiep left when her mom called for her. It was already ten o'clock. As each guest departed, I started to think more and more about Dad and what he would say or do to me. I climbed into bed and pulled the sheet up to my neck.

I shut my eyes and pretended to be asleep when Dad opened my door and turned on the light. I could feel my eyelids moving as I felt his body looming over me. "Amy, I know you're not sleeping," he said. I stayed still, determined to fool him. I lost all will, though, when he ordered, "Sit up!" I sat up, feeling his glare burning the top of my head as I looked down, rolling the sheet around my hand.

In a gentler voice he said, "I thought you wanted me to get out of the house and make friends, meet people."

"People," I said. "People. Not someone to marry."

"Who's talking about marrying? I mean, that might be a possibility far, far in the future. But not now. Besides, I thought you liked Auntie Sarah."

Of course, that wasn't the point. The point was that each time I looked at Auntie Sarah, I saw a person who didn't belong in our family. Sometimes when we sat together at the Soks' house all I could think about was how she knew nothing about Dad and me. She didn't know how Dad had gotten the scar down his face, or what his first job was, or what my favorite color was. For her to know everything about us, we would have to spend many, many years filling her in. This was not natural, I thought. A mom was supposed to know things about me without my having to tell her; and didn't the same go for a wife? I tried to explain this to him, but he didn't understand.

He sat down next to me. "I thought you knew a long time ago that your mom's gone, never coming back." When I didn't say anything he went on, "You knew it before I did." I looked over at him and found a blanket of sadness over his face, but all I could think about was Mom and how unfair it was that he was forgetting about her. I would not forget about her. "I love you, you know that, right?" he asked.

I blinked and nodded.

Dad stood up and walked to the door. "Remember," he said in Cambodian, "who you are." *Yes,* I thought, *I am Cambodian.* That was the only reprimand I received for my earlier behavior.

●

From my room I could hear Dad in the kitchen, dropping spoons into the sink and slamming the refrigerator door shut. I looked over at my clock . . . he had exactly fifteen minutes until Auntie Sarah came for dinner. This time there would be no other guests. I had refused to help him cook when he had asked me to; I thought it was nice enough of me to let her come.

I got up from my bed and walked to the kitchen, which smelled of oyster sauce and garlic. Dad was still wearing his old white San Diego T-shirt with the large ink stain on one sleeve, and now, specks of oyster sauce dotted the front. He looked tired and dirty, but I didn't feel sorry for him. Four chairs sat around the dinner table, which still had wet marks on it, and an old vase with fresh yellow roses from Mrs. Jackson's garden had been placed in the center.

"Are you having a romantic dinner for two?" I asked when he saw me. I waited until he turned around to roll my eyes.

He briefly looked over from the sink and in a calm voice answered, "No. We're having a special dinner for three, and you're our guest of honor."

I glared at his back. "A guest? She's coming to my house, and I'm the guest."

I stomped back to my room, all the while feeling my heart beating up in my ears.

A few minutes later he knocked on my door. "I'm taking a shower. Be sure to answer the door when *Meing* Sarah gets here."

Auntie Sarah was five minutes late, and when I opened the door I was prepared to tell her she had the wrong house. But I couldn't. Not when she stood outside my door carrying a small cake with white frosting and yellow flowers. Her short frizzy black hair rested around her head like a Chia Pet. She bent down to hug me with one arm. I didn't hug her back.

Since Dad had said I was their *guest*, I didn't bother to help him set the dinner table. Nor did I bother to pour the drinks or serve the food. I remained in my chair as both he and Auntie Sarah brought the rice and hot stir-fry to the table. She had asked him a couple of times where the plates were . . . then the spoons and forks . . . and then the glasses. I could have easily pointed to the cupboard and drawer beside the refrigerator, but I thought it was more entertaining to watch Dad trying to impress this woman whom he had asked to my home.

At first the only sounds at dinner were of the spoons hitting the plates, Mr. Jackson outside watering his rosebushes and shrubs, and the ticking of the clock from the living room. Once I even heard food going down Dad's throat when he swallowed.

Auntie Sarah was the first to speak. "Amy," she said. *What*, I thought, *are you going to tell me how pretty I am, or how sweet it would be to have me as your daughter?*

"Amy, how is school?" she asked. I ignored her until Dad said she was talking to me. Just as I opened my mouth to speak she started talking again. "I hated middle school. High school was so much better." I hoped she was right. At the rate middle school was going for me, I would have preferred to stay in the fifth grade for a couple more years.

"It's all right," I answered under my breath.

The sixth grade was just so different from what I had expected. Although our counselor at the old school had explained the changes to come, I was still surprised by them all. The school building itself had many wings, all of them connecting to the central one. I had six classes, each of them lasting fifty minutes and taught by a different teacher. And the kids—especially the older ones—were big, with breasts, hips, and shaved legs, or muscles, deep voices, and mustaches.

"When I started school I didn't speak English at all, and there weren't that many Asians. My hair was out to here." She extended her arms. "I got the hint that the white girls didn't like me because they thought I was going to give them lice, and the black girls didn't like me because they thought I was Chinese. Why that mattered, I didn't know. So I did everything by myself, ate by myself, studied by myself, and even did a group science project by myself. Now that is sad." I couldn't help giggling at the thought of doing group work by myself. She was right; that would look pathetic.

"What about riding the bus?" she asked.

I wondered how she knew I rode the bus. Quietly I said,

"The bus stops in front of the corner store. It's not so bad since Dad drops me and Sopiep there." And without knowing why, I started telling her how some of the kids who waited with us cussed a lot and sometimes smoked. And how Sopiep couldn't stand that. Then I said, "But listen to this. Some of them buy candies in the morning and sell them at school." I glanced at Dad, and he winked at me. I tried not to smile but wasn't successful.

"They're smart," Auntie Sarah said, and tapped her temple with a finger. "Oh, yes, kids now, they are businesspeople. Give them a dollar bill in the morning, and they'll show you a five at night." I put down my spoon to listen and to watch her. She was not shy at all about how loud she was. Her voice got louder as her eyes got bigger and her hand smacked the table. "My youngest brother, he wears name-brand clothes—like Polo and Guess—things I can't even buy for myself. And I know my mother can't. One day I asked him where he got the money to buy his jeans and shoes, and do you know what he said?" Dad and I shook our heads. "He said that he charges his friends to do their homework."

I started laughing until Dad glanced at me. "I'm sorry. I'm not laughing at him. I just think it's funny," I said.

"It's okay, sweetie," Auntie Sarah said. "It is kind of funny. But I don't tell him that." Then she continued with her story. "And he said that he's going to do that for the rest of his life. I asked him about college, and he said, 'Why pay to go to school when I can make money off someone else going to school?'" I started laughing again, and had to hold my stomach. The two of them started laughing, too.

When we finally quieted down, Dad said, "Amy, tell *Meing* Sarah about your *favorite* class." *Oh, yes, my* favorite *class,* I thought sarcastically.

Before I could start, Auntie Sarah stopped me. "Wait. I know this one. Is it health class?" I shook my head. "Then it must be gym."

"Yep. How did you know?" I heard my voice squealing.

"I don't understand why Americans want their kids to walk around without clothes in the showers. It teaches them all the wrong things," Dad said.

I didn't say anything and looked at Auntie Sarah. "Peera," she said, "I don't think they walk around naked. Don't they have on at least their towels, Amy?" I nodded.

"That doesn't sound so bad, then," he said.

"I guess," I said sheepishly, and started on my dinner again.

None of the girls exactly walked around naked in the locker room. No, they—mostly the seventh and eighth graders—walked around in lacy pink bras that showed their brown nipples and panties that rode up their butts. At first I had closed my eyes when someone nearby undressed. Once, when I'd opened them, I found a girl staring at me. "Are you praying?" she asked me. The girls around us turned to see if I was. "No, something was in my eye," I answered, and waited for them to look away before I took off my blouse.

One day an older girl asked why I wasn't wearing a bra. Until then, I had just assumed that I was still too young and wasn't ready for one. When I didn't say anything she went on, "You should buy one. If you don't wear it early, they'll hang when you get old." She put her hands at her stomach— "They'll hang down to here." I imagined having long, skinny papayas weighing me down. I asked her how she knew. "My mom," she said simply, and walked to the showers with a towel around her. For the rest of the day I had thought of ways of getting a bra, and all of them required having someone take me to a store. Even though the girls—some of whom I even liked—never gave me a hard time again, I started changing in a bathroom stall.

Auntie Sarah finished the last slice of the beef. "Okay, I'll eat it if you don't eat it," she had said to Dad, and put it in her mouth.

I watched her jaw working that piece of meat and saw it going down her throat. Mom would have never done that. She wouldn't have eaten more than two servings of rice, nor would she have eaten everything a guest had given her. But I didn't dislike Auntie Sarah for it. Actually, I liked that she didn't care about what she was or wasn't supposed to do in front of us. Mrs. Sok was the same way with her family.

Dad didn't ask me to, but I decided to help him and Auntie Sarah clean up. As I took the plates to the sink for him, I thought that the three of us looked strange in the kitchen. Although it was large enough for us all to be in it and move around, there was an unfamiliarity to the whole thing that made me just want to stand back and see if all the pieces were fitting. If Mom had been with us, Dad would have gone to the living room and turned the TV on while she and I cleaned up. Now he was at the sink, squeezing dish detergent onto a green sponge, and Auntie Sarah was at the stove, cleaning the top of it with a wet paper towel. None of us said anything as we did our own small task, and when I finished with mine and finally stood against a wall looking at them, I decided that what I saw remained strange . . . but not so bad.

"Okay," I said when Dad finished cleaning the pan, "I'm going to my room."

"What!" Auntie Sarah exclaimed.

I was stunned and asked quietly, "Huh?"

"I rented a Jackie Chan movie. I thought we could eat the cake that I brought and watch the movie together."

I looked over at Dad, who was trying to find dessert plates. "Don't the two of you want to spend time alone?"

Dad blushed and turned back around as Auntie Sarah uneasily tapped the counter. Then I realized how dumb my question was. Dad and Auntie Sarah were Cambodians, not Americans on TV—they didn't spend time alone. Doing so would have meant that they were doing something they weren't supposed to. I felt my cheeks burning with embarrassment.

"No," she said, and pointed at Dad. "Who wants to spend time alone with him?" For the second time that night I couldn't help laughing, and it felt good.

I sat between them on the couch, Dad smelling of Head & Shoulders and Auntie Sarah of baby powder. We had brought the whole cake out and cut big slices. "How did you know I like yellow?" I asked Auntie Sarah.

"Your dad. He talks about you all the time."

"Oh," I said, and ate my dessert.

The video was an action movie about Jackie Chan trying to expose a bad cop in Australia. He skied down snow slopes in the Ukraine and stayed under freezing cold water to save his life. In the process of fighting his enemies, Jackie would do silly things like swim away from a shark only to learn it was a seal, or strip down to his underwear, which had a picture of a koala bear on the front. Auntie Sarah's laughs were so loud they shook me in my seat. Sometimes she jumped in excitement and her arm touched me, sending warm blood through my body. In the middle of the movie I needed to go to the bathroom, but I was afraid to move because I didn't want to risk losing my seat to Dad.

I wasn't surprised when Auntie Sarah left as soon as the movie ended. It was only nine o'clock, but it wouldn't have been right for her to stay too much longer. When I was much younger I had heard Melissa's mom talk about a young woman in our neighborhood who visited single men until the *middle of the night*. From the tone she had used, I knew it wasn't a good thing.

"Are you going to come back?" I asked while Auntie Sarah put on her sandals with spaghetti-thin white strings.

"Of course," she said.

Dad walked her out to her car. He asked if I wanted to go with them, but knowing how sweet a private good-bye was, I shook my head.

16

It wasn't even three o'clock when gray clouds forced the November day to end and rushed us Mission Beach visitors home before showers started. No one wanted winter to come, so we had dressed in jeans and sweaters—Mrs. Youv even wore a jacket—to have one last beach day. Now we had to pack up our picnic, say good-bye to one another, and run to our cars. I climbed into the backseat as Dad and Auntie Sarah got into the front, and waved good-bye to Sopiep and her family as they backed out of the parking lot. While we waited in the long line of cars to exit the beach, Auntie Sarah turned around in her seat and asked if I had had fun. The scent of grilled chicken rose from her shirt and hair.

Auntie Sarah was a powerful tree trunk—big, uncomplicated, and comforting. Her steps were quick and fearless; even from my room I could hear her walk up to our door. With big round eyes, full lips, short frizzy hair, and deep pores, she only grew on me more when I discovered how simple everything about her was. Her favorite outfit was an old pair of black jeans and a Hawaiian floral shirt. She would run a pick through her hair once, put on quick strokes of blue eye shadow and glossy red lipstick, and then walk out of the bathroom as though she thought she was beautiful. She spoke in an easy, deep voice that carried no double meanings, and her laughs rang louder than even the men's.

I scooted to the middle of the backseat so that she didn't have to turn too far to see me. "Yeah, I had fun," I said.

I reached between the two front seats and turned on the radio before resting my head on her arm. Her black cotton-ball head bopped to the music. Her warm skin reminded me of how easily I could get lost in her comfort. I remembered the night Dad and I had first visited her family at her house. It had gotten late, but Dad hadn't wanted to leave. And as the night had grown heavier, so had my eyelids. I had sunk lower in the sofa and laid my head on her pillowy arm. I hadn't known we had left until I'd woken up the next morning in my bed.

The windows fogged up and turned our car into a co-coon. Above us the thunder drummed loudly as the rain continued to beat down hard. Dad stayed quiet, driving slowly and not taking his eyes off the road. I was getting used to riding in the backseat, watching him and Auntie Sarah and knowing that all three of us were heading together in the same direction. Back there, by myself, I didn't have to worry about making Dad laugh or wonder whether he was happy; Auntie Sarah did all that. I just sat in the back, bathing in the white, painless peace.

When we reached Auntie Sarah's house, where she lived with her mom and two younger brothers, Dad wanted to walk her to the door. But she said she didn't want him to get wet. She rubbed my knees and blew me a kiss. As she opened the car door, the raindrops shot at her and into the car like bullets. "Someone must be mad," she screamed before closing the door and racing to her porch. Sometimes I never wanted her to leave. I even wondered what it would be like to have her be part of our small family.

When we got home Dad took the cooler into the bathroom, and I followed him. He went on his knees and turned the water on in the bathtub. I leaned against the open bathroom door, running my hand through my hair and looking into the mirror as I played with the dead ends, deciding whether I should trim them off.

"When are you and Auntie Sarah getting married?" I asked.

He stopped scrubbing the cooler and looked at me over his left shoulder, apparently surprised that I had finally come to the conclusion that it was a sure thing—no longer a mere possibility.

It was completely obvious to me that Dad and Auntie Sarah were lost in the stage between acquaintance and engagement. It had taken me a while to get used to the idea that Dad wasn't married but had a girlfriend, although I wasn't allowed to say that word. They continued to call and visit each other often, and when they were bold enough they started going out in public as a couple to parks, the San Diego Zoo, and restaurants for noodles . . . but with me accompanying them. I was beginning to understand that they took me with them because the sight of an unmarried Cambodian couple eating or walking together down a street in public would look questionable. As much as they were accepted by our community—me included—neither he nor she, nor anyone else, used the words *boyfriend* or *girlfriend*. Those two words carried a stigma that anyone who considered himself or herself an educated, high-standard, and deeply traditional Cambodian was too moralistic for. So couples would go from acquaintance to engagement to marriage.

I knew all that without Dad's ever explaining it to me. And I knew he had to be thinking about the question I had just asked him . . . since all his friends were. At the beach while he and the other men had been away playing their ball games, the women had hung back. Too lazy to do anything else and eager to listen to adult gossip, Sopiep and I had stayed with them, sitting at one end of the picnic bench.

"Sarah," one of her friends had said in Cambodian, "when are you two getting married?"

I had no problem with everyone knowing that I liked Auntie Sarah now, but their assumption that I wanted her to be my mom still rang inharmoniously. It was a piece of music that someone had composed in a hurry and that could have been so much better with time. Yet I knew that if I had been born to her, I'd have been a lucky baby. I looked away and tried to talk to Sopiep, but she told me to hush.

"Don't be crazy," Auntie Sarah had answered, and pursed her lips. "I'm old now," she went on. She looked old, but she was several years younger than Dad. She had been engaged once when she was still in her twenties, but the engagement had been broken off when her parents learned that her fiancé had a gambling problem. She was so mad at them that she refused to marry the only other man who had asked her. For disobeying them, her dad had cursed her to life as an old maid. Lucky for her, he had taken back the curse before he died.

"You grew up here, but you talk like you've lived in Cambodia all of your life. You know, being in your forties in America isn't the same as being in your forties in Cambodia. You can still *do* things here," the same woman had said.

A full-fledged middle-school kid now, I got the idea of

what "do" meant. Everyone, including Sopiep and her mom, had chuckled. Although Auntie Sarah had refused to say anything more, the conversation had progressed to how many tables should be reserved at the restaurant, whom to order the cake from, and what traditions must be kept in a *proper* Cambodian wedding ceremony. No one had asked what I thought. I had smacked a bug on my arm before the women even acknowledged that I was around.

Dad still didn't answer my question about marrying Auntie Sarah. As he continued to clean the cooler the running water splashed onto his hair and over his shoulders to the floor. "Why do you ask?" he said finally. I didn't answer him. He turned the water off and towel-dried the cooler. "So, you really want me to?"

That wasn't the right question. He should have asked if I wanted him to be happy. Then I would have easily answered "Of course I want you to be happy. I want you to walk on clouds and have your cheeks wet with kisses every day." As Dad walked out of the bathroom I told him that whatever made him happy was fine with me. He didn't say anything— but in his eyes I saw that I had made him proud.

I brushed my teeth and washed my face. Looking in the mirror, I noticed, for the first time, bumps on my forehead that felt like gritty sand. *I'll have to wash my face with special soap like the other girls,* I thought. Then I saw my hair. It was almost at my shoulders, and the once ugly bangs blended with the rest. I decided to let it grow.

●

When Dad first told me the news, we were standing with Auntie Sarah on a cliff overlooking the beach in La Jolla. It was late morning but still cool. The clouds we stood in were slowly clearing up, and we had just seen a school of dolphins jump in the ocean below. With the fog wetting my face, I looked out, and even in the light of the morning, I couldn't see where the ocean ended and where the sky began. The world was quiet and peaceful, and so were my mind and my heart.

I hadn't yet responded to Dad's announcement of the wedding date. I'd been waiting for this moment, and now that it had finally arrived I just wanted to take it in completely. I'd been preparing myself for when Dad would finalize his love for Auntie Sarah, and preparing to accept the fact that if Mom ever did return, she wouldn't have him to return to, only me. I had thought it would be hard to accept that there would never again be Mom and Dad. But it wasn't. I was sad, though, for Mom. I loved her, and she would always be my mother. But what Dad did was only fair. He deserved to be happy, too.

The dolphins resurfaced, and I followed them with my eyes until they became one with the ocean. "I remember the first time you brought me here. It was when we got to San Diego," I said. Dad told me I had a good memory.

I couldn't help thinking that back then it had just been Dad and me against everything. Now there were three of us. And an army of three had to be better than two. I reached up to hug Auntie Sarah and realized that I would soon have my own mom again.

"I'm very glad," I said to both of them. I hoped they would understand from looking in my eyes all I wanted to say but couldn't. And when they didn't say anything, I knew they did.

A couple of nights before, Auntie Sarah had returned home with us after an early movie. Lately I had been leaving them alone in the living room, but that evening I watched TV with them. We were tired, and none of us spoke much. Dad said he was planning on buying a new car. Then Auntie Sarah replied that it was a good idea. I didn't know what to say, as I was planning the biggest apology of my life.

When Auntie Sarah got up to leave I said quickly, "I'm sorry. I'm sorry for being so mean to you that day when you brought me the dress. I'm sorry for being rude to both of you. I promise not to do that again."

Dad nodded at me, and Auntie Sarah simply said, "Don't worry about it, baby."

I knew I had done what I was supposed to. Yet I didn't feel cleansed or whole. It hadn't been an apology for breaking a dish or bringing home a bad grade; it was supposed to be an apology for hurting feelings and for doing something a Cambodian daughter wasn't supposed to do, being disrespectful to her father.

After Auntie Sarah left Dad and I watched TV some more, and again we didn't talk much. I could hear my heart beating.

"Dad," I said.

"Hmmm?"

"Dad, I am really sorry. I promise not to talk back, be rude, or yell."

He looked at me and again nodded. "I know. It's okay."

But I still didn't think it was okay, at least not for him. I stood up and went down on my knees in front of him. I felt my lips quivering as I folded my hands in a prayer form. "Daughter asks for forgiveness," I said in Cambodian. I didn't dare to look up at him, so I kept my head down. He turned the TV off and without saying a word, he pulled me up to sit next to him. And we sat there, in the quiet, for a long time. Now I knew for sure he finally understood my sincerity.

That night in my diary I had written: *I don't think anyone loves me as much as Dad does.*

The three of us didn't stay on the cliff much longer. In the car I asked Dad and Auntie Sarah about their engagement ceremony. "Both your dad and I think we're pretty old now. We think we're going to skip that step. We're going to Long Beach to buy wedding invitations, and that is probably how we're going to announce it to people," said Auntie Sarah.

"Does that mean I have to keep this a secret?"

"No. Our close friends will know. I guess what we mean is that we're not going to make any formal announcement until we get the invitations."

"Can we invite Mrs. Yen?" I asked.

Dad looked at me in the rearview mirror. "We've already put her down."

Before their trip to Long Beach, Auntie Sarah brought all of her nail polishes to our house. She was filing my nails while we waited for Dad to get home from work. "I think you should come with us," she said. I told her I was fine with her and Dad doing this by themselves. She finished filing my pinky and held my hand in hers. "Amy, I'm so lucky to be part of your life." She held her gaze on me until I turned away.

She spoke in Cambodian, and the sound of it was so soothing and comfortable that I thought warm milk was flowing through my body. It was then that I understood how beautiful and sacred our language was. How just the sound of it reminded me that a small piece of that ancient land, regardless of how far it was from me on a map, was in each ounce of my blood. How its words had earned me forgiveness from Dad.

I hadn't ever thought that anyone would want to be part of my life . . . maybe Dad's, but never mine. And after thinking of what I could offer Auntie Sarah in exchange for what she would be doing for me and him, I said, "After the wedding you and Dad can have my room." She tilted her head to one side, so I explained, "You and Dad will need a room. You can have mine." She pulled me into her arms and held me. I ignored the uncomfortable position, having sat cross-legged on the couch, and stayed there in her arms, determined not to leave her warm body until she released me.

"We'll look for a new house. You need your own room, too," she murmured into my hair. "When I was growing up, I never had privacy. I said to myself that once I had a daughter I'd make sure she did." She pulled me close to her again.

"A lot of girls are wearing bras," I said. "I know I don't need one now, but it will keep my chest round when I get older." As soon as I said it, I realized I had gotten lost in a place that I wasn't scared of, no matter how unfamiliar and strange it was. It was at that place and time, when everything was beautiful no matter how ugly it might be to others, that I knew I was safe.

Auntie Sarah sat me up. "When your dad and I get back, you and I will go find you one." Then she told me the story of when she got her first bra. Her mom had taken her to Sears, and she managed to get her mom to the girls' department. They found the underwear section next to an escalator going up to the second floor. Her mom didn't think she was ready for something like a bra, saying that girls in America were growing up too fast.

After putting down her purse and one bag, she pulled from the shelf a box with a small bra, told Auntie Sarah to stand up straight, took it out of the box, and held it against her chest. The white bra looked like a clean rag. "She didn't even let me take it to the fitting room," said Auntie Sarah. "People going up the escalator saw me . . . and I was so mortified. But she told me that if I cried she would just walk out of the store without me."

In late January, on a bright Saturday afternoon, Dad dropped me off at Sopiep's house. Mr. Sok, wearing black sweats, with a scarf around his neck, was heading toward his car when he saw us pull up. He walked to us and ducked his head in Dad's window. "So you're going to do it," he said in Cambodian. Dad gently nodded and grinned.

Mr. Sok told us he had to get new tires for his car and walked back toward his station wagon. Dad turned to me. All emotion left his face and gathered in his eyes, which were sparkling with happiness. He and Auntie Sarah would attend a Cambodian concert on Saturday evening with some of Auntie Sarah's friends who lived in Long Beach and then visit shops on Sunday. Auntie Sarah had told us that the bigger Cambodian community in the Long Beach area, which was very close to Los Angeles, would have better selections of fine Cambodian fabrics and jewelry for them to choose from.

I grabbed my overnight bag, wished Dad a great trip, and told him to say hi to Auntie Sarah for me, then went inside to find Sopiep. She and her mom were at their kitchen table with bowls, measuring cups, bags of flour, and a cutting board in front of them. Mrs. Sok was standing and kneading dough in a big plastic bowl as Sopiep continued to add more flour at her mom's command.

"Good, you can help us," Sopiep said when she saw me.

"Sopiep, let her get comfortable first. Amy, go put your bag away and have something to drink." With a floured finger, she pointed to Sopiep's room.

When I came back to the kitchen, Mrs. Sok filled a big pot with water and put it on the stove. I walked over to it, put my hands close to the pot, and let the new heat from the burner warm them. At the kitchen table I examined the ingredients: a bowl of yellow bean paste that had chopped green onions in it and the bowl of white dough that the two of them were working in. I knew Mrs. Sok was making the famous *biyn chaneuk* dessert. I had never liked it much because the sweet rice-based flour, when cooked, was always so sticky that it stuck to the roof of my mouth. Once, I had been so paranoid about choking on it that I had hyperventilated.

The dough was difficult to make, so not just anyone could knead it effectively. We novices could only help—adding flour to the bowl and standing by for other instructions. As Mrs. Sok finished with the dough, she gave us the job of rolling the bean paste into balls the size of jawbreakers. I dug my fingers into the mush and let them stay in the soft and moist cool paste.

"Gross," Sopiep said, "take them out."

I scooped out a small portion and rolled it into a ball between my palms. I liked the silky film it left on my hands.

"It looks like an egg yolk," Sopiep said. She showed us hers, and I knew it was too big.

Her mom looked at it and then teased, "What kind of chicken do you have?" We laughed as I divided the "yolk" into three smaller balls.

While we continued with our task, Mrs. Sok took a small portion of the dough, flattened it with her palms, wrapped it around a bean ball, and rolled the whole thing in her hands.

"Isn't the wedding this summer? Are you going to be in it?" Sopiep asked. I hadn't thought about that, and Sopiep was full of ideas of how I should look.

I imagined myself wearing a Cambodian dress for the first time . . . something yellow or light blue. Maybe I would even have long, painted fingernails. When I told Sopiep that I might have my hair put up in a French twist, she said that she could curl my bangs. Then her mom asked her why I would have her do my bangs when I would have a professional do the rest of my hair. As Sopiep explained her answer, I pictured myself dancing with Dad at the reception. He would tell me that even with Auntie Sarah in our lives, he would always understand my love for my mom, and then he would thank me for being such an understanding and wonderful daughter. And I would tell him that I would do anything for him.

When I made the last bean ball, Mrs. Sok rolled the left-over rice dough into tiny balls. And while Sopiep and I cleaned the table and bowls, she dumped all the balls into the boiling water. Then she took them out, each one looking glazed, and placed them in a bowl of cold water. After they cooled down, she put two balls each into three dessert bowls and poured a sugary brown ginger sauce over them. Mrs. Sok didn't eat hers, but instead stood watching us, asking Sopiep if she liked it and rubbing her head, stroking the mane down her daughter's back. As I bit into the sweet dessert, I knew that soon I would have what Sopiep had.

We were watching TV the next morning when the phone rang. Sopiep answered and told her mom it was

Auntie Sarah. After a minute of talking in the kitchen, Mrs. Sok told us she would use the phone in her room. I wanted to let her know that I would like to speak to Dad, but she wouldn't look at me, walking away as if she didn't hear me. I took the remote control from Sopiep and turned the volume down. As I watched the screen I knew, deep down in the pit of my stomach, that something was not right. And every time Sopiep laughed at the sitcom we were watching, I had to pinch myself to remember all the good things that were happening. I had a pretty home, a strong father, and, soon, a caring mother. But it became harder to remember as I watched the clock on the wall; Mrs. Sok was taking too long in her room. After two sitcoms, she finally came back out.

I jumped off the couch and asked, "When are they coming home?"

"Uh, they're already back." I didn't like how she hesitated a moment before answering my question.

"So soon?"

"Yeah. But let's go to the mall now. Ready, Sopiep?"

I sat on the floor and put on my tennis shoes. "*Meing,* everything is okay. Right?" I already knew that nothing was okay, but I was hoping for there to be a different truth. She didn't answer me and went to look for her purse. I followed her. "*Meing,* is everything okay?"

"Yes, Amy, your dad's tired. That's all. He needs rest. So you can go home this evening." I asked again if Dad was okay. "Yes." But she was slow to answer as I stood looking at her. I pushed my heels down to keep myself from getting mad at her for thinking I was too dumb not to know that something was wrong. I grabbed my overnight bag, and without saying anything else to her or Sopiep, I ran out the door.

I had walked the same steps from Sopiep's house to mine so many times that I didn't have to think about it. But on that day, I had to stop a couple of times, even at Maggie's corner, to see where I was. Even with the sun out, the day was turning dark around me. For a brief second I considered going back to Sopiep's safe world. But I understood that sooner or later I would have to face what was waiting for me at home.

17

CROSSING THE THRESHOLD into our living room, I reentered a world that I thought Dad and I had left. I smelled the familiar body odor before I saw Dad. He was sleeping on the couch with his shiny black dress shoes still on his feet, his legs hanging over one armrest. His shirt wasn't tucked in or buttoned, revealing three or four strands of hair that stood out on his bare brown chest. On the carpet next to an old soda stain was his travel bag, still zipped. And on the coffee table were empty Budweiser cans, a couple standing and some lying crushed. *Are you crazy? What are you doing with these?* I wanted to shout at him. But I couldn't, not after I had apologized and promised to be a better Cambodian daughter.

I found a small space on the couch, now so worn that the gray and white stripes had become the same color, and sat next to his unconscious body. "Dad," I said, and gently shook him. His hair and face were oily, and his lips were cracked like a dry riverbed. He looked so old. I wondered if he was still dyeing his hair. I rubbed the scar that ran down the side of his face and wiped my oily fingers on my jeans. "Dad, wake up." He parted his lips, and I turned my head away at the sour smell. "What happened?" I asked softly. "Get up. Where is Auntie Sarah? Why are you guys back so soon? You're not supposed to be back until later tonight." He brushed me away with a hand before turning onto his side.

I took off his shoes, buckled his belt, buttoned his shirt, and covered him with a light blanket; then I threw away the beer cans, even the unopened ones, straightened a picture frame, and drew back the curtains, whose frayed ends I had cut off with scissors. Then I filled a bucket with cold water and dish detergent and grabbed a dishrag. I moved Dad's bag to the side and started scrubbing the soda stain in the carpet. It had been there for almost a year, but until then I had never really noticed how dirty and tacky it made our little living room look. After the scrubbing, though, the sight before me was still *dirty*—a run-down house with gum in the carpet, a sticky kitchen floor, cooking oil on the counter, and hand-prints on the wall. Everything in sight pulled me back to what lay at the center of the room.

With a fresh hand towel I cleaned Dad's face, making sure to wipe the corners of his eyes and lips and wash his forehead and neck. Then I rubbed lotion on him, including his chapped lips. When I opened his bag I found everything inside just as I had arranged it when I helped him pack. On top was a towel: then there were white socks, underwear, pa-jamas, and a change of clothes for the next day. At one side of the bag were his toothbrush, razor, and comb. I pulled the comb out and ran it through his hair, flicking off dandruff with the tip of my finger. I was hoping he would wake up and tell me what had happened, but he didn't even budge.

During the night I checked on Dad several times and

asked him to eat dinner, but each time he just told me to leave him alone. Even when I told him Mr. Sok was on the phone, he ignored me. Only when I said I was going to call Auntie Sarah did he shout at me, *"Stop acting like you know everything! You're just a kid!"* and then he asked where I'd put his beer.

"Did you and she have a fight?" I asked. When he didn't say anything, I grabbed his arm and shook it, harder than I meant to. His eyes suddenly popped open. Trembling, I asked quietly, "Are you two okay?"

"Don't worry about it," he said, and shut his eyes once again.

Of course I'm worried about it, I wanted to scream at him. What if she had left us? The thought terrified me. Why had I come so close to getting something only to have it taken away?

Dad was still sleeping the next morning when I was ready for school. I stood in front of him and watched him for a long time, studying the length of his legs and the width of his chest. He slept curled on his side, and slowly I understood that he did that only because the couch wasn't long enough for his body. My heart ached and softened at the thought; not once in the year and a half that we'd been living in that home had he ever made me feel guilty for taking the single bedroom.

I knelt down beside him and caressed his arm. When he didn't get up, I said, "Dad, you're going to be late for work, and I'm going to be late for the bus."

He finally sat up, looked around, and scratched the back of one ear. There wasn't time for him to shower, so I went to get his work clothes from the hall closet. When I handed them to him, he threw them down.

"Walk," he said, and yawned. He didn't sound angry, but

tired and defeated; I hadn't seen that side of him since he had met the Soks. What happened? Had Auntie Sarah's friends given him a hard time about his past? She wouldn't have allowed that, though.

"I'll stay home. I'll take care of you."

He looked up at me, and I saw that the whites of his eyes had turned yellow with swirls of red. "Leave," he said in Cambodian, and pointed to the door. Without further protest, I called Sopiep and told her to meet me at Maggie's corner.

The brisk February morning made taking big strides easier for Sopiep and me. With just five minutes left, Sopiep and I still had three more blocks to walk.

"Did your mom and Auntie Sarah talk again last night?" I asked once I caught my breath.

"Yeah, my mom called her."

"And?" I tried to say it without showing how annoyed I was at her for making me ask for the details.

"All I heard was that she and your dad left the concert early and drove right home. Don't worry about it. I'm sure everything is okay." It was so like her not to understand that everything was not okay, that there was a real world with real problems.

"Did they have a fight?" I asked.

"I don't know."

"You don't know because you don't know the answer or you don't know because you don't know if they had a fight?"

"Huh?" She scrunched her eyebrows and turned up her lips. I wasn't even sure what I had meant. "Come on, we have to run," she said, and pulled on my jacket.

●

After school, I was relieved to see no car parked in the driveway and even more relieved when I found our home empty. I folded Dad's blankets and put away his clothes. Afterward I changed into my house clothes and went to lie on my bed, letting the bubbles of tension that had formed in my shoulders pop one by one.

It was just an hour later when I was getting ready for a bath that Dad came home. Surprised, I walked out in just my towel. Still in his wrinkled dress clothes, he plopped down in front of the television with a paper bag in his left hand. He hadn't bothered to brush his hair or wash up; the oil on his face had turned into a thick and dark film that I thought I could scoop off with a spoon.

I walked to him with the towel still wrapped around me. "Are you okay?" I asked.

He looked me up and down before speaking. "Go put on some clothes."

Although I was covered up, I suddenly felt naked and embarrassed. I skipped the bath, put on an old T-shirt and sweatpants, and spent the rest of the evening in my room. Every time Dad popped open a can of beer my heart dove into disappointment. And as the night went on, that disappointment grew.

Two nights later I heard Auntie Sarah's footsteps before I heard her knock at our door. I quickly opened the door and pulled her inside from the chilly evening. She smelled of soy sauce, and I knew she had brought us dinner. I took the plastic bag she held and moved to the side so that she could see Dad. He had been going to work, but he did nothing afterward but drink and sleep on the couch. I had tried to throw out the beer cans, but he ordered me to leave them where they were.

She went to sit on the carpet and gently shook Dad's shoulders. After three shakes he opened his eyes, sat up, and before acknowledging her, opened another Budweiser. "What are you doing here?" he asked in Cambodian after gulping down half the can. Auntie Sarah didn't look affected by his blunt tone. She told me to bring him something to eat. "I don't want to eat," he said as I walked to the kitchen.

I fixed a plate of food and went back to the living room. I stood a foot from them with the plate of hot rice and stir-fried chicken, not knowing what to do until Auntie Sarah took it from me. Dad stared straight ahead at the wall, and she gave me quick glances. And every time she did, I looked down at my feet. I had never seen Dad and Mom argue and didn't know what I was supposed to do. Auntie Sarah was not yet my mom, so I wasn't sure if I was supposed to take her side or Dad's.

"You need to eat," she said to Dad.

He hit the plate with the back of his hand, and the hot rice and chicken flew up before landing on her bare feet. She kicked her feet up, and some of the food flew on and over the coffee table. I moved in closer and got on my knees to scoop up the clumps of rice.

"It's okay, Amy, you can go and do your homework," she said, again not sounding as if she was affected by what Dad had done.

His childish behavior both infuriated and embarrassed me. I was not ready for anyone, including her, to see that our home was less than perfect.

As I got back up Dad tapped me on my behind with his foot, and even though the force was light, I fell forward. I felt rice, a clump the size of a quarter, warming its way through my sweats. "Don't tell my daughter what to do," he said. "You women are all the same." And he hit the cushion with his hands.

"I'm not telling her what to do," Auntie Sarah said patiently. "Amy should have something to eat, too. And I'm sure she has homework."

Dad didn't say anything, and for a long time the only sound in the house was the ticking of the clock. Although his silence permitted me to leave, I didn't move until I realized that they weren't going to talk seriously with me there.

At eleven o'clock Dad and Auntie Sarah were still in the living room. I had turned on the radio in my room to give them privacy when I heard her tell him to lower his voice. At first Dad hadn't done much of the talking, but eventually Auntie Sarah was able to coax him to speak. It was hard to stay in my room not knowing what was wrong with him and to accept that whatever was torturing him was something between him and Auntie Sarah. If that was true, then he no longer needed me for everything.

Sometime in the middle of the night I awoke to Auntie Sarah's voice. She had left my bedroom door open and the light from outside shone in, glowing behind her and highlighting her coarse black hair. Even with the radio still on, I could hear the shower running.

"We'll go shopping this weekend," she said.

"Everything is okay?" I asked.

"Yes. Your dad's fine."

"Are you two fine?"

"We two are fine."

"You're not going to leave us, even after you saw how much he can drink?"

Auntie Sarah played with my hair. "Nope. I'll always be here."

I wanted to thank her, to get on my knees and thank her for being so kind to us. "What was wrong?" I asked.

She hesitated before answering. "He just had a bad weekend." I didn't respond, almost hurt that she would assume that I'd accept such a trivial answer. "Amy, it's wonderful that you look out for your dad and take care of him. But it's not fair to involve you in adult problems."

"He and I have always taken care of our problems together."

"I know, he told me."

I wanted to explain further, but she started stroking my head. I liked the touch of her long nails caressing my scalp and twirling my hair. I no longer needed to prove anything to her.

18

THE UNIVERSITY TOWNE Center was my favorite mall in San Diego. Unlike the others, it was an outdoor mall. Sometimes there were clowns blowing up balloons for small kids in the food court, and at night a small band performed while people stood around sipping their coffee and swaying to the music.

"So yesterday, Dad said I can't go to the concert in Long Beach with Sopiep and her parents," I said to Auntie Sarah as we waited for our hot drinks.

"It's probably because he knows it's not all that much fun."

"Why not? Sopiep's parents go all the time. Anyway, he had said I could go next time the Soks went. And they're going next weekend."

"Amy, he said he *might* let you go."

"You're right, but I don't understand why he wouldn't let me go. You guys went." Instead of answering that question, she asked where I wanted to go for my first bra. I smiled and said, "Not Sears."

The afternoon wind made us walk quickly past many

shops, not even looking at their window displays, to the JC Penney at the other end of the mall. The underwear section was at the back of the girls' department. I was disappointed to see that there was only one rack of bras, none of which were colored or flowered, but I did my best to show Auntie Sarah my excitement. She took a white cotton bra out of a box and showed it to me.

"This one is pretty. Look at the pink flower in the middle," she said. It was softer and cooler to the touch than a T-shirt. "Do you want to try it on?"

"Do you think it will fit me right?"

"I wouldn't know unless I hold it up against you." We both looked around for an escalator and started laughing so loudly that a couple of people around us turned to look.

I took the box from her and gave her my jacket to hold before going into the dressing room. The bra was small, with two white triangular patches, straps, and the pink flower. I held it in my hand for a long time before putting it on, wondering when my own mother had gotten her first bra, and whether she had felt embarrassed like Auntie Sarah or sweet like I was feeling right then. And wondering, too, if she had known that she would miss sharing this moment with me when she decided to leave.

I told Auntie Sarah that the bra fit fine, and she handed me three boxes even though I said that one would be enough. "Don't be silly. You'll need at least three a week." I didn't want her to think I wasn't a clean person, so I took them to the cashier. I took out some of the money I had saved and handed it to the saleslady. "Amy," Auntie Sarah said, and pushed my hand away, "what are you doing?"

I didn't know what to say at first. "Ah . . . I'm paying for them."

"No, put your money away."

"Why?" I asked.

The cashier, a chubby older woman with wavy gray hair, waited for me. I didn't want to upset her by making her wait. But when I looked at her apologetically, she only smiled at us.

"Because I'm paying for them."

"You don't have to. I have money."

"I know. But you can use it to buy something else." And she handed her credit card to the cashier.

"Sweet daughter," the woman said.

I looked away from them and pretended not to hear her. I shouldn't have been so fortunate that a stranger would think Auntie Sarah was my mom, and that I was actually living a special day that was meant to be shared only between a mother and her daughter. But I was too embarrassed to correct the woman. Auntie Sarah didn't correct her, either, and instead said, "Thank you." Then she took the small package from the lady and handed it to me, and we walked off as if it were the most natural thing in the world.

●

I rewrapped my peanut butter and jelly sandwich and put it back into the brown paper bag before I started eating Sopiep's fried rice. "If you're starting to bring lunch to school, why don't you bring something you like to eat instead of that?" She nodded at my lunch bag. She had a good point, but after Auntie Sarah had taken me grocery shopping for my school lunch and paid for it, I couldn't just not bring it.

"I already told you why. Besides, we ate fish for dinner last night, and you know I can't bring the leftovers to school."

"Why not?"

"Because it would smell."

"But you ate it at home."

"I know. That's different. Fine, I won't eat your food anymore if you make such a big deal about it." I gently and intentionally put down the extra plastic spoon and opened my lunch bag once more.

"You know I don't mean it that way. And you know you can have whatever I have."

I grinned at her. "I know," I said, and waited a couple of seconds before picking up the spoon again.

"What *do* you do with those sandwiches?" Sopiep asked.

"I take them home and throw them in the trash."

"Why don't you just throw them away here?"

"Because," I said.

"Because why?"

I shrugged. "Because I feel guilty."

Sopiep hit the table with her hands, and her face looked as if she were in pain. The chocolate milk that she had just drunk drooled from both corners of her closed mouth as she tried to contain her laughter. "So you throw them away at home because you feel guilty for not eating them here?"

"Uh-huh."

After she wiped her mouth she asked about our project in language arts class. "Are you finished with your poem?"

I'd been putting it off because I hated writing. "No, but that's okay. I'm naturally creative at the last minute," I said to her.

"No you're not, Amy," Sopiep said, sounding motherly. "That's why you started on all your assignments early last year. It's due Monday. And you have to finish it by tomorrow because you know you can't do it this weekend."

Earlier in the week I had begged Auntie Sarah again to

talk to Dad about letting me go to Long Beach. She and I had been looking at bridal magazines because she wanted an American white gown to wear at the reception. I had shown her a picture of a sleeveless one and she shook her head, telling me it would make her arms look even bigger. "I don't know, Amy," she had said. "Your dad must have a good reason for not wanting you to go."

"What's the reason?"

"Maybe because it's far."

"Auntie Sarah." I rolled my eyes at her half playfully. "Remember, the two of you went. And when you guys were gone, we were just as far away then as we'll be if I go this time and you stay." She didn't say anything else and continued turning the pages. "Please, please talk to him." A couple of days later Dad had changed his mind and said I could go with the Soks.

As we left the lunchroom I said to Sopiep, "I swear I'll get it done before the trip." And I raised my right hand.

●

On Saturday afternoon Dad put his travel bag containing my things in the trunk of Mr. Sok's car. He rubbed my head and told me to be good. The weather had finally started warming up into the high seventies again, and the day was clear and bright, like a freshly washed and ironed morning. Even the flower buds were waking up to the new season. Dad wasn't smiling and looked worried, his eyes widening and turning dark.

"Dad," I said, "if you really, really, really don't want me to go, I won't go."

He pulled my hair behind my ear. "Remember the story I told you about how I left Cambodia? *Why* I left Cambodia?"

I nodded.

"Sometimes you see horrible things that you don't understand. But you can't give up. You still have to go on," he said solemnly.

I knew he preferred for me to stay home, but I hadn't thought my going was such a big deal to him. "Dad," I said resignedly. "I won't go."

He looked up at the sky and then around at the neighborhood before he finally turned back down to me. "Crazy," he said in Cambodian, "go."

He handed me some money and I put it in my purse with the rest I had saved. I was hoping we would go into the Cambodian shops in Long Beach so that I could find wedding presents for him and Auntie Sarah. Mrs. Sok had said she would help me pick out something special for Auntie Sarah. When I asked about Dad, she explained that usually in Cambodia, a wedding gift was meant for both people, no matter who would actually use it.

"Then please don't worry. Everything will be okay," I said to Dad. I got on my toes and kissed him good-bye.

On Highway 5 I saw the Pacific Ocean on one side and new business buildings on the other. Later we drove past a huge strawberry farm that had a PICK YOUR OWN IN JUNE billboard planted in the field. The land was dark green and went on until I couldn't see the other end of it.

"Those strawberries are this big," Sopiep said, and showed me her fist. "And they're sweet just like sugar, right Mom?" Mrs. Sok absentmindedly answered "Yes" before continuing her conversation with her husband.

I, too, turned absentminded as Sopiep pointed things out to me. I still hadn't written the poem for school, and it was due in two days. A poem was meant to be meaningful and straight from the deepest part of the heart, but how did a person put feelings on paper?

Asian and Mexican stores occupied both sides of Alameda Street in Long Beach. There were other businesses, too: several Vietnamese and Cambodian clinics, lawyers' and dentists' offices, and garages. I spotted the Cambodian stores with their blue signs and red letters right away. In a window of a grocery store hung a picture of Angkor Wat, our ancient and sacred temple in Cambodia. I had seen a painting of it on Mr. Yen's wall back in Florida. The eight-hundred-year-old temple was made of large blocks of stone, now aged into gray and black. Sitting on top of the huge temple were three columns that looked like budding lotus flowers. But what I liked most were the tall and skinny silver palm trees around it, which had withstood many years of harsh winds.

Mr. Sok parked between a white Lexus and a maroon 4Runner in front of Phnom Penh, a restaurant owned by his longtime friend. A fifty-gallon fish tank welcomed us in the lobby of the restaurant, and Sopiep pointed out a silvery white fish that was two feet long. The restaurant was filled with round tables occupied almost entirely by Cambodians. I immediately heard our language and tried to pick up on their conversations. Along the walls hung paintings; some were of country scenes and some were of women in Cambodia. I was shocked to see one of a woman who was naked from the waist up. At the back of the restaurant was a stage with band equipment and microphones.

Mr. Sok's friend came to greet us, and Sopiep and I *chumreab suor*ed him and said, "Hi, *Phou*."

Phou took us to his best table right below the stage. "They'll be practicing later for tonight," he said, and pointed to the empty stage. "The singer insisted on the extra practice." Mr. Sok told him that he didn't have to stay to talk since he had so many customers that afternoon. Before leaving, *Phou* reminded us to go to his house to get ready for the concert. "My wife is expecting you," he said, and handed Mr. and Mrs. Sok menus.

After the late lunch Mrs. Sok told her husband to drive me to Siem Reap, a store down the block. An older woman at the cash register near the door immediately greeted us. "*Neang,*"—a respectful term for ladies younger than oneself—"what are you looking for today?"

"Oh, my niece wants to buy her parents a present," Mrs. Sok answered the old woman.

"Well, what's the occasion?" she asked me. I wasn't sure what to say and turned to Mrs. Sok.

"No occasion," she answered. "Do you have any nice fabrics?"

I knew Auntie Sarah didn't have a new Cambodian gown, so I thought I might buy her fabric for one. The old woman opened her case and took out several samples for us. All were silky and shimmering, and Auntie Sarah would look beautiful in any of them. When the woman told me the price, I knew I didn't have enough. Mrs. Sok probably sensed my disappointment and told me she would help with the difference.

"Thank you, *Meing,* but no. I want it to come only from me."

"She doesn't have to know I helped." I still shook my head.

Next the woman took out a tray of *chonsang,* or towels. But these towels looked more like scarves. At the temple or any other religious ceremonies, women wore them like beauty pageant sashes. Mrs. Sok whispered that Auntie Sarah would need one at the wedding ceremony. I picked out a white one with eyelet at the ends. It was so thin and light that I could fold it to the size of my palm. Holding it in my hands, I knew it was the right gift, one she could wrap around herself and remember she'd gotten from me.

Phou's house was the biggest I had ever been in. It had a round driveway, a three-car garage, and French doors. Before getting out of the station wagon I looked down at my feet and saw my dirty white dress shoes. But when I saw that Sopiep's shoes also looked old, I didn't feel so backward. A young woman with a baby on one hip opened the doors and waved at us. After the three adults greeted one another, I learned that she was *Phou*'s wife.

We left our shoes in the front hall closet, and the brilliant marble floor immediately cooled our feet.

"Your house is so big and beautiful, *Meing*," I said.

She looked pleased and said, "We just bought the house, so it's still pretty empty." If I hadn't seen her I would have thought it was the voice of an American.

After a tour of the first floor, Mr. Sok walked back to the family room to watch television while *Meing* led the three of us upstairs to show us our rooms.

We were all dressed when *Phou* came home at seven. In our station wagon we followed him back to his restaurant. As we pulled into a parking space, a black bird landed on the windshield, and Mrs. Sok shrieked. Even when Mr. Sok hit the windshield it didn't fly off immediately but blinked at us until it was ready to leave on its own.

As I heard the music and saw the well-dressed people standing in line, the inside of me fizzed like a soda being poured over ice. We didn't have to wait long because *Phou* brought us to the door, and the ticket taker immediately let us in.

Most of the round tables had been put away, and in their place were rows of chairs. Again, Mr. Sok's friend walked us to our seats, right below the stage and just a few feet from the dance floor. Out of the corner of my eye, I could see a couple of older boys watching Sopiep and me. She must have seen them, too, because she pinched my arm. In my new black skirt and green sweater I felt like money, a new bill right off the press. I rubbed my arms, thinking about the soft bra I was wearing underneath the sweater. I could feel my lips spreading into a smile.

I had seen the singer before on karaoke album covers. As she sang, she also danced, showing us her long thin fingers with red fingernails. When she finished her slow dance song, she started on a *romvong* one, and flocks of people gathered on the dance floor. The men had on dark-colored pants with dress shirts, and the women wore dresses and looked to have spent a long time putting up their hair. It amazed me that with so much in common each of us still led separate lives. How I could have easily been one of them on the dance floor. How, after all, one of them could have been Dad or even Mrs. Yen.

The two older boys who had watched us earlier walked up to Sopiep and me and asked if we wanted to dance. I knew they hadn't asked in the correct manner, so I just looked at them and shook my head. Amazingly one boy understood and asked Mr. Sok if he could dance with me. His friend saw and did the same thing. Mr. Sok said yes, but I was still hesitant. I had forgotten to ask Dad if I could dance. Without his permission I thought that a yes decision would enter me into a realm of betraying his trust. And at the same time I felt that I would be losing a part of myself by simply dancing with this skinny boy who tried to look older in an adult haircut. I told him no, and Sopiep, after glancing at me, said the same thing to his friend.

I wasn't sure why I felt so loose and carefree; maybe because I had been asked to dance or maybe because Dad wasn't present or maybe because the raven had blinked at me. Whatever the reason, it didn't matter. What did matter was that the world had finally turned on its axis for no one but me. The world, represented by these people in this restaurant, was seeing me.

With Mr. and Mrs. Sok dancing so often, Sopiep and I stayed back to watch them and enjoy the food the waitress brought us. I must have drunk three glasses of coconut juice before I realized that I had to use the bathroom. Sopiep and I stood up, smoothed down our skirts with our hands, and walked to the restroom.

I was in the stall when I heard a familiar woman's voice. At first I wasn't sure, so I stopped moving to listen more closely. I quickly flushed the toilet. But when I got out, the person the voice belonged to wasn't there. Leaving Sopiep behind, I left the bathroom and pushed myself through groups of people, searching for her, for the voice. The same voice that had haunted me for almost three years. A woman elbowed me in the stomach by accident as she tried to get out of her chair and a man blew cigarette smoke in my face, but I didn't stop pushing. I tried to tell myself I was imagining things. But I knew I wasn't.

And suddenly there she was, just two steps in front of me, her back to me. I saw the slenderness of her waist and how the back of her elbow came right at her midsection. She was so close that I could have reached out my hand and touched her, pulling out the silver clip to release her hair down her back. I wanted to run my hands down that hair, to get lost in its dark waves. I didn't realize I had moved until I saw my fingers on her shoulder, tapping it. "Mom?" I said. She didn't turn around, so I said it again. And for a split second I thought that I was actually crazy for calling out to this woman. Maybe it wasn't *my* mom after all.

But it was. When she turned around I lost my breath. Even in the dimly lit restaurant with the noisy crowd, she appeared brighter and younger than I had remembered. She didn't say anything, but in her startled eyes I saw her recognition. I could see myself reflected in them. They were the same eyes that I sometimes woke up to, the ones in the photo that sat on top of my dresser, and the ones that had said that she would pick me up from school. We were back in Florida in our little home with the red roof and the oak tree in the yard, and we were back under her blanket, napping in the warmth of the summer sun.

"Mom," I said again. I opened my arms and walked in closer. But just as I was about to hug her a man holding a small child walked up. The little girl, about one year old and with curly black hair and chubby cheeks, tried to grab me with fingers that looked like a baby doll's. The man saw me, still standing with my arms wide, and pulled *my mom* to follow him. She went with him without a fight, and without once turning back to look at me.

"Who's the kid?" I heard him ask her as they walked away. But I didn't hear her answer.

19

I FOUND MYSELF a place between the Soks' old station wagon and another car in the parking lot. The night had fully set in, and the February air was dark and moist. Some kids walked by and saw me sitting on the ground with my knees under my chin, rocking myself for warmth, but they didn't seem to think much of it. How I envied their lives. Far down a street somewhere a car screeched, and behind me the music continued with the drums rolling and the singer now launching into a cha-cha. One of the kids around the restaurant corner had just said a Cambodian curse word, and someone else coughed. No one seemed to understand what had happened to me. My whole life had been crushed, and still no one knew. My vision turned blurry, and then a second later, the single tear that trailed down my cheek turned to many.

I looked up at the black sky and tried to console myself with thoughts of Dad, Auntie Sarah, Sopiep, and Anthony. But they didn't matter; only one thing mattered: I was motherless. And not like other kids whose mothers left because they died. Those kids were lucky; they could walk around with their heads still held high. I wanted to scream to God that he had been unfair to me. What had I done, I asked him, to deserve to be orphaned by a mother who had stopped loving me? I hadn't even thought that was possible. Wasn't there something in the blood we shared that was to connect us forever, even after death?

I couldn't erase the image of my mom. Her beautiful eyes. Her lips. The smoothness of her forehead. She had looked straight at me and acted as if she didn't know me. But how could she not? Didn't she remember that I was her little girl, the one she used to pick up and kiss? The one she hugged and cuddled with in the afternoons? And now why was there another little girl in a lacy pink dress and hair bow? A little girl who looked like her? My heart ached at the thought of her carrying the baby in her arms and calling her Daughter.

It wasn't long before Sopiep found me. I turned away from her and stared at the muddy tire beside me. I tried to wipe my face but couldn't brush the tears away fast enough. My hands had gotten so wet that I couldn't do anything but let the tears fall freely.

"Amy, why are you crying?"

Her soft voice and her touch on my shoulder didn't stop my tears. For some reason, knowing that she had a mother only brought on more. Soon, the crying turned into screams and wails that poured out of me as if I had held them in for ages. They took over my whole body as I shook in her arms.

"Stop, it's okay, it's okay," she said. But the more she lied, the louder I got.

I looked up to breathe in some fresh air and pull off the hair that stuck to my cheeks. Several young people stood around Sopiep and me, probably wondering what was wrong with the big crybaby. But I didn't care. I didn't care that my eyes were swelling up or that salty snot was dripping from my nose. These people were not my mom.

An old lady asked Sopiep in Cambodian, "What's wrong with her?"

"I don't know," Sopiep said.

"You should get her mom," the lady said. I looked up and glared at her until she moved back.

Sopiep stroked my back until I hit her hand. I didn't want her, with her perfect mom, to sympathize with me. She let go of me and left, and I fell limp against the car. Then, not knowing why, I stretched myself flat on the ground, feeling the cold concrete numbing my back and legs. I pulled my sweater up and cleaned off my tears. A couple of kids had gotten closer and looked down at me, staring. I looked past them to the night sky: not a single star. *I might as well close my eyes forever,* I thought.

"Amy, Amy, tell *Meing* what's wrong."

I opened my eyes to Mrs. Sok. The terrified look on her face made me hurt more than Sopiep had. Where was my mother? Wasn't she supposed to be the one to mend my broken heart? Mrs. Sok tried to pull me up, but my legs didn't want to stand on their own, and I fell back to the ground, feeling only a bit of pain as my behind hit the concrete.

"Amy, hush, did anyone hurt you?" *Did anyone hurt me?* I laughed. "Sopiep, go find your dad," she said.

Mrs. Sok tried to pull me up again, but when some men stepped in to help her I started to kick and punch them with my weightless fists.

"If she were my daughter I'd kick her until she faints," someone said in Cambodian.

"Shut up!" I screamed at the person, the only response I could think of. And when I said it in English, a couple of people walked away, first mumbling that I was crazy. "I am crazy!" I yelled back between my wails. This got a few more people laughing.

I barely saw Mr. Sok stand over me when he came. By that time, he was just one figure among the many who wanted to see the show. So like Cambodians, I thought. Watching you and waiting for the moment you would fall. How I had used to loathe them when they did that to my mom. How, now, I wished they would do it to her again so that I could join them.

Mr. Sok felt my forehead and told his wife that I was hot. "Amy, tell us what happened," he said gently.

"No," I said quietly.

Before putting me in the station wagon, he told Mrs. Sok he would get his friend's wife so that we could go back to their house. My throat felt raw, and it hurt to open my eyes. Several minutes later Mrs. Sok climbed into the backseat with me, and Mr. Sok and Sopiep got into the front. The sound of the key turning and the engine starting made my heart race once more.

"No!" I screamed, and jolted up. I put my face up against the window and pounded on it as if to break it open. Some of the bystanders had gone back into the restaurant, where the music was still playing. Not once had the music stopped for me. The restaurant grew smaller as we drove away, but I still heard the music. I heard everything . . . everything but somebody saying *"Amy-a."*

By the time we reached *Meing's* house and she let us in, my crying had diminished to a whimper. Mr. Sok carried me upstairs and left his wife and me in the room alone. She put me in bed and sat beside me, asking again if someone had hurt me. I looked at her and opened my mouth, but I didn't know where to begin, so I shook my head. She pulled the sheet off my legs and pushed up my skirt, feeling and looking at my inner thighs. I knew what she was doing, what she was thinking, but I didn't stop her. When she was satisfied that there were no bruises, she pulled down my skirt and covered my legs again. As she touched my forehead, my heart ached, as if it were compressing.

When Mr. Sok returned he asked if I wanted him to call my dad. I didn't answer; I hadn't thought about Dad. I didn't even know what I would tell him or how he would take the news. "Call him," Mrs. Sok sternly told her husband. He left again. The next thing I knew he instructed his wife and daughter to pack because we were going home.

"No!" I hollered. "I'm sorry. I'll be okay." But they didn't believe me.

I didn't even thank or say good-bye to the restaurant owner's young wife when we left. I had heard her ask about me, but Mrs. Sok said that she didn't know what was wrong. I just looked at her baby and absentmindedly shook its little hand before walking out her French doors. I opened the car door and sat on my knees in the back, again with my nose pressed against the window. Mrs. Sok pulled me down and put an arm around me. The car started, and we got on the highway, following the sign for south, San Diego. This highway, I realized, would take me away from Mom and everything I knew about her, forever.

●

I woke up the next day hot in my own bed. My face felt tight and swollen, and my head and throat ached. My comforter and another blanket were tucked all around my body. The back of my left leg itched, but everything on me was so heavy I didn't bother to reach down to scratch it.

Dad opened my door and came in. At the sight of him I panicked, because I still hadn't thought of a way to break the news about Mom to him. "How are you feeling?" he asked.

I wasn't ready to talk. I managed to turn onto my side and face the window; the light from outside burned my eyes until I shut them again. He walked to the bed and told me I had a fever. I felt him standing over me and waiting for me to talk, but I couldn't.

Dad gave a deep sigh and said, "You have to take these." I opened my eyes to see two white pills and a glass of water. I sat up to take the medicine, and then he told me that he had made me something to eat.

He went out and brought a tray with bowls of rice porridge and Chinese sausages. I looked up at him, feeling my lips trembling and turning into a deep frown. The sausages, baked with their chunks of fat and cut into oval slices, made me remember how I had hoped for Mom's return the day after she left us. I shook my head and pushed the tray away. Dad sat down. I couldn't look at him. I was too embarrassed. Embarrassed that I had had to be brought home in the middle of the night, embarrassed that he was going to learn the news about his wife, and embarrassed that finally I was going to have to accept that my own mom had left me, for someone else. I knew that once I told him, he would say it wasn't my fault. But I feared I wasn't going to believe him.

Dad touched my forehead with his palm. "We have to talk." When I crouched lower in bed he said, "I know what happened." I was grateful that he was speaking in English; I needed this fence that separated words from feelings.

"I'm sorry that Sopiep's parents had to bring me home last night. I told them I was fine. Are they really mad?"

"No, they're not mad at all," he said quietly, almost distantly.

"Are you mad?"

"No, I'm not. And I'm not talking about that, Amy."

He stood up to close the curtains and remained at the window. He was definitely older. From my bed, I could see more white than black in his hair, and extra wrinkles on his face. His neck sagged a little, too. Even his arm muscles had become less tight.

Dad tried to smile and came back to sit on my bed, but his eyes were too far away to console me. He rubbed his left cheek. "Amy."

When he said my name I knew that *he* knew. But his face was expressionless, like a wall whose fingerprints and history had been whitewashed. I wanted him to be affected like I was, to hurt inside so much that it was sometimes hard to breathe. I wanted and needed to know that he and I were in this together . . . that I wasn't alone.

"Amy, did you see your mom?" I didn't answer him.

"I saw her, too, when we were at the concert," he continued. I looked at him blankly. Then slowly he said, "That's why we came home early."

I didn't know what to say. He didn't take his eyes off me; they wanted something from me.

"Amy, that's why I didn't want you to go. I heard that the Cambodians around the Long Beach area go to concerts whenever singers come to town, so I thought you would have a good chance of seeing your mom there."

My head began to feel hard again, as if the walls were closing in on me. "Why didn't you tell me?" I asked.

He began speaking fast. "What would I have said? 'Hey, Amy, your mom is living with a new family'?" I hadn't meant to cry again, but he mentioned the word *family,* the word that included the baby girl in the arms of Mom's new husband. "I don't know." He shook his head as he got up and walked around the room.

"Well, you shouldn't have let me go," I screamed. "What kind of father are you?" As soon as I said it I regretted it, and I hoped he knew that.

He waved a finger at me. "Amy, we're not Americans."

My voice cracked. "I know, I know. You don't have to tell me that. I know we're Cambodians. I see that every day in the mirror. Look at my hair." I held some of it and showed it to him. "Does this look like *American* hair?"

He told me to lower my voice and not to be disrespectful. "Americans aren't bad, Amy, they're just different from us. They do things differently and believe in different things. For instance, they focus too much on feelings."

"That's not so bad," I said quietly. I used the bedsheet to wipe my eyes.

He came to sit on my bed again. "I know. But that's just not me. I came to America a long time ago, but half of my heart is still in Cambodia. Khmer blood runs in me, and in you. I don't want to lose that. It is the only thing that ties me to my parents, your grandparents, and the land that I was born in." He put a hand over his eyes and rubbed them with his fingers. I'd always known he loved Cambodia, and I used to think he had left part of himself there. Now I knew that he had brought Cambodia with him here. "I didn't know how to raise you when you were little. Plus, your mom was so young. I did what I thought my own parents would do."

"Did they break up, too?"

"No, they didn't. But when they were alive they made me learn things about life the hard way. And if they hadn't . . ." He hesitated and took a deep breath before continuing. "If they hadn't, I don't think I would have survived after we were separated and they were killed. Do you understand?" I nodded. I understood well that he had lost his family and been able to start a new life by himself in a new country. But understanding it didn't relieve any of the pain or anger. "And, Amy." He put his hand under the blankets and grabbed mine. "I didn't think I would be able to hide the truth about your mom from you much longer. I figured the sooner you saw it for yourself, the sooner you could move on." And with that he kissed me, got up, told me that I needed to eat, and left.

Dad was partially right. Whether or not I had known about Mom, the fact remained the same: she would still be there, two hours north of me, with a new husband and baby. And because of that, I didn't think I would ever be able to go on.

In the middle of the night, my stomach felt as if it were dissolving and slowly oozing its way up my throat. I got out of bed as fast as I could and ran to the bathroom, kneeling in front of the toilet. It came freely, as if it knew the route. And I couldn't stop. It poured out of my mouth like a dirty waterfall. Greenish, yellowish mush that had spoiled within me. I flushed the toilet and rested beside it. How funny, I thought, that something that was part of me just minutes ago could be flushed and disappear, forever.

I spit into the toilet to clean out the bitterness in my mouth and then lay against the bathtub. Everything in the bathroom was just as it had been before the previous night. The ceiling hadn't changed. The shower curtain still had the brown mildew stain. And the mirror still needed to be cleaned. Dad was snoring in the living room. And outside, I was certain, the night was still black and starless. Regardless of how I felt, everything went on. Yet I didn't want to go on. I was cut into pieces, and the ones that mattered—the ones

that once made me eager to wake up or to laugh or to care—
were scattered into the air, never to be found again.

In the morning before leaving for work Dad told me I
didn't have to go to school.

"Make sure you take the medicine every four hours," he
said, and patted my head. I didn't say anything to him and
closed my eyes again.

I spent much of the next several days sleeping and looking out the window. I cried less, but the tightening in my
heart was still there.

Many people visited me. Auntie Sarah had come that
Sunday night and every day after that. She said almost the
same thing on each of her visits. "I know you're mad," she
would start. When I didn't respond, her voice would turn
pleading. "Talk to me. You can say whatever you want. It will
make you feel better. Amy?" I heard her, but I didn't know
what to say. All my life, all eleven years of it, I had had to
know what to say and what to do. But for the previous couple of days, being a lost traveler in an endless cave and not
knowing anything gave me a peace that I didn't want to give
up. Anyway, telling her, or anyone else, that I hated my mom
was wrong.

One day I heard a sniffle in Auntie Sarah's voice. "Amy,
don't be mad at your dad. Be mad at me." She moved in
closer and kissed me. Her frizzy hair tickled my face. I didn't
understand why this woman cared so much about me when
my own mother didn't. How long would she be around until
she decided one day that she would just leave, too, and make
another family for herself?

"I'm not mad at him, or at you," I said finally, quietly.

Mrs. Sok called almost every evening. I would hear Dad
tell her that I was getting better, especially if I had eaten and

kept it down. "But she won't talk," he'd say. "I just don't understand that girl."

On Tuesday after school Sopiep came with a stuffed an-
imal. Seeing her, a friend, should have raised my spirits, but
it didn't. She was the last person I wanted to talk to. And
since she probably knew by now what had happened on the
trip, I wanted to see her even less. "He'll keep you company,"
she said as she tucked the stuffed dog inside the blankets
with me. I pulled it out and gave it back to her.

"I'm fine," I said, and pulled the covers back up.

She took it and held it in one arm. "You didn't miss
much in school. We've only been reciting our poems." The
stupid poems. I hadn't even written one. "I did good. It was
no big deal, though. Everyone who wrote one got either an
A or a B."

"I'm tired," I said to her, and closed my eyes. Before she
left she said she would bring me my homework.

When I slept I had terrible nightmares. One night I
woke up with sweat running down my face. Even the back of
my neck was wet. I thought I was going to suffocate under
the blankets, so I pulled them off. I needed water, immediately. Finding my way in the dark, I walked out to the
kitchen. I opened the refrigerator and poured a glass of water. My throat was screaming for the cold water to quench
the fire. But as I drank it, I realized that the water was warm,
almost hot. And I didn't want that. I wanted cold water.
"Water in the refrigerator is supposed to be cold!" I
screamed. "It's only natural." I threw the glass on the floor
and it shattered. The kitchen light went on, and I looked up
to see Dad standing just a foot from me. I ignored him and
stepped over to the dish rack, grabbed a plate, and threw it
against the wall. He told me to stop, but I couldn't. When he

tried to walk toward me I threw a glass right near his feet. I didn't stop until I broke every single plate, bowl, and glass in the dish rack and on the table into pieces, never to be mended . . . just like me.

"Amy." He gently pulled my hand.

I wasn't sure what I was trying to prove, but I dug my heels into the kitchen floor anyway. Then his grip around my hand tightened, and I followed him to the couch. He sat down and pulled me to sit close to him. The only light in the house was from the kitchen, some of it spilling into half of the living room. "Amy, tell Dad what you're feeling," he said.

"I can't," I cried.

"Tell Dad," he urged me in Cambodian.

I told him about the night I had seen my mom. How she had stood before me without saying a thing, not even my name. And how she had walked away without looking back even once. "I think my heart broke, and I don't think it will ever be right again."

"And," he said softly and pulled me closer to him. I could feel his heart beating.

"And I . . . hate her." There, I'd said it. He put his arm around me, and I laid my head on his chest. We were out at sea in a boat just for two, swaying in the deep ocean. And I was safe. "I hate her for leaving me, for forgetting me. Like I don't exist, Dad," I cried louder. "I don't exist in her eyes." And I continued crying, but unlike the many times before, it didn't hurt. It was loud and bubbled easily out of me.

When my crying quieted down Dad said, "But you do. You are here, right now, with me. And I love you."

"I don't understand why *she* stopped loving me."

"But she does love you."

I didn't believe him. "You know, she's a liar. She used

to tell me, do this, it's the right thing to do. Don't do that, it's the wrong thing to do. But look at her. She left her daughter!"

"But it wasn't because of you."

"I don't care. I still hate her. Maybe I always hated her, from day one, when she lied and made me wait for her at the school. I waited for her, Dad. Deep down in my heart, I never stopped waiting for her to come back even when I told you she was gone." There was a silence as we sat together in the dark living room. Soon I heard my own heart beating. "Then I figured when you and Auntie Sarah get married, Mom would at least have me to come back to. I hate her so much that thinking about her makes me shake."

"That's okay."

"It's not okay. It's wrong to hate your own mother," I said.

"If that is how you feel, it's not. But someday you won't hate her."

"Yes I will, I'll hate her forever." I pounded once on my thighs.

Dad rubbed my shoulder. "Amy, your body is your first home. You don't want it so heavy with hatred that it holds you back from living. You want it clean and beautiful, so that peace is welcome. In this house where you live"—he poked at my chest—"there is too much goodness to let you hate someone forever."

I looked into Dad's eyes, and for a moment I was a little girl again in a time when I didn't know anything but the things my mom and dad told me, the only things that seemed to matter. Part of me wanted to stay a little girl and not to be hurt. But the other part knew that sooner or later I would have to grow up.

The following Monday morning I got up, dressed for school, and made sure to grab my schoolwork before leaving the house with Dad. Over the weekend, I had completed all the homework that Sopiep had brought me. I apologized for having been rude to her, and she said she understood. I must have looked at her funny because she said, "Seriously, I do."

"But you still have your mom," I said.

"Well, you have Auntie Sarah. My mom loves me because she has to. But Auntie Sarah doesn't have to love you. She loves you for who you are. Once I even overheard her tell my mom that she's only marrying your dad because she's crazy about you."

"You're lying."

"I am not."

"Then why didn't you tell me this before?"

"Because." She shrugged playfully.

"You're a good friend," I said. And she told me I was right.

At school when I turned in my work, all my teachers asked if I was well. "That was one bad fever. You were out for a week. Did you go to the hospital?" my math teacher asked.

"No, my dad took care of me at home."

"Maybe you'd have gotten better quicker if you went to a doctor."

"Maybe," I answered politely.

When Mr. Hunnicut saw me walk into his class he said that whenever I was ready I could read my poem. I was the only one left, and he needed to complete the grades.

I stood at the front, looked in my diary for one last time, and closed it. All eyes were on me. Even the rowdy boys in the back were waiting for me to recite my poem. I had a feeling that most of the students watching me would be disappointed with what I had to say. It was only a couple of lines, written quickly just the night before so that I could get my easy A. I hadn't wanted to spend too much time thinking about it—wanting, instead, to spend the time cleaning my home.

Black bird brings sadness
leave me and never return
Mother, oh Mother

EPILOGUE

It was late spring, and Dad, Auntie Sarah, and I threw down a blanket on the cliffs. We had just finished looking at a house and had grabbed some pork sandwiches from the Vietnamese restaurant for our picnic. The two of them had thought it would be a good idea to buy a house so that after the wedding, which was just a month away, we could start living in it. We'd gone to look at seven houses, and our favorite was a two-bedroom ranch with a garage and a small yard. Auntie Sarah had said she wanted to have a garden to grow mint and lemongrass and maybe a couple of fruit trees. And Dad said that he would grow gardenias and jasmine in the front, right outside my window.

Auntie Sarah handed me a sandwich and I popped open a can of Coke. The sweet pork and fresh green onion tasted good, especially after I washed it down with my drink. After we finished eating Dad wanted to take a walk along the cliffs and watch the hang gliders. I told him to go ahead with Auntie Sarah.

When they left I lay on my back, resting my head on my

hands. The sky was bright baby blue, and the spring wind was soft as it brushed my face. I felt light, free, and lucky to see the things around me. Below I could hear waves gently crashing against rocks, and once in a while I could smell the salt of the ocean. I turned over and looked out at the water. It was wide and powerful.

I sat up and opened my bag, taking out the small package I had loosely wrapped the night before. I pulled out the framed picture of my mom and looked at it for one last time. Then I threw it over the cliff, feeling no regret. But it didn't make it to the ocean; instead, it broke on some rocks. Maybe I shouldn't have been, but I was satisfied to know that she lay shattered and lost. Maybe someday, I would pray for her to be found.

I heard Auntie Sarah's loud laughter and turned away from the ocean. She and Dad were holding hands and walking toward me, smiling. Had I been younger I would have run to them and taken their hands so that I could be in the middle. But now, I decided to stay back. I understood that I would always be as much a part of them as they were of me, no matter where I was.

I stood up, waved to them, and watched their happiness come my way.

MANY LY was born in Cambodia in 1977 and came to the States in 1981. She grew up in St. Petersburg, Florida, and attended the University of South Florida, graduating with a teaching degree in 1997. After teaching seventh- and eighth-grade language arts for two years, she married her longtime love, Danith Ly. They moved to La Jolla, California, so that Danith could finish his studies. It was there that Many first began writing. They now live in Pittsburgh, where Danith is a professor at Carnegie Mellon University and Many is an area coordinator for the Greater Pittsburgh Literacy Council. Not too long ago, Many and Danith adopted their first "baby," Pluto, a beautiful mutt.